Among the Olive Groves

Chrissie Parker

First published in 2014

This novel is a work of fiction. Names and characters and events are fictitious and a product of the author's imagination and any resemblance to actual persons, living or dead, is entirely coincidental.

ISBN-13: 978-1500601751
ISBN-10: 1500601756

Dedication

To Christopher and Frank Betts, who worked as dispatch riders in Bristol's Home Guard during World War Two.

To my brothers Matt and Si, the surfers.

To my cousin Sandra Beavis, who lives the Zante dream.

CHAPTER ONE

Cornwall, England, 1991

Kate Fisher ran. Her legs pounded the ground, each blow sending shockwaves through her feet and up into her shins, but she pushed through the pain and continued on.

This wasn't supposed to happen. It couldn't be happening. Not today.

Today was supposed to be a happy day, a momentous occasion filled with laughter and celebration. Instead her world had crumbled around her and she had been unable to stop it.

The terrain along the clifftop was rough and uneven. Tufts of thick grass and rabbit holes threatened to trip her and send her tumbling to the ground, but Kate was smarter. She knew the area well and jumped lightly over them, leaving them in her wake. The tangy smell of salt hung in the early morning air and she could feel the ocean spray dusting her already sweat-soaked skin. Her hair was whipped by the strong Cornish winds and small tendrils stuck to her sweaty forehead, but she didn't care.

As she finally rounded the headland, the beach came into view. A large expanse of golden sand that arced its way along the shore, clinging to jagged granite cliffs; cliffs that had shaped the landscape for thousands of years making the countryside what it was today. Searching the crashing waves below, she looked for him, scouring the tumble and froth in vain. Moments later, a surfer appeared on the crest of a wave and she watched as he expertly rode it to the shore.

Determination coursed through her and she pushed her body to its very limit. With lungs aching and muscles screaming, she picked up speed, each step bringing her closer to him, as the tears began to fall.

CHAPTER TWO

Zakynthos, Greece, 1938

Elena Petrakis walked through the olive groves, it was a place she loved. Her slender fingers traced the bark of the trees as she went, and her feet displaced small blades of lush grass and the occasional wild flower. She loved mornings like this, mornings where the sun shone brightly overhead and the sky blazed a brilliant blue. It was a hot and steamy summer, the sea was calm, the olives were growing plentiful and war was now a memory. The islanders lived in paradise in the middle of the Ionian Sea, with nothing but the beauty of nature to keep them company. It was idyllic.

Elena was lost in her own world. Her small

frame danced in time to the tune she sang. Her long brown hair, falling in small tendrils from her headscarf, flowed in the gentle breeze and her bright green eyes, all knowing just like a cat's, didn't miss a thing.

She loved the island. It had always been home and she knew of nothing else. She lived in the mountains with her parents and brother, helping her mother around the house, sneaking out when she could to explore the picturesque land that was surrounded by vibrant turquoise waters. Her parents never knew where she was from one moment to the next and, despite their frustration, they loved her more for it. They liked that she was a free spirit and, as long as Elena remembered the traditions of her heritage, she could do as she pleased.

Elena was nineteen, almost an adult but in many ways still like the mischievous and happy child she had always been. She had always taken an interest in the world around her and had grown into a strong-minded young woman, who lived life to the full. She was part of the island and it was part of her. She couldn't imagine being anywhere else.

As she reached the end of the olive groves, she climbed the stone wall and sat on top, staring down at the world below, quietly singing. As far as her eye could see, the ground was interspersed with rows of thick, twisted and gnarled brown tree trunks. Their branches held plentiful leaves, and budding green olives, growing heavy with the promise of a good harvest. Wild flowers and grass grew in abundance, while lizards either stalked the undergrowth chasing their next meal, or leisurely basked in the heat of the summer sun.

It was then that she saw him, walking towards her through the trees. A boy not much older than herself. Elena had seen him around the island before but only ever at a distance, and he had always fascinated her. He was taller than her, handsome in a Greek sort of way, with brown hair that fell untidily about his face. His skin was tanned from the intensity of the Zakynthian sun and, whenever she saw him, his clothes were always smart and tidy, unlike hers. Today he wore the clothes of a working man and she wondered why that was. She remained on the wall, swinging her legs, singing a little louder now, watching like a cat as he drew ever closer.

Angelos Sarkis was checking the olive trees when he heard the sweet melodic voice; it carried on the light breeze and wrapped itself around him like a comforting blanket. Intrigued, he stopped working and followed the sound. With growing curiosity, he dipped under the branches of a tree, and took in a scruffy girl, sitting on the wall. He was very tempted to stop, but knew he did not have the time, so he continued walking, a brief smile passing across his lips as they locked eyes.

“Hey you! Sing with me!” she shouted as he

walked by. Angelos tried his best not to stare, but her beauty shone brighter than the sun overhead. He had to stop. He was lost for words and just stood like a fool gaping at her, as though an angel had descended before him, trapping him in its heavenly spell. Elena grinned, jumped down and ran over to him. It was only then that he noticed her feet were bare.

"Do you realise you are barefoot?" Angelos asked, perplexed by this strange vision. He wondered who she was and why he had never seen her before.

"Yes, I hate shoes. I prefer to feel the earth against my skin." She stood before him, smiling, trying to sum him up. "Come, sing with me!"

Angelos shook his head. "No. I can't sing."

"Everyone can sing. Come, sing with me!" She playfully danced around him, continuing the song she had sung a few minutes earlier. She was full of energy and her spirit was infectious. Despite himself, Angelos found himself singing, albeit very badly.

As soon as the song had begun, it was over and she stood before him once more.

"Elena Petrakis," she said holding out her hand. Her formality made him laugh.

"Angelos Sarkis," he replied, shaking her delicate hand. Every part of her was beautiful.

"Sarkis?" she raised an eyebrow. It was a name she knew well.

"Sarkis," he nodded.

"Hmm. You are very handsome, Angelos. Tell me about yourself."

"What do you want to know?"

"Everything!" she giggled, running rings around him making him feel dizzy.

"Do you ever keep still?"

"No. Never! If you keep still, then life stops. You have to keep moving, Angelos, or the grass will grow under your feet and your life will cease to have meaning."

Angelos laughed loudly. "How old are you, Elena?"

"I am almost twenty. Why do you ask?"

"You are much too wise for your age."

"You sound like my father!" she laughed. "Come, let us go to the beach."

She grabbed his hand, and Angelos had no choice but to follow her, his work forgotten. Elena ran, weaving between trees, heading for the lane, her bare feet kicking up dust as she pulled him along behind her. They felt the wind on their faces, the sun on their skin and, for Angelos, the thrill of spending time with a beautiful girl, something he rarely did.

Running along the rough track, they eventually found themselves on Xigia Beach, a small expanse of coarse sand dotted through with pebbles. It was silent other than the gentle swish-swish of waves washing back and forth along the shore. Angelos stood and watched as Elena ran to the water. She dipped her toes into the waves, and squealed as the cool viridian waters washed over her warm, sun-kissed skin.

"Angelos! Join me."

"No thank you. I will just sit here." He plonked himself down on the sand and watched as she continued to dance in the shallow waves, like a child who was seeing the sea for the first time. As he stared out across the water towards the neighbouring island of Kefalonia, his mind began to wander. He really should not have stopped work. He was supposed to be checking the groves for his father. His father. Angelos's stomach tensed. If Loukas Sarkis knew his son was sitting on a beach, spending time with a girl instead of working, he would be furious, and Loukas was not a man to cross. Angelos jumped to his feet.

"Elena! I must go."

She spun around and ran up the beach, her face filled with disappointment.

"You must?"

"I must."

"But why?"

"I am supposed to be working. My father owns the olive groves. He would be cross if he knew I was here."

"Pah! Work is for fools."

Angelos sighed. "I am sorry Elena. It was lovely to meet you but I really have to go." He turned and walked up the beach. Elena ran after him and grabbed his arm.

"I am sorry. I did not mean that you are a fool."

"It is okay. Maybe I will see you again another time?"

"Maybe," she said, shrugging her shoulders.

He sighed again. "I have to go. But I will see you again, Elena." Without a second glance, he ran off up the rough track and back towards the road. At the top, he could not help glancing back at the girl who had stolen his heart. He knew he would see her again, even if he had to scour the island for her, for Angelos Sarkis had fallen head over heels in love.

~

Elena silently crept along the wall. She was desperate to look at the Sarkis house. She had heard the name before; most islanders knew who the Sarkis family was. They were one of the wealthiest families on the island. Loukas Sarkis owned many of the olive groves, a business he had inherited from his father. She now understood why Angelos looked and dressed the way he did. He was a cut above her and her family. Too good for her.

Sighing, she sunk to the ground and leaned against the wall. She did not have many friends, and she liked Angelos. He had a pleasant smile and spoke *to* her rather than *at* her like most people did. Finding out who he was had been a shock, and she knew that Loukas Sarkis would never allow them be friends. Picking at the grass and watching the birds flit from tree to tree, she heard a bang. Elena sprang to her feet and peered over the wall to see Angelos and his father leaving the house. Studying them, she took in the elder of the two. There were similarities between them but, whereas Angelos was good-looking and had a pleasant air about him, Loukas looked gnarled and beaten, like one of his ancient olive trees. Like many of his kind, a fondness for ouzo, too much sun and the weight of business had begun to take its toll.

At the gate, the two men parted, Loukas in a donkey-drawn cart and Angelos on foot.

Elena continued to watch. As Loukas disappeared around the bend in the road, she ran to catch up with the younger man.

Sneaking up behind him she tugged at his shirt sleeve. "Good morning, Angelos."

"Elena! What are you doing here?" Anxiously, he scanned for his father.

"I came to see you. Do not worry; I waited until your father had left. Why did you not tell me who you were?"

"Why does it matter?"

"Because I want to know everything about you."

"You are very sweet, Elena, but I have to

work and I do not think it would be appropriate for us to be seen together."

"Why?" His attitude irritated her. "Why Angelos, are you worried about what people will say? The landowner's son running about the island with a peasant."

"I never said you were a peasant, Elena!"

"You did not, but others do. I can see how it would bother you. You are a Sarkis, destined to own the island's best olive groves. You live in a nice big house and wear fancy clothes and do not have time to spend with the likes of me, a lowly island wretch. Good day, Angelos Sarkis, it was nice to meet you!" She turned and stormed off down the road.

Angelos watched her go, torn between work, and the beautiful spirited girl he wanted to get to know better. His heart won out and he ran after her. Catching up to her, he took her arm.

"Stop one minute."

"No. I have said all I have to say."

"For goodness' sake, Elena. Stop and let me speak!"

She heard his tone and whirled round, coming to a standstill. "What?"

"Do you know you are very beautiful when you are angry?" he laughed.

"Is that all you have to say?"

They walked silently side by side along a narrow road, lined with trees and hedges. It was a typical island morning; the sky was a vibrant cornflower blue, with barely a cloud in sight. A light breeze wafted around them, birds sang and vegetation blossomed. Angelos was first to break the silence.

"Where do you live, Elena?"

"In the mountains with my mother, father and brother. My brother is younger than me. We do not have a lot, we are not very rich, all of our money comes from my father working on the land or in the olive groves, but we are a happy family. I love them very much; I do not know what I would do without them."

"Being rich is not the most important thing in the world. Being happy with who you are and what you do in life is far more important."

"You think so, Angelos?"

"Yes."

"But you are rich! Does it not make you happy?"

"You think I am rich?"

"Yes. Your father owns many olive groves and much land. Look at the big house you live in. You must be rich!"

Angelos laughed, shaking his head. "It is true that we have money, and that we can buy many things that others cannot, but we are not rich, Elena. We have no gold or jewels or a motor vehicle. We work twelve hour days almost every single day of the week, sometimes more. I rarely see my mother or father other than at the dinner table or at work. I would rather be poor than be who I am. I hate it. My father only cares about work."

"You do not like your life, Angelos? You are unhappy?"

He looked away from her. He was a man, and there were things he could never tell her, things he could never tell anyone. It had been a mistake to come out with her today. "It has been nice seeing you again, Elena. Enjoy the day."

With that, he was gone, leaving Elena standing alone and confused, wondering how she had managed to upset him.

~

Elena lay under the large olive tree. Its branches hung low and wide, giving more than adequate shade on the humid summer day. She closed her eyes and began to drift off to sleep, the rustling sounds of the trees above and click of cicadas in the undergrowth relaxed her. It was two weeks since she had seen Angelos and she had given up ever spending time with him again. They were from different worlds, worlds that would never safely collide.

During those weeks, she had run through the mountains with the other village children, climbing trees and searching out undiscovered places to play and hide, but it had bored her. She was nineteen years old and too old for childish games. She wanted the company of someone her own age, and her mind had slowly crept back to Angelos. She had woken early that morning and crept down to the olive groves, where she had lain ever since, desperately hoping he would turn up. So far she had been disappointed. The day was hot and sleep overtook her. She dozed under the tree in a deep dream-filled slumber.

Angelos strode purposefully through the groves, checking the branches of the trees as he went. It looked like the harvest would be a good one this year. Up ahead, he spied someone asleep under an awning of branches. Stepping closer, he pulled up short and smiled. Elena. He had not seen her for weeks and he had missed her. He regretted walking away from her the last time they were together, but there were things in his life he could not talk about to anyone, and he had come perilously close to revealing them to her.

He crouched next to her and ran his fingers through the loose brown waves that fell across her shoulders, before sitting with his back to the tree.

"It is a lovely day for a sleep," he said loudly.

She stirred and sat up quickly, startled to find someone next to her.

"Angelos! You made me jump."

"You are lucky I found you. My father hates people trespassing on his land."

Elena almost said something rude but bit her tongue, not wanting to upset him. "How are you?"

"Good. You?"

"Good."

"I am sorry I ran out on you the other day. Can we start over?"

Elena nodded, smiling.

"Hi, I am Angelos," he said and held out his hand.

"Hi, I am Elena." She took his hand and shook it, before collapsing into giggles.

"Hello Elena. So, friends again?"

"Yes, friends."

"Good."

Elena jumped to her feet and pulled him from the ground. "Come on, let us go to the beach!"

He rolled his eyes, and followed in her wake, all thoughts of work abandoned. She was an unpredictable force of nature but, as far as Angelos was concerned, he did not care. As long as he was with her, she could do whatever she wanted. Love was like that. There were no boundaries and he for one was glad they were friends again.

CHAPTER THREE

Zakynthos, Greece, 1938

Elena and Angelos became inseparable over the summer. Angelos found it hard to slip away from work, fearful that his father would find out, but he took a chance and met Elena whenever he could. They walked to the beach, sat on walls watching the lizards, and ran through olive groves singing. Angelos was deeply in love with Elena, a love that grew stronger with every passing day, but as yet he had not acted upon it. There were so many obstacles in the way, and the last thing he wanted to do was hurt her. Elena enchanted him and he felt breathless whenever she was around. Elena seemed oblivious to Angelos's feelings, and treated him as a friend. He did not care though. He was just happy to spend time with her.

As the heat intensified over the summer, they lounged on Xigia Beach and swam in the clear sea. They dived down through sunlit dappled waters, to see who could reach the sea bed, a never ending yellow mass of rippled sand. Swimming through the water, they watched as fish moved seamlessly past them, oblivious to the humans invading their peaceful underwater existence. They enjoyed the feel of the cool ocean against their suntanned skin, and the freedom of the unspoiled nature that surrounded them.

One afternoon, while languishing in their favourite cove with the sun beating down upon them, listening to the gentle waves brushing the shore, Elena turned to him.

"Tell me about your family, Angelos."

"Why?"

"Because they are your family and you never talk about them."

He shrugged. "They are normal, like yours."

"Hardly. From what little I know, my parents are nothing like yours."

Angelos sighed, shaking his head. Elena's green eyes flashed in the sunlight, as if luring him in. He spoke, knowing he must answer if he wanted to keep her company.

"You would not like them. My mother is quiet, a worrier, like a timid little mouse. She rarely speaks when my father is around. My father owns many of the olive groves on this side of the island, as you know. He employs many people at harvest time, and thinks he is a great man, but he is ruthless. He has a temper and I worry that I will turn out like him. It scares me sometimes. He expects me to take over the business when he is gone. I am his son, his only child, and the Sarkis name is very important to him. Sometimes I think it is more important to him than his actual family."

"Do you love your parents?" Elena asked.

It was a question he was unable to answer. "What is love?"

They were silent for a moment, each considering the question.

"Love, Angelos, is when you care deeply for a person. Love means you will always be there for them. Love means you would protect them, fight for them and even, I suppose, die for them."

"If that is love then, no, I do not love my father. He is a mean man and I disagree with him and everything he does. I think maybe I love my mother a little, but she is cowardly, so I cannot fully love her."

"So you do not truly love anyone then?"

Angelos stared at the one person he did truly love. The person he loved with all his heart, cared deeply for, would always be there for and would always fight for. But how could he possibly tell her? He knew all about Elena's family. They were so very different to his and he knew his father would be furious if he ever discovered their friendship. His family was akin to gentry. Elena's were poor mountain folk, scraping a living wherever they could. His father would never approve of any kind of relationship between them. Angelos wanted to tell her that he loved her, but friends they would remain and nothing more. It made him sad.

"Angelos?"

"No, Elena. There is no one I love."

Elena jumped to her feet, fire flashing in her eyes. "Then you too are a mean man, Angelos Sarkis! You are just like your father!"

She stormed up the beach leaving him sitting there. Angelos wanted to run after her but, if he did, he would have to give in and declare his love for her and that would only bring hurt and pain. Lying back on the warm sand, Angelos closed his eyes and wished he had never been born.

~

A few days later, Angelos was sitting at the kitchen table pushing his half eaten breakfast around his plate. He had not seen Elena since their argument and he missed her. Pigi, his mother, stood at the sink rinsing the breakfast dishes. Loukas, his father, sat at the head of the table, silent and stony. Until Loukas gave his permission, Angelos was unable to leave the table, which frustrated him. It was as though his father controlled his entire life and he hated it. Finally

Loukas stood, nodding permission to his son, and Angelos followed suit. He deposited his plate on the side next to his mother before planting a delicate kiss on her cheek, patiently waiting for his father to leave for work so that he could race towards the beach and search for Elena.

"You are coming with me today, Angelos. We have work to do, the olives need our attention," Loukas said, placing a battered hat onto his head, the only protection he got from the sun while walking the groves.

"Yes, father." Reluctantly, Angelos followed Loukas into the bright sunshine. The donkey was already harnessed to the small cart. Angelos climbed up next to his father, and felt the gentle bobbing back and forth motion as they set off. Silence settled upon them, only occasionally interrupted by the clopping sound of the donkey's hooves on the lane and the twittering of birds in the trees.

The two men worked silently side by side for hours, only stopping to eat some village bread and olives, and to drink some wine when the sun was directly overhead. Once they had finished, they returned to work. It was tedious and backbreaking, and Angelos was beginning to hate the daily grind of working out in the baking sun.

A tuneful melody came to them suddenly on the passing breeze. It was a sound that Angelos recognised and it made his heart soar. His sweet angel had found him and was calling for him. The noise irritated Loukas and he marched off to investigate. Sensing trouble, Angelos followed. As they rounded a line of trees, they saw Elena, sitting on the wall, singing her heart out.

"You there!" Loukas shouted. "Get off my wall!"

Elena looked up, and smiled. A single melodic note stuck briefly to her lips before floating away on the breeze, to be lost forever.

"Hello! You must be Angelos's father." She jumped from the wall and walked up to them. As usual, her feet were bare and her hair was tied back with a headscarf. Angelos smiled shyly.

"I am Loukas Sarkis, and you are on private land, peasant."

Angelos groaned. He wished his father would not treat everyone like a second class citizen. Elena ignored the insult. These may be his groves but, as far as she was concerned, the beauty of the surrounding nature belonged to everyone. Walls were there to be climbed and gates to be opened.

"Is this your grove? I like it; it is one of my favourites. I like sitting under the trees and watching the lizards bask in the sun."

Loukas was furious at the cheek of the girl. He had seen her many times before, running around with no shoes on, climbing walls and trees, trespassing where she should not. She was poor mountain folk, nothing more than a gypsy. He could see from the look on his face that his son was already acquainted with her, which unsettled him. It was something he would have to put a stop to. A few well-aimed lashes of his belt would ram the point home.

"I do not care." Loukas stepped forward and took hold of her arm. "You are on my property, girl. You need to leave," he snarled as he marched her past Angelos and up the grove to the main road. Angelos trudged behind them, feeling sorry for Elena. He wished his father was not such a monster. At the road, Loukas released Elena and climbed into the cart. Angelos knew the working day was over. Loukas would now abandon his grounds to seek solace in a bottle of ouzo. Left with no choice, Angelos climbed up beside Loukas. He was desperate to turn and smile at Elena, but he did not dare. His father frightened him too much.

~

Lying on the beach, Angelos stared up at the never-ending sky. The bruises from his father's belt had turned from black and deep purple, to a dull shade of green and yellow, and no longer hurt as much. Despite his punishment, he still sneaked out when he could, desperate to see Elena, but she had stayed away. It had been almost a week since he had last seen her. Sighing, he knew he should be going home. His father's leash had tightened since that day at the groves and he did not want to become a punch bag for his father's wrath again.

As he stood, he caught sight of her. She was leaning against a lone tree, watching him. *How long has she been there?* He wondered. Slowly he walked towards her, and calmness washed through him. Elena ran to him and threw her arms around him, hugging him tightly before stepping back.

"Angelos, my friend! Where have you been? I have missed you so much."

"I had to work. My father was so angry with me for talking to you."

"I have decided I do not like your father very much. He is a horrible man."

Angelos laughed. He could not help it. She was always so frank and honest. "Do not tell anyone I said this, but I do not like him much either!"

"Angelos! That is no way to talk about him; he is still your father!"

He shrugged. In his head, he had too many horrible images. Too many reminders of beatings to believe his father cared about him, and to see the way he had treated Elena made him mad. Elena was not a peasant. She was a beautiful young woman, with a strong personality.

"Come Angelos, we will go for a walk and talk properly."

"I cannot. I have to get home."

She pouted, crossing her arms and tapping her foot. "I thought we were friends."

"We are, but my father is expecting me."

Elena rolled her eyes. "We do not want to upset your father now, do we?"

"Elena..."

"Okay. Okay. But you must meet me tomorrow."

"Okay. Tomorrow. I promise."

Angelos planted the lightest of kisses on Elena's cheek before running up the road.

~

Angelos kept his word. As he pulled on the bicycle's brake, Elena was already sitting on a gate, swinging her legs and singing. Her own battered old bicycle, that had seen better days, was propped against the wall.

"I knew you would come!" she squealed. She jumped down and ran over to hug him. Angelos awkwardly hugged her back, still finding bodily contact with her difficult; it stirred feelings in him that he could not even begin to comprehend. They climbed onto the bicycles and pedalled their way through winding lanes, lined with wild flowers and trees. Angelos always marveled at how Elena enjoyed everything she did. Today he was even more surprised.

"You are wearing shoes! I thought you hated them."

"I do, but I cannot cycle without them. The pedals hurt my feet too much."

Angelos laughed and weaved the bicycle around her.

"I will race you! All the way down the hill to the beach!" he shouted.

A mischievous smile crept across her face. "Prepare to be beaten, Angelos. I am very fast!"

They pedalled hard and sped down the hill. A wide smile spread across Angelos's face as he watched Elena. She had stopped pedalling and was allowing the momentum to carry her. She stuck her legs out and the wind whipped her long hair out behind her. Remembering the race, Angelos pedalled furiously to overtake her.

"I am going to beat you!" he shouted back at her, but as they reached the bottom, he deliberately slowed a little allowing her to overtake him. He did not care if he lost; he was content just to see her happy and having fun. At the bottom of the hill, they wound along the lanes until they reached a cove. Leaning their bicycles against a tree, they ran across the pebbles to a small wooden jetty. A rowing boat was tethered to the end of the jetty.

"Come Angelos! Let us go for a boat ride!" She was already running along the precarious slats of wood, clapping her hands in delight.

"I do not think we should, Elena. It is not our boat."

"There is no lock on it. It means it can be borrowed. Oh come on Angelos, it would be so much fun!" She was grinning, clapping her hands and jumping up and down like an excited child. "Please, for me."

Angelos knew he was unable to resist her. Shaking his head, he stepped onto the jetty and walked towards her.

"Okay. But I row."

She twirled her hair in her fingers. "Can I have a little go?"

"We will see," he said as he lifted her in one swift motion, depositing her into the bottom of the boat. The bobbing motion made her feel unsteady. Angelos released the rope and stepped in. The boat rocked with the added weight and they both had to balance themselves to prevent it from tipping. Angelos took up the oars and directed Elena to sit opposite. Pushing off from the jetty, he powered the oars back and forth, swiftly increasing the distance between them and the shore.

The sea around them sparkled vibrant hues of blue and turquoise in the sunlight. Trailing her hand over the side, Elena allowed the water to pass through her fingers. She felt as though she were touching the very heart of the ocean. With strong powerful strokes, Angelos got them out to sea and up the coast in no time at all. Finally, he stopped and pulled the oars back in, leaving them bobbing gently on the sea's glassy surface.

"I have never seen the island from here before," Elena said quietly. "It looks so beautiful."

"Have you never been out in a boat before?"

She shook her head. "I have never been given the chance. That is why I love being your friend, Angelos. I learn so much from you."

He smiled at her and admitted, "I like spending time with you, too."

They gazed at the shoreline as the boat continued to rise and fall with the gentle swell of the ocean. They both loved their home, and knew they would never want to live anywhere else. Who would want to when they lived in paradise?

"I am getting hot," Elena said, fanning herself. "I thought it would be cooler here on the sea, but it feels just as hot as on land."

"It does," Angelos agreed.

Without another word, Elena pulled off her sundress and heaved herself over the side of the boat, wearing nothing more than her undergarments. It had happened too quickly for Angelos to be embarrassed.

"You are a beautiful woman, Elena Petrakis, and yet you act like a boy! What would people say if they saw you now?"

"Pah to them!" came the voice from the sea. Moments later, Angelos felt a splash of water as she dived under into the deep recesses of the aqua waters. Rolling his eyes, he stripped to his underwear and jumped in after her. She surfaced in front of him, laughing.

"You have left the boat! Is it safe? It might

float away!"

"No, it will be fine. The sea is calm, as long as we do not swim too far, we will be okay."

As quickly as she surfaced, Elena was gone again. Angelos watched her gliding through the water, her hair streaming out behind her. She reminded him of a mermaid, slinky and exotically beautiful, enticing him to let go of his heart and soul completely, and follow her to the murky depths to be lost in her siren clutches forever. He managed to resist, but only just.

They swam through the waters, enjoying the feel of the ocean upon their skin. They took turns seeing who could dive the deepest and to see if either one could reach the bottom. Neither could, but Angelos came the closest. Every time they came back up to tread water, he was barely able to catch his breath before she was off again. Once more, he plunged down after her, gently caught hold of her ankles and pulled her back to him. They broke the water's surface, laughing.

"You caught me! I am now yours," Elena said teasingly.

Angelos was about to speak when something caught his eye. Putting his finger to his lips, he gently instructed her to submerge herself in the water. Gently treading under water, they watched in awe as a loggerhead turtle gracefully swam past, its flippers moving effortlessly in the water, its wide eyes all-knowing. It was captivating. As it swam away, they surfaced gasping for breath.

"That was wonderful. I am glad you were with me to see it."

"Me too," he said and, in that moment, he wanted so much to kiss her. They were completely alone with nothing but the sky, sea and marine life for company. He wanted to wrap his arms around her, run his fingers through her long hair, and bury his head in her neck. But he was too scared. If she rejected him, he would lose his friend forever and he just could not bear to live without her.

"Angelos!"

He was brought quickly back to the present. The boat was drifting away from them and they were in danger of losing it. They powered through the water and eventually caught up to it, but Angelos's perfect moment was lost to the sea. Elena hoisted herself into the boat and sat in the hull, allowing the heat of the sun to dry her skin. Catching sight of her in nothing more than her undergarments sent Angelos dizzy with desire. It took every ounce of strength he had not to take her then and there.

Once they had dried, they pulled on their clothes and reluctantly returned to the cove. After securely tying up the boat, they jumped onto their bicycles and started the long and tiring journey back up into the hills.

~

Elena and Angelos continued to defy Loukas,

meeting up in secret whenever they could. They explored the whole island, from Keri in the west, to Agios Nikolaos in the north. One hot and sticky day, they decided to cycle to Vrahionas in the mountains. The weather made for a tiring climb, but it was worth it. At the top they could see for miles across the island they called home, to the mainland in the east and to Kefalonia in the north.

"I feel like I am queen of the world up here!" Elena exclaimed, holding out her arms and spinning. "I can see so much and my kingdom goes on forever! Bow down Angelos, and worship your queen."

Angelos laughed at her exuberance. Playfully, he pretended to doff his cap and bowed.

"My queen. I am your loyal subject."

"Good. Now as my loyal subject, pass me my lunch. I am hungry!"

Angelos unfurled a battered old rug he had found in the closet at home and lay it out on the ground, motioning for her to sit. After opening the small basket, he passed her some bread and olives. They ate hungrily, and washed it down with some wine, before lying back on the blanket and staring up at the clear bright sky.

"Do you ever want to marry, Angelos?"

"Why do you ask?"

"Because I am interested. Now answer the question."

"Sometimes I do. Other times I look at my parents and think that I would rather not. I do not think they are very happy and I would hate to end up like them. What about you?"

"Yes, I do want to marry. I want a strong man. Someone who loves me for me and for the same things I believe in. I do not want a man for his money or possessions. I want a man for him."

"And have you found him yet?" Angelos asked hopefully.

"Maybe. Maybe not," she said with a shrug.

"That is no kind of answer, Elena Petrakis!"

She laughed. "I know, but I have not decided if the man I want is worth marrying."

Angelos felt his heart flutter. He wondered if it was him she was talking about or another man. He desperately hoped it was him. He would give anything to be able to make her his wife, but sadly he knew too much stood in their way. His father would never agree. If he found out they were still friends he would be furious. Why was life so hard?

"What are you thinking, Angelos?"

"Nothing."

The sun had moved across the horizon, and he knew they should make a move. It was a long bicycle ride back to their homes. While packing up the basket, Elena suddenly grabbed his wrist and a fleeting look of worry passed across her face.

"Promise me you will always be there for me, Angelos."

"I promise. You know I will."

He watched as the relief washed over her face, brightening her eyes once more. But it did not hearten Angelos; instead it left him with a mix of fear and dread. He should not be making promises he might not be able to keep.

~

The hot and hazy summer slowly turned to early autumn, bringing cooler temperatures and thunderstorms. Angelos and Elena bravely sat on Xigia Beach watching as forks of bright hot lightning hit the sea, between great rolling cracks of thunder that rattled the earth. They had both been warned by their parents to take shelter when the storms hit, but they were both too young to listen and felt they were invincible. Nature's storm ranted and raged in the skies above, reminding those who lived on the island that it was she who was ultimately in charge.

When Angelos could get away, they continued to swim in the sea, splashing and laughing together, enjoying the movement of the water around them. They ran hand in hand, through the olive groves, hiding behind trees, jumping out on each other and falling to the ground in fits of laughter. They cycled mile upon mile, racing each other, weaving chaotically along roads, feeling the thrill of the speed as they went down some of the steeper hills. Both of them knew the island so well that they were able to sneak through fields, woodland and back roads to avoid being seen. Angelos was worried about being caught by his father or one of his father's friends, but the island was good to them and helped them to keep their secret.

Towards the end of September, islanders were woken in the middle of the night by a low rumbling sound that steadily increased in volume. The ground violently shook and pitched, shattering glasses, cracking building walls and splitting the earth. They were used to earthquakes but this one was bigger than normal and it sent Zakynthians running from their homes with fright. Elena's family slept outside for the next week, too frightened to stay indoors in case another earthquake came and brought the house down upon them. Elena was so worried about Angelos. She wanted to run to him, to check he was okay, but she knew it was not possible. She just had to wait and hope. Good news finally reached her a few days later when she learned he had escaped with only a few cuts and bruises.

As the earth returned to normal, the olive harvest arrived. Angelos found his time with Elena limited. He was reduced to working long hard days, assisting his father and the labourers to help bring in as much fruit as they could. Sometimes while he was shaking branches to release dozens of the small oval fruit, he was sure he could hear the far off lilting sound of Elena singing. It carried to him on the breeze. No one else seemed to notice and he wondered if it was his memory playing tricks on him. Or was she really there, hiding nearby watching him, cat like, stalking her prey, her green eyes glinting with mischief? He held onto the thought of seeing her soon and it got him through the long backbreaking days.

Before too long, the harvest was over. Autumn had rapidly changed to winter, signaling the end of the year. The island was still as beautiful and serene as ever, but the world beyond was rapidly changing. Angelos and Elena's quiet and happy existence would soon be gripped by a terror that would take over the lives of millions and change the world forever.

CHAPTER FOUR

Cornwall, England, 1991

The rugged granite coastline of Cornwall was bathed in bright sunshine. The waves swelled and rushed towards the shore, crashing onto rocks and sand, showing how powerful the mighty Atlantic Ocean really was. The sky was blue, unusually so for late spring, and splashed through with an occasional wisp of white cloud, surprising the residents of Newquay as they woke to a new day.

Kate Fisher sat in uncomfortable silence across from her parents. The Fishers' dining room was, as it had always been, an eclectic mix of her mother's homeliness and her father's chaotic clutter that had not yet been tidied away. Her mother was always nagging him for it and yet he never seemed to listen. The dining room table was set for three people, something her mother always did whatever the meal-time. Place and drink mats, cutlery and other culinary items graced the surface, sometimes making Kate feel as though she were eating in a hotel. But it was her mother's way and she had come to accept it.

The quietness of the room was all enveloping. Kate had no words, and she hated the awkward silences that descended when her parents had something to say but could not work out how to say it. It was worse this time. She knew it was something serious, and she sat wracking her brain wondering what it was that she had done. Try as she might, nothing sprang to mind.

This time she had not been suspended from school.

This time she had not run away from home for three days leaving them frantic with worry.

This time she had not crashed the car.

Today was her twenty-first birthday.

It was supposed to be a happy occasion, a time for joy and celebration. So why did her parents look as though someone had died? Impatiently, Kate drummed her fingers on the table. The sound echoed around the room. Her father looked up, startled, like an animal caught in glaring headlights. Taking hold of his wife's hand, Brian Fisher slowly cleared his throat.

"Um, well, firstly happy birthday, Kate."

He pushed an envelope across the table and she smiled. She picked it up and tore at the paper. *You're 21!* screamed the card's lurid colours. She opened it and read the simple statement within: *All our love mum and dad.* No money, no cheque and, by the looks of it, she realised as her eyes quickly scoured the room, no other present either. She felt deflated; it looked like she really had done something grave this time.

"Thanks," she uttered, not feeling thankful at all.

"Right. Well," her father continued, "We have this, too."

Uncomfortably, he pushed a brown envelope across the table towards her. As she went to lift it, he slammed his palm on top of it. Shocked, Kate sat back. What on earth was going on? Her mother looked like she was about to burst into tears, and her father had never been so on edge.

Was it bad news? Oh god, were they dying or something?

That was it! They were dying!

Tightness gripped her chest and her palms became sweaty.

"Dad. You're scaring me. What's going on?"

He buried his head in his hands, not knowing where to start. It was her mother who finally took the reins.

"The envelope is yours, Kate. But you can't open it until we've explained everything to you. It's so hard and we didn't want to do this today, but we have to. We have no choice."

Her father raised his head to look at his daughter. Pulling himself together, he continued on behalf of his wife.

"There's no easy way to say this Kate, so I'll just come out with it: you're adopted."

They're not dying! Thank goodness for that! Kate breathed a huge sigh of relief.

Wait a minute. What did they say? Adopted? What?

Quizzically, she looked back and forth from one parent to the other. Had she heard them correctly? She pinched herself on the arm, daring herself to wake up, but she knew from the pain that she was already awake and that the unfolding nightmare was real.

"Did you just say that I'm adopted?" she squeaked. Time slowed and she struggled to breathe. This could not be happening. It was so unfair. It was supposed to be a happy day. It was her birthday! Why were they doing this to her today?

"Yes," her father said apologetically.

Kate let out a long, deep breath, turning the news over in her head. This explained so much. The reason why she loved her parents but had never felt close to them. Why she looked nothing like them and acted so very differently, so much so that it was as though she were from a different planet. Why Granny Fisher had always been really odd with her and referred to her as *that* child. To be honest, Granny Fisher had hated everyone, but she had always been particularly venomous towards Kate.

It all made perfect sense now.

"I'm adopted?" she asked again with a trembling voice.

"Yes," her father repeated.

"Adopted." The room swam slightly and she gripped the table for support. Seeing her daughter's distress, Margaret Fisher reached across the table and took Kate's hands in her own.

"We don't love you any less, Kate. We are, and always will be, your parents, but when we got you, the first decision we made was to tell you about where you came from. We decided that twenty-one was a good age. You have a right to know. What you choose to do with that information is up to you. The contents of this envelope may help a little more."

Kate was completely dumbfounded. She stared blindly at the plain brown envelope. Her heart was thudding and she did not know what to do. She had two choices. Tell her parents that it did not matter, she was not interested and she loved them. Or, open the envelope and find out who she really was. Confused, she looked up at her parents.

Her adoptive parents.

Adoptive parents.

It hung heavily in the air around her,

weighing down upon her. She was not theirs. She did not belong. She was alone. A rush of anger, hurt and disappointment washed over her like a swollen river bursting its banks.

"I'm sorry. I can't do this."

Standing, she knocked over her chair and bolted from the room. Moments later the front door banged and Brian and Margaret watched as their only daughter ran down the front path and away from the house as fast as her legs would carry her.

~

Kate ran. Ran, and ran, and ran, pounding her legs on the harsh and unforgiving ground, putting as much distance as she could between her and the house. The streets of Newquay were still fairly quiet, and she passed very few people. If anyone saw her, they would assume she was just another early morning jogger.

Her rhythm became steady, her breathing deep. Her muscles screamed with pain, but she kept on running, taking her frustration out on the pavement beneath her. With each step, she heard her brain repeat the same word over and over.

Adopted. Adopted. Adopted.

She tried to banish the words but they refused to disappear, and instead continued to taunt her with every step. She navigated the town's winding streets, eventually finding herself up on the rough grass-covered and rabbit-holed clifftop heading to the one place she loved the most: Fistral Beach.

Keeping an eye on the lone surfer as he expertly rode the frothing waves, Kate thudded down the steps onto the slipway. She felt the ground change as sand flew from beneath her feet. Her momentum continued as she ran past the International Surfing Complex and along the wide arcing beach. The stitch that had nagged in her side for the last few minutes finally became so painful that she had no choice but to stop.

Standing on the vast shore, she gasped and panted for breath, her lungs aching from the harsh punishment. Sweat ran down her face, mingling with tears. She had not realised that she had been crying. Finally, getting her breath back, she glanced around her and took in the beautiful English seaside town she called home. The long, wide sweep of soft sand, the deep blue pounding waves of the Atlantic Ocean, the stately looking red brick of the Headland Hotel that sat upon the cliffs. The town, the place she had been born. She loved it all. But had she actually been born here? That one statement from her parents turned her world, the world as she knew it, upside down. Was her life really what she thought it was? Or had it all been an elaborate lie?

Settling herself onto the sand, she crossed her legs and sat staring out across the choppy sea, watching the lone surfer, waiting for him to come to her.

Her poor parents; she should not have run out on them like that. They must be worried sick. She felt so sorry for them. They were always so protective of her and now she knew why. It must have been dreadful for them, to have adopted her, brought her up as their own, only to tell her twenty-one years later that she was not really theirs. She had to admit that they had their faults, but despite those faults she loved them very much. She would never intentionally do anything to hurt them, and yet she found herself wondering who her real parents were.

What had caused them to give her up? Where did they live? What did they do for a living? Did they ever think about her and wonder how she had grown? There were so many questions that began to fly unheeded about her head, threatening to overwhelm her and she had no idea how to answer any of them. She had decisions to make but she did not know if she was strong enough.

"Katie!"

She looked up to finally see him: her best friend Fletcher Donovan running towards her. He was glistening with dewy drops of water. Small crystals of salt had already begun to cling to his drying skin. The surfboard slung under his arm was thrown to one side as he lifted Kate in one swift movement. He swung her around, making her feel as though she were on a merry-go-round and she instinctively threw her arms out to the side, enjoying the motion. Moments later they crumpled to the sand, giggling, and Fletch planted a kiss on her cheek.

"Happy birthday, bestie!"

She could not help but laugh. He always brought out the best in her, always made her feel better, and was such a fun person to be around. They sat back on the sand staring out at the tumbling waves.

"So why is the birthday girl sitting alone on the beach?" Fletch could see she had been crying. Something was wrong, and it concerned him.

She looked up at him, taking in his messy blonde hair and brilliant blue eyes, and the hemp pendant she had given him a few years ago, that still hung around his neck. He had been her best friend since childhood, the person who had always stood by her and been there for her.

"Come on, Katie. If you can't tell me, then who can you tell?"

She sighed. He was right of course. She had to tell someone, and maybe he could help her decide what to do?

"I'm adopted," she said, looking up at him. Immediately she saw it. That look. What was it, shock, confusion, fear? She could not quite place it. Was that what her parents had seen in her? Oh god, she hoped not.

For once, Fletch seemed lost for words, but finally after an awkward silence, he managed to speak.

"You're what?"

Sighing, Kate explained everything.

"And now you're here, alone on the beach, licking your wounds while your mum and dad pace up and down with worry."

"Something like that," she groaned. She knew she'd handled it badly, but what was she supposed to have done? Hug them and thank them for such an amazing birthday present?

"Come on. I'm coming back with you. We can talk to them together," he ordered.

"But..."

"No buts!"

Fletch dragged Kate up off the sand and marched her back up the beach to the International Surfing Complex, where he hurriedly changed before taking her home to face her parents.

~

Fletch was right. The Fishers had indeed been frantically pacing, going out of their minds with worry. Kate was often unpredictable but they knew this time it would not be so easy to sort things out. Relief washed over them as they heard the front door bang. Kate, followed closely by Fletch, entered the dining room and sat at the table, opposite her parents.

"Good morning, Fletcher. Cup of tea?" Without even waiting for a response, Margaret Fisher had already begun to pour from the brown teapot sitting at the centre of the table. She poured a second one for her daughter and pushed it towards her with a weak smile.

Kate caught her mother's hand.

"I'm so sorry, Mum. I shouldn't have run out like that."

The mood lightened in an instant.

"It's alright. We understand. It must have been a huge shock," Margaret said.

"It was." Kate noticed that the brown envelope was now on the side, and she pointed to it, "I don't know what I want to do about the envelope yet. But I'd like to hear your story, if that's okay?"

Her parents looked at each other, and her mother nodded.

"I'll leave you to it," Fletch said.

"No," Kate cried and grabbed his arm. She needed the support. She needed him here. "I want you to stay, if that's okay with Mum and Dad?"

Her parents nodded. They liked Fletcher. He was a sensible boy, and there were far worse people their daughter could have chosen for a friend. They were glad she decided to run to him. As she drank her tea, Margaret began her tale.

"Your father and I had been married for three years. For those three long years we'd been trying to have a child, but sadly none came. We didn't know what to do. I was afraid it was me, your father was afraid it was him. But neither of us spoke about it. We became grumpy and distant with each other, until one day, unable to put up with either of us anymore, Aunt Cheryl sat us down and demanded we talk to each other. She wouldn't let us leave the room until it had all spilled out," Margaret paused to drink some tea.

"Once we'd learned why we were both so unhappy, we set about getting help. We were lucky, since Aunt Cheryl was married to a doctor and he put us in touch with the right people. Even though the process was long and drawn out, we eventually got accepted and, not long after, you came into our life. We were so happy. Our little bundle of joy." Margaret looked up, tears filling her eyes. "Even though you were adopted, it never felt like you were someone else's. The moment we saw you, we fell deeply in love with you. Our beautiful little Kate. Our daughter. We loved you so much. We always will."

Kate blossomed with love. She had never heard her mother talk like this before and it touched her deeply. She rushed around the table and hugged her mother, rocking her gently as Margaret sobbed in her daughter's arms. It hurt Kate to see her parents go through this. They were so brave telling her, when they could have just kept it to themselves, but they had chosen to be honest with her and that counted for a lot.

"I love you too, Mum. I love both of you. I always will." She smiled up at her father and placed a hand on his to show him how much she cared. He smiled back at her, eyes filled with pure unconditional love, and it melted her heart.

"I don't understand why you told me, though. If that's how you feel, why didn't you just keep quiet?" Kate asked, sitting back down.

Brian explained, "It was the right thing to do. Like your mother said, we love you, and you will always be our daughter. But we felt you had the right to know who you are and where you came from. We don't have all of the answers but we do have some."

Kate turned to look at the envelope. She did not know what she wanted to do. She looked at Fletch and searched his face for an answer, but none came.

"It's your choice, Katie. Only you can decide. Not me, not your mum or your dad, just you."

She knew he was right. She looked around the table, and then at the envelope again. She already knew what the answer would be. Her parents had done so much for her, and they had always loved her without fault. She did not need to hear about her past. Brian and Margaret may be adoptive parents, but they had loved and cared for her, put food on the table and clothes on her back, put up with all of her childish misdemeanors and that was all she needed to know.

"It changes nothing. I'm Kate Fisher. My birth mother abandoned me a long time ago," she said as she looked up at her parents, realising for the first time what they meant to her, and what sacrifices they had made in their lives for her. "I love you both very much and you are, and always will be, my parents."

Tears fell and Kate stood and walked around the table to where her parents sat. Leaning forward, Kate held them tightly, clinging onto them for dear life, not wanting to ever let them go. They were her parents and that was all that mattered.

As Margaret held her daughter, stroking her hair lightly with her hand, she felt relief wash through her. They thought they were going to lose the thing that was most precious to them, but they had not. Their daughter still loved them and was not going anywhere. They knew telling her would be a big risk, but they had wanted to do what was right, and it was right that Kate was given an opportunity to know about her past.

"We love you too, Kate, before, now and always."

Fletch silently crept from the room to make another pot of tea, allowing them to be family once more. In the hallway he removed a small present from his pocket, and placed it on the table by the front door. It was a dolphin pendant that Kate had seen in the window of her favourite shop months earlier. He knew that she would love it. He then walked into the kitchen to boil the kettle. *What a shock to get on your birthday*, he thought as he stared out of the window. He could not even begin to imagine what kind of turmoil Kate was going through.

Maybe today was not the day to tell her he was in love with her after all.

CHAPTER FIVE

Cornwall, England, 1991

Kate slammed the door behind her, and threw her coat and bag over the stair banister. It had been a long day, and work was always tiring. Good, but tiring. She worked at the local Tourist Information Office. It was a varied job and she enjoyed meeting new people and being part of the tourist industry. She thought it was much better than working in a supermarket or the local chip shop. Her parents had been very proud when she announced two years earlier that she had gotten a job there. Many teenagers struggled to find work, but Kate had plugged away, applying for job after job, finally succeeding. The pay was not great, but she enjoyed it and it had prospects and that was all that mattered.

She could hear her mum clattering around in the kitchen, and her father laughing at something on TV in the living room and it made her smile. It was just how it should be. Things were finally back to normal.

In the end, she had managed to have a good birthday. The four of them had spent the rest of the day at Holywell Bay, and Kate had realised during that afternoon that she could not imagine her life without her parents. She had been really lucky being placed with such a lovely couple. Family was not about who gave birth to you, it was about who brought you up, who looked after you, who saw you through the scrapes and she had to admit that she would not change them for anyone. They were her mum and dad and always would be.

She stepped into the living room and placed an arm around her dad's shoulder, hugging him lightly. Walking back into the kitchen, she kissed her mum's cheek before sitting at the table. Her mother shouted for her father as she put dinner on the table and, once they were seated, they began to eat. Absentmindedly, Kate shuffled through the day's delivery of post: a bank statement, a magazine and a card addressed to her. The card intrigued her and she ripped at the envelope. What looked to be a belated birthday card fell on to the table. It was old and printed on strange raised paper, unlike anything she had seen in the shops. Inside was an old banking passbook.

Curiosity peaking, she opened the card and began to read.

My dearest Katerina,

Happy Birthday!

You are now twenty-one and you have your whole life ahead of you, and I am truly grateful to your parents, Brian and Margaret Fisher, for that. They are such nice people. I like them a lot and I know they will look after you and raise you well.

I hope that by now they have told you about your adoption. I asked them not to tell you until you were a little older, the only thing I asked of them was that they keep your name, Katerina. So I hope this card will not come as too much of a shock. You probably have so many questions and I am sorry but I am unable to answer them all. You see, I am very ill and I only have a little time left. The doctors tell me there is nothing more they can do for me. I am losing the will to fight and no longer have the strength left to eat, move or speak, it has been hard just to write this card.

There is so much I wish I could tell you, but time is escaping. I can tell you that we are of Greek descent, but sadly, I know nothing about our family. I too was adopted. You have to understand that the war did terrible things to people and it changed lives forever.

This card contains a bank passbook, it is all

the savings I have, it was part of the divorce settlement with your father. It is now yours, but there is one condition attached.

You must find out everything you can about our family, who we are and where we came from. All I know is that my mother's name was Elena and she lived on one of the Ionian Islands. Please Katerina, it is my dying wish. Make things right for our family.

I love you very much and will always carry you close to my heart.

Your loving mother,

Athena

"Bloody hell!" Kate muttered.

"Language, Kate!" her mother said sternly. She caught the look on her daughter's face and felt the fear ripple through her body.

"What is it?"

Kate refused to hide it from her parents and passed them the card. The room fell silent and still. It was an age before anyone spoke.

Eventually Kate sighed. "What on earth am I supposed to do? How am I supposed to find out about something with little or no information to go on?"

Her parents looked at each other and shrugged. They had no idea how to handle this.

Finally her father spoke. "It's up to you Kate, and whatever you choose, we'll support you."

Kate scanned the card again, and felt the hurt and anger surge through her. How could this woman just abandon her at birth, die a few years later and then get someone to send her a birthday card telling her what to do! Who did she think she was? Kate wanted to just throw it in the bin and forget about it, but how could she when the words *'It is my dying wish'* jumped out at her and pulled at her. She was confused and it made her angry that this woman was now trying to dictate her life from the grave.

"Where the hell are these Ionian Islands anyway?"

"I think they're off mainland Greece," her father replied factually.

"Well I couldn't go, even if I wanted to," she said stubbornly with an air of finality to her voice. "I can't get time off work."

Brian and Margaret knew that was an end to it. Once Kate made up her mind, there was little chance of persuading her otherwise. They said no more and turned their attention back to dinner.

Kate leaned over and opened the kitchen bin behind her. She dropped the card and passbook in it. *Let it end up in a landfill*, she thought. She had had enough and no longer cared. Her birth mother was selfish and had no right to tell her what to do.

Enough was enough.

~

Kate snuck out of the house just as dawn was creeping over the horizon. As she reached the beach she stopped, searching the crashing ocean waves. The previous night had been fractious, plagued with nightmares, making her wake suddenly in sweat drenched sheets that twisted around her, tying her in knots. She kept thinking about the card and what it meant. In the depth of night, she suddenly remembered that her birth mother had called her Katerina. She thought it over. Her parents had always just called her Kate. Katerina sounded very foreign.

At three am she had crept downstairs to the kitchen and lifted the bin lid, but it was empty. Her mother had already taken out the rubbish and the bins were out on the pavement for the Council to empty the following morning. There was no way she was going to start rummaging in dustbins in the dead of night. Resigned, she had tried to go back to sleep but just tossed and turned. Eventually she was stirred by the crashing and banging of the bin-men as their household rubbish and her birthday card disappeared into the back of a rubbish truck, lost to her forever. Feeling annoyed, she decided to head to the beach to see Fletch.

A surfer suddenly appeared from the foaming chaos, bringing her back to the present. His board flipped expertly along a wave, making it look like the easiest thing in the world, before it finally got the better of him and he wiped out. Running onto the sand, Kate headed towards the rough, surging waters, waving wildly to catch Fletch's attention. Moments later, he had left the sea and was walking up the beach towards her.

"You're up early. Coming out to catch some waves?"

"No, you know I hate all that," she laughed, as she sat on the sand.

"So what brings you down here then?" he asked, as he sat next to her, flicking water from his hair in the same manner a dog would after swimming in a river.

"She sent me a card."

"Who did?"

"My birth mother."

"She did?"

"Yes. She's dead. She died not long after I was born. But she instructed a solicitor to send the card on her behalf. Oh Fletch. I have no idea what to do. She told me she wants me to go and look for my real family because she never knew them. She even said the words *it's my dying wish.* I thought it was all over."

"So what are you going to do?"

"I have no idea." Kate looked out across the ocean, while waves rolled and crashed, never ceasing. Like life, they continued on around them, moving forward, never stopping.

"You have to do what feels right for you,

Katie. No one can tell you otherwise. Don't let pleas from some dead woman you never met force your hand. If she cared that much, she would have handled things differently, but she didn't. It sounds like she was trying to lessen her own guilt, without any thought for you."

"That's a bit harsh, Fletch."

"Is it? We've been friends for a long time, Katie, and I care for you a great deal. More than you will ever know. I hate the turmoil you went through when your parents told you about the adoption. I hated seeing you hurt."

"I know. But what if I do have family out there? Shouldn't I find them?"

Fletch was angry. He liked Brian and Margaret very much but wished that they had just kept their secret to themselves or told Kate when she was little, so that she could have dealt with it better. He could understand why they had wanted to tell Kate, but he hated seeing the girl he loved as a shadow of her former self. She pretended she was okay with it all, but he knew it was hurting her deeply and that she was still struggling to come to terms with it. There were dark circles under her eyes, a sure sign that she had not been sleeping well. The news that she had received a birthday card demanding she do a dead woman's bidding just made him even more furious. Who the hell did the woman think she was? Dead or not, it was totally unfair. He could not bear to see her like this.

"We've been over this so many times, Katie. I can't tell you what to do. You have to work this out for yourself. I care about you, I really do, but we can't keep having the same conversation over and over again. It's beginning to do my head in," he said with exasperation. "Whenever you have a problem you always run to me expecting me to fix it for you, and I can't keep doing it. You have to figure this one out for yourself." He stood, grabbed his board and raced back into the waves.

"Fletch!" Kate shouted. But he ignored her, disappearing into the tumble and froth. She sat there for ages in the hope he would cool off and come back, but he did not. Eventually she stood and ambled back up the beach.

She felt let down.

She felt confused.

She felt angry.

She felt sad.

If this was how Fletch reacted, then there was no hope. No hope at all.

CHAPTER SIX

Zakynthos, Greece, 1939

It was early spring. The cooler winter temperatures began to give way to warmer weather, flowers were blooming and trees were blossoming. Scudding clouds had changed from a dirty grey mass to fluffy white cotton buds. Islanders loved spring. It was a season of possibilities, summer was on its way and anything could happen.

Angelos found Elena sitting on the beach, staring out across the hazy sea. She had a faraway look in her eyes and her face was a mask of anxiety. It was not something he had seen in her before and it concerned him. He sat next to her, smiling, but her frown remained.

"Elena?"

She smiled, but the light never reached her eyes, as they remained focused on a point far out to sea that was only visible to her. His concern only grew. Lifting her hand, he cradled it in his, trying to grab her attention.

"What is it, Elena? Are you ill? Has someone hurt you?"

"No."

"Then what is it?"

She sighed and turned to look at him, "What do you think of the war they are predicting, Angelos? Do you think it will affect our tiny island?" He had learned long ago that Elena was always this blunt, and she believed in being straight with both her questions and answers.

"I do not know."

Angelos cared little for life off of the island. They were so far removed from the rest of the world on their little haven of paradise that world events did not matter. His father had mentioned something about the uneasy politics of the new German leader but Angelos had not really listened.

"I hope not. I love this island and its people. They mean a lot to me, and I could not bear it if we were invaded," Elena said.

"Are they going to? Surely they learned from the Great War?" Angelos was confused. Was the world really about to go to war or was Elena being dramatic?

"There is a man called Hitler. They say he is to be feared. He spouts rhetoric and creates a lot of unease. I heard he has been in prison and yet the people of Germany have chosen him to lead them. Why would they do that? What kind of politics is this?" Elena's face clouded again and Angelos caught a glimpse of something, a fleeting fear. Moments later it was gone and her smile returned, her eyes glinting with merriment. It worried him how she was able to hide everything away as if it had not happened.

"Come, we will go for a walk."

They walked up the lane, watching the birds dip and weave as they chased insects.

"I am glad spring is here again. I love seeing the sun shining, the birds flying, the flowers and trees growing," Elena sighed. She looked utterly content, unlike the Elena he had found on the beach earlier. It amazed Angelos how quickly she could change.

"Me too, although summer means more hard work for me. Father is extending the groves and needs my help."

"Is that what you will do with the rest of your life, Angelos? Obey your father and live your life the way he dictates?"

"Elena! Must you be so blunt?"

"What?"

"I know you dislike my father, but he is a well-respected man, and he expects his son to follow in his footsteps. I do not know what I want to do with my life yet. What is the harm in helping him and learning the family trade?"

"Nothing, if you are happy to be his slave for the rest of your life."

"I am not his slave!"

"Yes, Angelos, you are. When was the last time you said no to him? When was the last time you refused to work for him? When was the last time you were brave enough to tell him about your friendship with me?"

"I hate it when you are like this."

"Like what? Honest?" Elena crossed her arms in defiance. "I am sorry if my honesty makes your relationship with your father difficult! Touvlo!"

"Did you just call me an idiot?" Angelos asked, glaring at her. She really was impossible sometimes.

"You know I did. So why do you ask?"

"I am not going to be insulted, Elena, not even by you." He walked away from her seething with anger. Why was it that his father always brought out the worst in them? As he walked along the lane, he heard a small whistle from behind. A familiar tune. He ignored it. Continuing on, the whistle stayed with him and eventually turned into a lilting song. He stopped and sighed. He loved her too much to stay angry with her. He turned just in time to feel her arms wrap around him in a tight embrace. He hugged her back, holding her to him and not wanting to ever let her go.

"Go on. Say it."

"Say what?" he asked.

"I am an idiot."

"I would never call you that."

"No?"

"No. Never, but can we just agree not to talk about my father again, Elena? Things with my father are difficult enough, without him coming between us as well."

She smiled and stood on tiptoe to kiss his cheek. "I promise. What shall we do now?"

"Beach?"

"Yes!"

Hand in hand, they ran along the lane, the argument behind them and best of friends again.

~

Elena skipped through the streets of Macherado, a small village in the southern part of the island. Her hair was tied back with ribbons and she was wearing her best dress, a heavenly vision in green and brown. Her feet were still bare and dusty, but it did not matter to her. It made her feel comfortable, and she no longer cared what others thought. The day was a beautiful bright sunny one and Macherado was holding the Festival of Agia Mavra, an important religious ceremony followed by a banquet and traditional dancing in the village square.

The village was already filled to the brim and Elena wound her way through the throng of people in search of Angelos. She hoped he would be there, she had not seen him for ages. His father always kept him so busy. Despite promising not to talk about it with him again after their argument, Elena had to admit that Loukas Sarkis made her angry. He treated Angelos badly. She had seen the bruises Angelos had suffered at the hands of his father, although she never discussed it with him and she hated Loukas for it. She wished there were something she could do, but she was just a woman, and too weak to stop a man like Loukas.

Despite searching, she could not find Angelos anywhere and she was left feeling disappointed. Sitting on the wall overlooking the town square, she watched as the locals milled around taking in the events of the day. She had missed the religious ceremony but had really come for the banquet and dancing anyway. She loved the dancing; she liked watching the men move in their traditional ways, their faces serious, their bodies tall and straight. She wished she could be like the women as they twirled and whirled, matching the men as much with their beauty as anything else. It was as if they had been left with no choice but to dance. She wanted so much to join in, but she could not. She was wary of Loukas seeing her, and perhaps keeping her away from Angelos, so she remained where she was, staring in awe.

Suddenly, she caught sight of Angelos's father across the square. He was standing next to a shy looking woman, who had the same facial traits as Angelos. His mother? She searched for Angelos, but the dancers kept getting in the way and she could not see if he was with them. Suddenly a pair of hands cupped her eyes, and everything went dark.

"Yassou! Guess who it is?!" a deep voice teased.

Gently releasing the hands from her face, she spun round. "Angelos! I have been looking everywhere for you! Where have you been?"

"I know. I am sorry. I had to try and escape my father. You know he watches me like a hawk. Come, let us get away from here."

"Really?"

"Really."

Reaching out, Angelos caught her in his arms as she slid off the wall. Their eyes fleetingly met, and time stood still for the briefest of moments, but it was over in an instant. Releasing her, he took her hand and led her through the mass of people and into the quiet back streets. It was not long before they were sitting under a tree on the outskirts of Macherado, listening to the sound of the festival as it carried on the passing breeze. A pair of butterflies danced in the sunlight, lost in their own world, while cicadas chattered in the long grass and ants scurried along the path. The weather was hot and the sky was clear and bright.

"I saw your father and mother," Elena said, playing with blades of grass, pulling them from the ground allowing the breeze to carry them away.

"They always come to the festival. I did not want to, but I have not seen you for ages. I hoped you would be here."

"Your father does not like me, does he?"

Angelos was silent for a moment. He did not want to have another argument with her about his father, but he had learned honesty was always the best policy with Elena.

"No. I am sorry, he does not. But if it makes you feel any better, my father dislikes many people."

"Well if that is how he feels, then there is nothing I can do about it is there?"

Angelos laughed at the defiance on her face. She threw a handful of grass at him in protest, before changing the subject.

"Do you think the world will end up at war, Angelos? I worry that it will."

"Why do you worry so much about it?"

"I do not know. I just cannot stop thinking about it. The world should be peaceful, Angelos. We should be able to live side by side, we should all get on, no one should dictate to others the way that man Hitler or your father do!" The anger within her bubbled and rose to the surface, and continued to seethe.

Angelos had never seen her this angry before, and it shocked him. “You are comparing my father to Hitler?!”

“Why not? They both bully people and try to force them to do what they want.”

“I know my father has his faults but it is not fair to talk about him like that, Elena!” It was the same argument all over again and it hurt him deeply. Angelos was the first to admit that he did not get on with his father and that he hated the way Loukas treated him and his mother, but to compare him to a man like Hitler? That was low, even for Elena.

She caught the look on his face and realised she had gone too far. She reached out and lifted his hand to touch her cheek. “Oh, Angelos. I am so sorry. I do not think. I speak without using my brain, sometimes with no regard for others and I should not have said that. He is still your father. It was unfair of me.”

Angelos’s heart melted. Just the feel of her delicate cheek on his fingers chased the hurt and anger away. He could never stay mad at her.

“It is okay. I forgive you.”

“Good.”

They were silent for a moment, while Elena picked at the grass and Angelos stared out across the lush landscape.

“The flowers are beautiful this year, those are my favourite,” Elena said pointing to a nearby bush of pretty fragrant star-shaped flowers called bougarinia.

"They are?"

She nodded, and Angelos grinned. "Well, if they are your favourite, then you shall have them."

He stood and gathered great handfuls of them. Then, sitting opposite, he began to separate them and work delicately with his hands.

"What are you doing?"

"It is a surprise. Wait and see."

Intrigued, Elena watched as he carefully split the stems, before connecting each flower to the other in a long chain. Leaning forward, he placed the circle of flowers over her head, letting them hang against her chest.

"A flower necklace! Angelos you are so clever! It is the best present I have ever received."

Leaning forward, she kissed him lightly on the cheek, making him blush. Music still wafted on the air, so she jumped to her feet and held out her hand. "I like this song they are playing. Dance with me."

Without hesitation, he stood and took her hand in his, pulling her to him, careful not to crush the delicate flowers. It was the first time he had ever held a woman so close. He could smell her hair and feel her cheek against his and desire rippled through him. As delicate hues of pink and orange began to colour the horizon, bringing with it the close of another day, Angelos and Elena shared their first dance.

~

Angelos sat under the veranda in his parents' garden. He felt uncomfortable, but his father had insisted he be there. Loukas Sarkis was entertaining town officials and other business owners. A large long table was laid out with food and drink and they were all laughing merrily. The ouzo was free flowing and Angelos watched as Loukas showed off like a prize bull. He realised in that moment how much he despised his father. How had he ever come from this man? He was nothing like him at all. And his mother? Glancing over at Pigi, he was just as embarrassed. She was sitting in a corner, twisting her hands together, her mouth twitching. Every time Loukas poured himself another glass of ouzo, she twitched a little more. Angelos wished she would learn to stand up to him a little more instead of being the doormat she was, but it was too late now. She would never change.

Angelos wanted to get away and find Elena. It had been over a week since he last saw her and a month since that glorious night dancing at the Agia Mavra Festival in Macherado. Whenever he saw her now, he wanted to kiss her. He wanted to marry her and spend the rest of his life with her, but he knew that it would never happen while Loukas still lived.

"Angelos. Do you hear me, boy?"

Loukas's voice shattered his thoughts, and he turned his attention to his father.

"Yes, Father?"

"More ouzo!"

"Yes, Father."

He stepped inside to find the bottles his father had saved up for special occasions. Returning to the veranda, he plonked them on the table and sat back down. He hoped the meal would end soon, but it seemed they were all going to drink themselves into a stupor.

"You have a good son, Loukas," Stelios Makris said, while topping up his glass. As a town official, Stelios kept very close company with Loukas. It was a favourable relationship all around.

"He is okay, but he disobeys me too much, Stelios," Loukas spat.

Angelos felt uncomfortable; he hated being spoken about as if he were not there.

"You should not disobey your father, Angelos. He is the person that feeds and clothes you. You would be nothing without him," Stelios slurred, and pointed his sloshing glass at Angelos as if trying to push his point home. "What is it you do to disobey him so?"

"He runs about with that Petrakis yeeftisa!" Loukas growled.

"Ah, the mountain gypsy! I hear she wears no

shoes and has sex with farm labourers on the beach. You should choose your friends better, Angelos. You could catch something nasty." Stelios laughed at his own joke and the other men fell about patting him on the back.

Angelos felt his blood boil. He hated hearing the woman he loved being talked about in such a disrespectful manner. They had no respect for anything other than titles, money and ouzo.

"She is not a gypsy!" he shouted. "You know nothing about her!"

"Hold your tongue, son, we have guests!" Loukas barked. The boy was asking for twenty lashes if he carried on like this.

Angelos knew it was futile. It did not matter what he said, they would still have the same opinions and continue to talk about her as if she were a mangy dog on the street. He lowered his gaze, and stared into his glass, wishing he were anywhere but home.

He felt Stelios's arm about his shoulder, a stench of ouzo wafted around him. "It is okay, Angelos. I understand a boy's urges, but what you need is a nice girl. My Maria needs a nice man. How about it, Loukas? They would make a good match," he suggested with a laugh.

Loukas allowed the information to sink in. It was not a bad thought. Maria Makris was a quiet girl, plain looking and not very bright, but she would make a good wife for his son and get him away from that Petrakis girl once and for all.

"Maybe, Stelios. Maybe." Then changing the subject, Loukas said, "Now gentlemen, shall we talk business?"

Angelos sat in stony silence and let his mind wander, drowning out the incessant crowing of the men, allowing only thoughts of Elena to enter it.

~

The following evening, Angelos crept down to the beach, desperate to see Elena, he could not get the harsh words Stelios had uttered about her out of his head. The shadows of day's end continued to lengthen as he crept through the lanes. Then he saw her. She was lying on her back by the shore, singing sweetly. Quietly, he crept closer hoping to surprise her but she sat bolt upright, looking left and right.

"You are getting more and more like a cat every day!" he laughed.

Springing to her feet, she ran to him and jumped into his arms, her limbs snakelike about his neck, her legs clamped about his waist. As he put her down, she took his hand and pulled him to sit next to her on the sand.

"I have missed you, Angelos. It has been too long." She smiled at him but realised that something was wrong. "What is it?"

"My father had a business meeting yesterday. Stelios Makris was there. He said some horrible things about you."

"Ignore him. He is a pig!" she spat.

"I know, but there was one thing he said Elena. I am sorry but I have to ask you."

She pushed back and stared at him. "What? Come on, out with it."

"He called you names and said that you sleep with farm labourers on the beach every night and that you are diseased." Angelos was ashamed. He felt awful for talking about it, but he loved her too much. He needed to know if there was any truth in what Stelios said. He refused to share her with anyone.

"That pig! Let me go there right now and tell him who is the diseased one!" She was on her feet in an instant and Angelos had to stop her from marching off in fury.

"Talk to me, Elena. Why would he say such a thing?"

"Stelios Makris gets bored with his wife and likes to have sex with anyone who will give it to him! He tried it with me last year and I told him to leave me alone. Ever since, he has spread vicious rumours about me." Elena sank dejectedly to the ground and sighed, her heart heavy. "Just because I come from a poor family living in the mountains, people think they can treat me and the rest of my family badly. They think we are all there for their amusement, to do their bidding. I hate it, Angelos. I am a person with feelings just like them. I may not have money or breeding but I have a right to be treated fairly and they treat me like dirt! I promise you, Angelos, I have never done that with anyone and I am certainly not diseased. You do believe me, do you not?"

Angelos saw the tears as they clouded her eyes, and the rawness of her breath catching in her throat told him all he needed to know. She was his and no one else's, and everything Stelios had said was a lie.

"Come here," he said softly, holding out his hand to her. She took it and they sank to the sand draped in each others arms. "Do not let them get to you. I am here for you and always will be. Friends forever, Elena?"

"Friends forever, Angelos."

CHAPTER SEVEN

Zakynthos, Greece, 1939

Elena ran from her house, kicking up dust as she wound through the mountain roads, desperate to find Angelos. Her heart was thumping, not from the exercise, but from pure terror. Eventually she located him in one of the groves, he was alone, the only one left working. Fear was etched in her eyes, and she was breathless from the long run.

"Angelos! It has happened! Hitler has invaded Poland! We are going to lose our island!" She was beside herself, so he stopped work and pulled her to him, hugging her tightly. He could not bear to see her like this. She was normally such a happy soul, despite her fiery temper.

"Shush, my love, all will be well." He tried

his best to reassure her. “They will not make the same mistakes as they did in the Great War. It will all be over in a month.”

“I hope you are right, Angelos. But I fear Hitler so much. He has an evil face. I worry that he will crush us with his might and rule over us for all eternity. I just could not bear it.” She wept and Angelos had no idea why it affected her so much. They were all scared, they were all worried. The impending war that had seemed so far away and unthreatening suddenly became very real, and it cut through to Elena’s very soul and petrified her.

Angelos continued to hold her tightly and it was then that he finally spoke of his true feelings for her. The threat of war heightened everything. It made life more real, more urgent.

“Oh, Elena. I care so much about you, my little one. I wish you would learn not to carry the burden of the world upon your shoulders.”

“I cannot help it Angelos. At least I know the world is a better place with you as my friend.”

“I am always here for you. You know that.”

“I know.”

They were silent for a moment, and then Angelos spoke, his words unheeded.

“I am in love with you, Elena Petrakis.”

Surprise washed over her and she gazed into his brown eyes, which were surrounded by long dark lashes that matched his hair colour. He spoke words that she had hoped to hear for so long but thought would never come. Even though she heard him say them out loud, she still could not believe it.

"You love me?" It came out as barely a whisper.

"With all my heart. I have done since the first day I met you. I have wanted to tell you so many times, but I never knew how. It is such a difficult situation. My family would not approve and if we ever wanted to be together, life would be even more difficult than it is now, but I cannot deny my heart Elena. It yearns for you every single day. I feel lost without you, and I miss you when you are not around. I want to love you so much that I fear my heart will break."

"Angelos. My beautiful Angelos. I love you too, so very much, but we both know I am the wrong girl for you. Your father does not approve. It would never work. We would both end up brokenhearted."

"It is a chance I am willing to take. I cannot live a lie any longer."

Elena pulled away from him and leaned back against a tree, studying him carefully. She really did love him, but she knew they could never truly be together. She did not want to lose her heart to him only to have it broken a few months later. As brave as she was, she was frightened to death of Loukas Sarkis. She knew how vicious he was and how he would react if he learned about the two of them being together. It was impossible. Her heart was screaming at her to love Angelos back but her head was telling her to pick up her feet, run and never look back, to forget about him and begin again. She did not know what to do.

Angelos took the choice away from her. Stepping towards her, he took her hands in his, and stared intensely at her, trying to fathom what was going on inside her head. Feeling his hands around hers grounded her, made her feel at ease.

"What are you thinking, my love?"

"That however much we love each other, there is too much that could break us apart."

"It is true, but I have come too far, Elena. I cannot lose you now."

Angelos was so close now that Elena could feel his warm breath on her neck. In the sky above them, hues of pinks and oranges had given way to the falling inky blackness of night and stars were appearing in the heavens above. Angelos gently ran his fingers up and down her arms, his touch making her shiver with excitement. Leaning in, he kissed her neck, little butterfly kisses that moved to her throat and then finally, to her lips. Unable to resist, she threw her arms around him and allowed him to kiss her, strong urgent kisses that left her reeling and begging for more.

Angelos could not remember how it happened, but it was not long before they were lying under the canopy of a spreading olive tree, with their hands entwined. Elena's eyes shone brightly in the moonlight, begging Angelos to love her and he surrendered. As the night-time breeze wafted around them, and lizards crept silently in the undergrowth, Angelos and Elena slowly became one. They took each other heart, body and soul, eventually drifting off to sleep, wrapped in each other's arms.

~

In the following days, Angelos's smile was brighter than the sun itself. It did not matter what anyone said or did to him, all he could think about was that glorious night with Elena under the heavens. Life on the island was slow and steady. Men worked hard on the land, fished or toiled in the groves. Women cleaned their house, looked after their children and supported their husbands. They slept when they could, drank wine to fortify themselves during long summer days filled with backbreaking work, and ate plentiful amounts of village bread dipped in olive oil, accompanied by onions, olives and the occasional bit of meat or Zakynthian cheese if they were lucky.

Angelos's life was no different, he worked just as hard. During the day he toiled in the groves obeying his father, and fulfilling his duty. But at night he snuck from the house using the darkness as a shield to secretly meet Elena. One night, while lying upon a blanket under a tree with the faint smell of pine, grass and earth enveloping them, Angelos turned to Elena and gently brushed the hair away from her face. Her body was a silhouette in the darkness of night, but her eyes gleamed brightly.

"Have I told you how much I love you?"

"Yes, you tell me every time you see me," she giggled.

"Have I told you how very beautiful you are?"

"Yes, every time you see me."

"And have I told you..."

She smothered his mouth with a loving kiss, pinning him to the ground. "Be quiet!"

"I am sorry," he said and held her tightly, feeling her skin against his, never wanting to let her go. "I cannot help it, I do love you and you are so very beautiful."

"I love you too. I will always love you."

"Would you ever marry me, Elena?"

She rolled onto her back, considering the question, as she gazed up at the stars.

"I would marry you tomorrow if I could."

"But?"

"But it is not possible. Your father would never allow it; we both know that. We are too different. I am not suitable to be the wife of a landowner's son."

Angelos sighed. "I would give it all up in a heart beat. If I were forced to choose, you or my father's plan for me, I would choose you every time."

"I know you would, but for now, can we just not be, Angelos? We both know that we love each other and that should be enough. We should not need a declaration to prove how we feel."

"I know. But I would marry you all the same."

"I know you would." She rolled to face him and placed a hand on his warm chest. "Enough talk of marriage, it will be light soon and we should think about going home."

"As always, you are right."

As he went to stand, Elena grabbed his arms and held him tightly once more before having to separate. As they embraced under the private canopy of nature, dawn began to tint the skyline, heralding the start of a new day.

~

Life on Zakynthos did not change much; islanders went about their business and the olive harvest went ahead as normal. But the threat of war still hung heavily over their heads. Two days after Hitler invaded Poland, both Britain and France declared war on Germany and the Second World War officially began. Each day, Angelos and Elena desperately searched for news, fearful that they might be invaded. But the war remained at a distance, their little island left in peace, and finally they began to relax and breathe a sigh of relief. Paradise was still theirs and their love was stronger than ever. They were lucky and were defying all odds, but for how much longer?

CHAPTER EIGHT

Cornwall, England, 1992

Kate sat on Fistral Beach staring out at large rolling waves that crashed and thudded along the coastline. Late spring storms had intensified, bringing heavy rain that fell like stair rods, soaking everything in sight. The winds were whipping the sea into a frothing frenzy and the local surfers loved every minute of it. Sitting on the wet sand, water seeping into her jeans, Kate desperately searched the ocean for a glimpse of Fletch but could not see him anywhere. The wind swirled around her, seeping into crevices in her coat, chilling her bones, making her pull it tightly around her. The rain that had ceased for a few hours now began to fall again in small splashing droplets, wetting her already messy hair and running down her face and neck. She would be completely soaked by the time she got home, but she did not care. She needed to see him.

Two surfers ran out of the waves, threw their boards to the sand and high-fived each other. Kate rose to her feet and ran down to see them.

"Kate!" A tall skinny blonde man smiled at her with surprise.

"Hi, Jase. Have you seen Fletch anywhere?"

"No, not for months. Last I knew he was in California."

Kate felt her stomach flip. California? What on earth was he doing there? She did not even know he had gone. Had she really been that caught up in her own world for the past year? How could he not tell her he was leaving? Had he been that angry?

"I saw him before he left. He said there was nothing to keep him here, so he packed up his surfboard and rucksack and said he was off to see the world. I think Shane got a postcard a few months ago, but no one's heard anything else since."

"Right. Thanks."

Kate left the surfers and plodded up the beach. Why did Fletch leave so suddenly and why had he not come back? Was it all her fault? Was it because of the argument they had had? Whatever it was, she wished he was still here. She missed him so much and she really needed a friend right now. Tomorrow was her birthday. A whole year since she had learned she was adopted. She had been fine at the time, telling Mum and Dad that she did not care about her birth parents. But then Athena's birthday card had arrived out of the blue.

Ever since, the words had stayed in her head, tormenting her at night when she tried her best to sleep, interrupting her thoughts during the day. Was Athena right? Should she have put everything to one side and done her best to find out about her birth family? She was so confused and did not know what to think or do for the best. She was angry with Athena for doing this to her, angry with her parents for being so bluntly honest with her and angry with herself for being so weak.

Now she was angry with Fletch. He had been the one constant in her life, the one person she could always trust and turn to, until he abandoned her and left her to deal with everything on her own. Stomping along the wet and stormy beach, she allowed the now heavier rain to lash her face and body. She no longer cared what happened. She was so angry. No, worse than that. She was bloody furious, and she had had enough.

"Everyone can just go to hell!" she screamed.

As if the world heard her, a flash of lightning soared brightly across the sky, quickly followed by a cracking rumble of thunder that shook the ground. Kate knew coastal storms could be dangerous so she picked up speed. Running along the sand was hard work, and took every ounce of strength she had. She reached the International Surfing Complex just as lightning flashed overhead again. Flinging herself under the wooden decking, she sat on the cold wet sand, shivering, as the bad weather worsened and continued on around her.

She was not a fan of storms, but she did feel a little safer under the decking. The wind had really whipped up now and she knew she would be stuck there for a while until it passed. Resigned, she settled herself in and watched as the tempest raged. The waves rolled and crashed, like a sea of white horses galloping to the shore in endless droves. A few hardy, and some might say idiotic, surfers remained in the water, taking their chances, but the rest had abandoned the sea in search of safety.

Forks of bright white and pink lightning lit up the inky black sky, landing forcefully on land and water. Thunder quickly followed, crashing loudly, making everything around her shake. The clouds were dark and forbidding and they continued to drop a wall of intense, never-ending rain that drenched everything in sight. She sat hunched under the decking, shivering, watching in awe as nature's spectacle swept the coastline.

A lone surfer caught her eye. He was the last out of the water and was sprinting towards her with his board tucked under his arm. A fork of lightning descended, and landed barely a few feet from him, making him jump. Panicked, he threw his board to the ground and picked up speed, heading in Kate's direction. Moments later he threw himself under the decking and was sitting next to her.

"Shit that was close," Jase said. "Do you think my board will be okay?"

"You're an idiot."

Jase looked sideways to see that she was smirking.

"It cost me a lot of money!" he said petulantly.

"It's your own fault for staying out there so long. You should have come in when it started."

"What are you, my mother?"

"No, thank god."

They sat in silence for a few minutes as the storm continued to rattle around them.

"So you and Fletch..." Jase shouted over the din, not really knowing what to talk about.

"What about us?"

"Were you guys, like, going out or something?"

"No. Nothing like that. He is…was my best mate."

"Ah okay."

"Why do you ask?"

"No reason."

Another fork of lightning came down on the sand not far from them, leaving the air zinging with electricity, as a simultaneous crash of thunder bellowed overhead. Without thinking, Jase and Kate grabbed hold of each other out of pure fear. The storm was directly above them and spitting venom for all it was worth. Kate tried to speak but her words were carried away on the wind as soon as she opened her mouth. They had no choice but to stay where they were until it blew itself out. Kate was grateful for the company, even if it was a dumb surfer who had stayed in the waves too long and almost got himself fried.

~

Just over an hour later, the storm was finally moving away and the rain had let up. The clouds parted and a faint beam of sun shone through. The calm after a very intense storm.

Kate and Jase stepped from under the decking, thankful that they got through it unharmed.

"I better go and rescue my board."

Kate nodded. "I better get back. I'm soaked. See you."

"You wanna go for a drink?"

Surprised, Kate turned and asked, "What…you mean now?"

"Um. No, not right now. Later?"

Kate stifled a chuckle. "I don't go out with surfers."

"I meant as friends," Jase said uncomfortably.

Asking her out for a drink had surprised him. While the storm had raged, he had felt okay sitting next to her, but now he felt discomfort. He did not want to push her away by saying the wrong thing.

"Where?"

"In town?"

"No, but thanks for asking though."

Jase was confused. He had expected her to say yes. Normally girls did.

"Okay, not in town. Why don't we go to the new pub on the main road out to Holywell?"

"You have a car?"

"Of sorts. Look Kate, do you want to go for a drink or not?"

"Yes, Jase. Pick me up at my house at seven."

"Okay. Where do you live?"

"That's easy. Work it out."

Kate turned and walked up the slipway leaving a puzzled Jase scratching his head in confusion.

~

Kate was sitting with her feet up, watching TV, when the doorbell rang. Concentrating on the screen, she let her father go to answer it.

"You have a visitor, Kate."

She looked up to see a clean and tidy Jase standing before her. She glanced at the clock; he was ten minutes early, too. She could not help feeling a little impressed. She rose from her seat, with a smile planted on her face. He looked disappointed to see her lolling about in faded hole-ridden tracksuit trousers and a ripped T-shirt.

"You're not ready?"

"I just need to change. I won't be a minute. Sit." She motioned to a free chair before running from the room. She had not actually expected him to turn up. She groaned inwardly; she really hoped he did not want anything more than friendship. Scrabbling around her room she found a clean pair of jeans and her favourite t-shirt, and slipped them on before slotting her feet into her trainers. She was going for a drink with a friend and nothing more. As she shook her hair out and looked in the mirror she caught sight of the silver dolphin pendant Fletch had given her on her twenty-first birthday. She really missed him and wished she knew where he was. It upset her to think he had left the country without even saying goodbye. Shaking the thoughts from her head, she grabbed her bag and ran down the stairs.

Sitting in Jase's battered car in uncomfortable silence, they left Newquay and drove towards Holywell Bay. Arriving at the pub, they parked before taking a seat inside. As Kate sipped her drink Jase spoke.

"That storm was mad, wasn't it?"

"Yes. Mum and Dad were worried. They know I hate storms."

"You really don't like them?" Jase asked with

surprise.

"No. They scare the life out of me."

"I'm shocked. You were so calm, I'd never have known. My sister doesn't like them either. She usually hides under the duvet."

"It was mind over matter, and you were there. If I'd been alone, I'd probably have been a wreck, too. Thanks for staying with me."

"It's okay. I didn't fancy staying out in it either. That bolt came a little too close for my liking." He paused, taking a sip of his drink. "You really miss Fletch, don't you?"

"Yes. He was the only friend I had, and now he's gone. I feel so terribly lonely." She dipped her eyes to stare into her glass. "Sorry Jase. I don't mean to sound depressing."

"It's okay." He stared at her, taking in the silky tresses that fell thick and long, framing the pretty features on her face. He had pined after her for so long but had never been brave enough to tell her how he felt. She had always been at the beach with Fletch. Fletch the supremo surfer. The man everyone wanted to be. The man who had one of the most beautiful girls in town at his side constantly, and yet he never did anything about it. So Jase would seek solace in other girls, mostly tourists, or those going off to university so they would not get too attached to him. But all the time, it was Kate he wanted to be with, but he had not stood a chance while Fletch was around. Then suddenly Fletch had gone and here she was, free and available. It had taken Jase an eternity to feel brave enough to ask her out for a drink. What if the storm had not struck? Would he still be pining after her, too afraid to reach out?

"Jase?"

"Sorry Kate, I was miles away."

"Anywhere nice?"

He shrugged and swiftly changed the subject. "So were you serious about not wanting a relationship with anyone?"

"I don't know," she admitted. Kate liked Jase. He was funny and not as geeky as most of the guys who rode the waves at Fistral, but she knew he was not boyfriend material. It was common knowledge that he was the *love them and leave them* type and she did not want to get hurt. She definitely wanted a friend though. She had a big hole in her life and wished she had someone other than her parents to talk to.

"My life's a mess, Jase."

"You? I doubt that very much. You have great parents, a nice house, a job you love, and your car is almost brand new! I would say that's pretty good. I rent a small room in a house with a bunch of people I barely know, I have no job, I spend all day in the sea and my car is on its last legs and held together with bits of wire."

Kate could not help but laugh. When he put it like that, her life did sound pretty good. But she could not help the feeling of uncertainty that nagged at her every day. Her life may look great from the outside, but underneath, it was all a lie.

"If I tell you something will you promise to keep it a secret, Jase?"

"Of course."

"I mean it. If I ever find out that you told anyone, I will never speak to you again."

He knew from the tone that she was deadly serious and he nodded with assent.

"It's my birthday tomorrow and I'm dreading it. A year ago I learned that the Fishers aren't my real parents."

"You're adopted?"

"Yep. They told me on the morning of my twenty-first birthday. It was the worst day of my life, and it knocked me sideways. I told them it didn't matter, and it didn't until I got a card a few days later from my birth mother. She died when I was very young, but had instructed someone, I think her solicitor, to send it. The things she said sent my brain into a tailspin. I haven't been able to deal with it since. I'm a mess, Jase. I tried to talk to Fletch about it last year. He's the only other person I've ever told, and he just abandoned me."

She suddenly realised she was crying, and looked up at Jase. His face was filled with confusion. Embarrassed, she stood up, "I'm so sorry Jase. I shouldn't have..." she fled from the pub, only to remember that she had nowhere to go. They had come in his car. She kicked the wall in frustration, then sat down on a wooden bench.

Jase appeared and sat next to her. “You can’t get rid of me that easily, Kate. If you want a friend, I’ll be your friend, and I promise I won’t tell anyone what you told me.”

“I thought I’d scared you off.” Kate managed a small laugh.

“You’ll learn in time that it takes a lot to scare me.”

“Thanks Jase. I really could do with a friend.”

“I know, and I’m here for you, whenever you need me. Do you fancy going back into town and getting some fish and chips? I’m starving.”

“Sounds like a great idea. Let’s go!”

~

“Come on Kate!”

“No. I look like a fool.”

“I’m sure you don’t. Get a move on or we’ll miss all the good waves.”

It was a very early morning in the height of summer, and for three months Kate and Jase had been good friends. He stayed true to his word and had not told anyone her private business. He became the shoulder to cry on that she so desperately needed. He was the friend she could hang out on the beach with, eat fish and chips while trying to avoid dive-bombing seagulls with, and now, after much persuasion, he was about to give Kate her first surf lesson. Fletch had been trying to get her to surf for years, but she had always refused. She was not sure why she changed her mind now, but maybe Fletch was the reason. Over the last few months, she had continually broken convention where Fletch was concerned, almost as if she were rebelling against him and his very ideals.

"Why did I ever agree to do this?" Kate said, storming out of the changing room, decked out in a figure hugging wetsuit. Checking herself out in the mirror she groaned. She looked awful.

Jase was taken aback. She was the sexiest looking surf girl he had ever seen.

"You look fine. Grab that board and follow me."

They ran down the beach towards the rolling surf, boards tucked under their arms. Jase had already shown Kate the basics on land, and today she was being let loose in the water for the first time. As far as he was concerned, she was ready. Kate, on the other hand, was dreading it. Wading out to sea, they pushed their boards through and over the waves, soon finding themselves almost waist deep. It was a battle. The waves were strong and kept trying to knock them off their feet. Hauling themselves onto their boards, they paddled farther out, the breakers now behind them and on their way shoreward. Kate found the whole process unnatural and hard going. She did not realise how many muscles were used during the art of wave riding. She knew she was going to ache like mad tomorrow. Suddenly Jase stopped paddling and instructed her to do the same and turn her board so that they were facing the beach. They lay there bobbing on the ever-moving water, Jase looking back over his shoulder waiting for the right wave.

Suddenly without warning, he shouted.

"Paddle, Kate! Paddle, paddle, paddle!"

Frantically, she did as instructed, feeling the board moving swiftly towards the shore caught in the continually moving tide. Suddenly, she felt a wave catch her, sweeping her forward. She thought back to her training and pulled forward trying to jump up, but she drastically misjudged it and fell head first into the tumbling waves. She felt like clothes in a washing machine, tumbling every which way. Water rushed past, deafening her. Her board, still attached to her ankle by the leash, swirled in the waters and banged into her leg. Kate was disoriented not knowing where the surface was. Overcome with mild panic, her head finally broke the surface and she gulped in air, coughing up unwanted seawater. Scanning the horizon, she looked for Jase, but could not see him. Clinging onto the board for dear life, she calmed herself down before summoning all the energy she could to climb back onto it, where she lay like a washed up seal. She watched the other surfers expertly ride the continuing waves, and felt disappointed that she had wiped out the first time. A few minutes later, Jase paddled back towards her grinning.

"How did it go? I lost sight of you."

"I wiped out, really badly. I'm not sure I like this surfing business. I must have swallowed half the ocean."

He laughed. "Do you know how often I wipe out? You'll get the hang of it. Come on, try again."

They spent a merciless hour, trying wave after wave. Eventually with muscles screaming, eyes stinging and feeling slightly nauseous from swallowing far too much seawater, Kate did it. She managed to stand and ride the waves for a few feet before losing her balance and falling into the relentless churning water. She stumbled out of the surf, threw down her board and lay on the sand groaning. She was going to be so sore tomorrow.

"I saw that Kate, your first wave!"

"I'm bloody knackered, Jase. How do you do it?"

"With a lot of practice! Why did you never learn before? Most kids who live round here learn to surf or at least bodyboard."

"I don't know. Fletch wanted to teach me, but I told him that it wasn't my sort of thing."

Interesting, thought Jase. Fletch had not been able to persuade her. Maybe Fletch was not as perfect as everyone thought he was. Maybe Jase was the right man for her after all? Despite agreeing to be friends, Jase still secretly harboured thoughts of their relationship becoming more but he was too scared of telling her for fear of losing her. It was better to be friends than not have her in his life altogether.

“What are you thinking?” she asked.

“Nothing.”

“You’re such a liar, Jase Smith!” She reached out with her arm and pushed him over.

“Right, that’s it!” He went to grab her but was too slow and she jumped to her feet. Scrambling up, he ran after her, chasing her along the beach. Just as he reached her, she ran into the waves and turned, sending great handfuls of water into his face. Not letting a bit of seawater deter him, he ducked under and grabbed her legs, flipping them up and pulling her down into the sea. Despite the water going up her nose, she resurfaced, laughing.

“I’m all wet again now.”

Jase brought his hands down into the sea, sending a big splash up into her face.

“Even more now!”

“You are in so much trouble!” Wading forward, she tried to grab him, but he was too quick and beat her to it, holding her hands by her side so she could no longer splash.

“Are you going to stop now?”

“No,” she said mischievously.

“Please?”

“Make me!”

Without another word, he pulled her to him and planted his lips on hers. Rather than pulling away as he had expected, she wrapped her arms around his neck and kissed him back. They stood in the swirling Atlantic Ocean, arms around each other, savouring the kiss, much to the amusement of the other surfers, who cheered. When they parted, Kate looked at him.

"I thought we were going to stay friends?" she asked.

"We are. But I thought maybe we could be friends with benefits. After all, I like you and you like me." He held up his hand before she could speak. "Hear me out. I know you already said you don't do relationships, so really this seems like the best option for everyone."

He thought he would make it easy on her. If she was adamant about not wanting a relationship then this was the next best thing. He would get what he wanted, to continue spending time with her, and eventually she would fall for him and he would get what he wanted most of all.

"Do I have any say in the matter?"

"No. None at all."

"Well in that case..." She pulled him to her and kissed him again. "Okay then. Friends with benefits," she said before pushing him away and wading out of the sea and up the beach to get changed.

CHAPTER NINE

Cornwall, England, 1992

The summer seemed to go on forever and Kate enjoyed every minute of it. For the first time, her life truly felt like her own. She loved spending time with Jase and she was beginning to fall for him. She resisted telling him her true feelings; she did not want to scare him off. She had seen how some of the surf boys were with their girls. If the girls got too close or too clingy, they were dropped faster than you could say paddle.

She continued to surf and became very adept at it. She loved it and could not understand why she had not learned to do it years earlier. She enjoyed being in the water and felt at home there, and did not know what she would do if she ever stopped. It gave her a freedom that nothing else could.

Over the months, she and Jase had also driven the length and breadth of Cornwall. They had visited Land's End, where Kate had stood under the large signpost staring out across the sea in the direction of New York. Another time, they hired a boat at Helston and took turns to row up and down the river. They also drove to Jamaica Inn and explored Bodmin, getting lost on one of the tors as the mists descended.

Kate had never enjoyed herself so much. Her job also kept her occupied. Tourists arrived in their droves in the height of the season and the Tourist Information Office was very busy. She enjoyed talking about the town she loved; its beaches, the harbour, the surrounding area and exciting places to visit further afield.

Thoughts of Athena dwindled and she finally managed to start sleeping properly. Fractious nights filled with bad dreams were behind her and she felt more relaxed and able to concentrate on other things in her life. Her parents had picked up on her better mood and stopped nagging her about living her life, and it seemed that things were finally back to normal again. She, for one, was very glad and she had Jase to thank for it. She could not have been happier.

~

It was late in the evening on the August bank holiday weekend, and Kate, Jase and the other surfers were sitting around a huge campfire they had illegally built on one of the smaller beaches. They were enjoying the balmy weather before the colder autumn temperatures arrived. Some of the surfers' girlfriends had already left, dispatched back to their hometowns or universities after a long summer of fun, most likely never to be seen again.

Kate was enjoying a can of beer, thinking about how she had been so busy with work in the last few weeks, and she felt she had been neglecting Jase a bit. She was glad they had been able to come out and relax. Looking over at him while he talked football with Shane and the others, she smiled. It had been such a great summer. She had enjoyed his company and she definitely wanted a relationship. Tonight she planned to tell him.

The noise of another car arriving punctuated the air, and it was not long before two girls in skimpy dresses and sandals made their way along the sand towards them. Kate did not recognise them; they definitely were not part of the surfer community.

Walking past the gaggle of boys, the girls waved with their fingertips and gave them their best smiles. It annoyed Kate. No doubt they were holidaymakers and Shane had invited them. Glancing back at the boys, she caught the look of horror that passed across Jase's face, and Kate felt a chill go up her spine. Did he know them? If so, who were they?

The two girls came over, sat next to Kate and introduced themselves.

"I'm Sherrie and this is Chelsea."

Definitely tourists, Kate thought. She wished they had chosen to sit elsewhere, but did not want to seem rude.

"Kate."

"Kate." They nodded and then turned to each other to talk about the amazing hair salon and shops they had visited earlier in the day. Kate groaned. She was not that sort of girl and she wished they had not sat next to her. Standing, she went over to the boys and sat next to Jase.

"You okay?" she asked, linking her arm through his.

"Yeah. Why?" he snapped, pushing her away.

"No reason. I just thought I'd ask. There's no need to bite my head off."

"Sorry. I didn't mean to," he smiled weakly.

"I see the tourists have arrived. Who invited them?" Kate whispered, motioning towards Sherrie and Chelsea.

"I don't know."

Something was wrong. Kate had never seen him this irritable before. "What's up?"

"Nothing."

"You could have fooled me."

"Is that so," he grumbled as he grabbed another can of beer, opened it and took a long slug.

"If you're pissed off, why don't you just tell me?" Kate was confused. He had never talked to her like this before and she wondered what she had done to upset him.

"For god's sake! Life isn't always about you, Kate."

"I didn't say it was!"

"Well you sure act like it most of the time. Why don't you just piss off and leave me alone!"

"Jase!"

He turned to her and glared, cold flint-like eyes that told her he had nothing more to say. With tears stinging the back of her eyes, she stood, and stumbled over the log they had been sitting on. Feeling embarrassed and hurt, she walked up the beach to her car, pulled her keys from her pocket and climbed in, slamming the door hard, venting her frustration on it. Fumbling with the keys, she eventually managed to start the engine and sped away from the beach.

She had no idea what had happened. Jase had never ever spoken to her like that before. Tonight he was nasty and downright hurtful. She was at a loss to know what had upset him so much. She would let him cool off and speak to him in a few days, but until then he could go and rot. As she pulled up to her house, she reached into the passenger well for her bag, but it was not there. Groaning, she realised she must have left it at the beach. She needed it, since her house keys and other important stuff was in it. And given the mood Jase was in, he could not be relied upon to bring it back in one piece. She would have to go back for it. How humiliating.

After pulling into the car park, she sat in the car for almost fifteen minutes trying to summon the courage to get out. To run off was one thing, but to do it and then return just over half an hour later was embarrassing. Eventually she shrugged. If Jase had a problem, that was down to him. She would get her bag and hightail it back out of there. People could think what they wanted. She no longer cared. Storming back down the beach, she climbed over the log, reached down and grabbed her bag.

"Oh. You're back," Sherrie said nervously.

"Only to get my bag," Kate said, not that it was any of the girl's business.

"Well I don't know where Jase is."

"Okay then," Kate said dismissively, and turned and walked back up the beach. She stopped. What an odd thing to say. She walked back over to Sherrie, while scanning the bonfire and its environs. She could not see Jase at all, and come to think of it, Chelsea was missing, too.

"What did you mean by that?" Kate

demanded.

"Nothing," Sherrie smiled sweetly.

"Where is he?" Kate whispered hoarsely.

"Who?"

"Do not fuck with me, Sherrie. Where is Jase?"

Shane heard the raised voices. He knew there would be trouble the minute Sherrie and Chelsea arrived. He felt sorry for Jase. He had not known Chelsea would turn up. Jase had told her over a year ago that it was over, but instead of being honest with Kate about his relationship history, he had overreacted and Kate had stormed off. Shane felt sorry for her too. He stood and took hold of Kate's arm. "Come on Kate, calm down. Leave her be."

Kate shook his hand away. "Where is he, Shane? I won't ask again."

Shaking his head, Shane pointed in the direction of the tufted dunes. Kate strode purposefully towards the rising banks. Her head was telling her to run away, but she needed to find out what was going on. Climbing the dunes she looked left and right, searching for him. She had almost given up when she heard them. Slowly rounding a dune, her heart plummeted. Jase was on top of Chelsea. They were naked, writhing and sweaty, and she was screaming for him never to stop.

As Kate vomited, Jase caught sight of her and he stopped dead, frozen like a deer caught in headlights. Untangling himself from Chelsea mid-act, he jumped to his feet and ran over, trying his best to pull on his shorts.

"Oh shit. Oh god Kate. I didn't mean..."

Wiping her mouth with the back of her hand, Kate glared at him. "So what exactly did you mean?"

"I..."

"I thought you liked me, Jase. I thought you were the one who was desperate for a relationship!"

"I was. I am! But you didn't want one!"

"Not back then, but things change. I've changed. I was going to tell you!"

"So why didn't you?"

Kate sighed again. This was not her fault. None of it was her fault. She could not have this conversation while he stood there sweaty and filthy from cheating on her with someone else. And she certainly could not stand there pretending everything was okay while Chelsea sat naked on the sand, twirling her hair and enjoying the show.

"I'm sorry, Jase. I'm going," she cried and turned to leave.

"Kate, please," he begged, running after her.

Kate rounded on him, fury spilling out of her.

"Who the hell is she anyway?"

"My ex-girlfriend. I didn't know she was in town."

Kate gave a hollow laugh. "So I was just

another in a long line of friends with benefits. It's nice to have known you, Jase."

She stormed back towards her car and climbed in. Through falling tears and with shaking hands, she drove, and carried on driving for hours, all of the pent up emotion eventually leaving her body. She was so furious with herself, for allowing herself to trust him only for him to throw it all back in her face. She had lost Fletch, and now realised she had tried to replace him with a mirror image, but it had turned out to be a poor reflection. Jase would never come close to Fletch, so why did she ever think he would?

She wondered where Fletch was right now. If she wished hard enough, would he hear her desperate pleas and come running? Now she had lost Jase, all her old fears and inadequacies came flooding back in an instant, crashing over her like a torrent, drowning her in the detritus she had picked up along the way.

CHAPTER TEN

Zakynthos, Greece, 1940

Angelos's prediction of the war ending quickly did not come to pass. German armies were still advancing across many countries, threatening to overwhelm them, and the world was in a state of fear and uncertainty. But none of it mattered to Angelos. He had Elena and, in his eyes, she was even more beautiful than ever. He was desperate to marry her, but knew it was impossible. His father would never allow such a union. Elena told him she wanted to enjoy life first before she settled down. She loved him very much, but needed time, and did not want to rush their relationship, so he took things slowly.

The pair continued to sneak about the island.

They climbed in the mountains, walked through pine-scented woods and ran among the olive groves. Sometimes Angelos would stand before her, gazing at her beauty, and he would fall in love with her all over again. They kissed often and spent as many nights together as they could, but in winter it became more difficult. It was colder and they could not lie on the blankets under trees. They had to sneak into outbuildings and hope that they were not caught. Neither of their parents would have been happy if they had known what they were doing. It was against tradition, it was immoral, but they took their chances anyway. Young love wrapped them around its little finger and the grip was tight.

Elena was still obsessed by the growing war, even though some people called it the phony war. With every news bulletin she became more anxious and needy, asking Angelos so many questions that, in the end, he had to stop her, his head spinning in confusion.

"Do you think anyone will ever kill Hitler?" she asked one bright February day. They were sitting on the harbour wall in Zakynthos Town. She had wanted to see the boats, and so Angelos relented and had ridden there with her. He worried about being seen with her in Zakynthos Town. In the hills and around the beaches it was easy to hide, but in the town, the risk of being caught greatly increased, and many of his father's business acquaintances lived and worked there.

"Angelos! Did you hear me?!"

"I heard you," he sighed, taking her small delicate hand in his, rubbing his thumb across the back of it. "I really do not know Elena, but you must stop worrying about these things."

"How can you say that?! The whole world is tearing itself apart. People are dying!"

"I know, my love. But we are still safe, there are no Germans here. We are alive and well, we are free people and you have to stop worrying."

"I cannot help it. I do not want to bring a child into a world of hatred and suffering." She began to cry, and Angelos placed his arms around her, holding her tightly.

"Oh Elena, by the time you marry and have children, the war will be a distant memory."

Elena sobbed in his arms, great heaving sobs and he had no idea why she was so upset. Suddenly without warning, she shrugged him away and stood. "You do not understand!" she yelled as she walked away.

Angelos went after her, eventually catching up. He took hold of her arm and spun her around, then held her close again before wiping the tears from her face. He tried to read her, but she was a closed book.

"What is wrong, Elena? Whatever it is, you can tell me. You can trust me."

"I cannot," she wailed.

"You cannot trust me? After everything we

have been through?"

"I cannot tell you. You are a man. Worse, you are a Greek man!" She slumped onto the wall, staring out across the beautiful blue waters of the harbour. "You will hate me and leave me. I do not want to lose you! I love you too much!"

Angelos laughed, and Elena shot him an icy glare. "My beautiful Elena. I love you, too. Whatever it is, you can tell me. I may be a man, but I still have a heart. I told you, whatever happens I am always here for you." He sat next to her, and took her hands in his, forcing her to look at him.

"I am...oh god." She started crying again. "I am having a baby, Angelos," she wailed.

"You are?" He was so happy to hear the news. He was going to be a father! He lifted her to her feet and swung her round, planting a kiss on her lips.

"You are not angry?" She was shocked. She knew it changed everything. Their lives would no longer be the same and the baby would either bring them together once and for all or force them apart forever.

"Why would I be angry?"

"We are so young, Angelos. We are unmarried. You have your whole life ahead of you. I will be called names…well, more names than I am now. Your father will be furious. Our parents will try to stop us from seeing each other and then there is the war." She sobbed again. "Our child will grow up in a world of hate and suffering and I do not want that!"

"I do not want that either. But we love each other, and as long as we do, then our child will have everything it needs."

"But our parents..."

"We will just have to try and talk to them, make them see how much we love each other and that we are meant to be together. It will be okay. I love you and I will never, ever leave you."

"You promise, Angelos?"

"I promise, Elena."

Little did Angelos know that it was a promise he would never be able to keep.

~

Winter slowly turned to spring and the world was still at war. Much of Europe continued to call it a phony war, as little had happened over the winter, but just as everyone began to relax with hopes of a quick solution, Germany invaded Norway and Denmark. It did not stop there. German troops advanced toward France at a frightening pace. Daily news bulletins were filled with the horrors of war, and the suffering of countries that had already fallen to the might of the Germans. Zakynthians began to worry about their future.

It was a warm day. Elena and Angelos sat on

their favourite beach, watching gentle waves wash back and forth. She was blossoming and trying her hardest to hide it, but it was becoming increasingly difficult. Neither had found the courage to tell their parents about the baby, and they were running out of time. They needed to do it soon, or someone would guess. Elena stared out to sea lost in her own thoughts. Angelos loved watching her when she was like this; she was so beautiful and it brought joy to his heart. But today was not a happy day, terrible news had broken on the airwaves the day before. Germany had attacked the Netherlands and Belgium, bringing them into the grip of the world's fast growing enemy. The rest of Europe was now even more at risk of falling into Germany's clutches and seemed incapable of stopping them. Angelos realised it was now or never.

"We must tell our parents, Elena. I want to marry you, I want to be a good father to our baby, and for us to be a family, but we have to be honest with our own families. We are running out of time."

She looked up at him with beautiful eyes that sparkled like emeralds and nodded. Both were dreading it, but they had to do it. There was no other option. They agreed that Angelos would tell his parents that night, and then they would sit down together and tell Elena's the following day. As they lay back on the sand, they held each other tightly, forgetting about the war and all it threatened to bring with it. Safe in each other's arms, they relaxed as they listened to the waves swelling in and out, enjoying the glow of the sun as it slowly sank for another day.

~

That night, Angelos returned home filled with anxiety. He knew exactly what he had to do but felt nervous and sick. It was more than anxiety. He was fearful of his father's reaction. The Sarkis family had just finished eating, when Angelos sat before his parents and explained everything: his feelings for Elena, the baby they were due to have, and how he wanted to marry her. His mother quietly wrung her hands and glanced nervously at her husband. Loukas was silent and still, fury personified.

"This girl is a whore and a peasant! What were you thinking, Angelos? Have you not shamed us enough already, running about the island with her?!"

Angelos had no answer. He knew Elena's family was poor but they were like so many of the other islanders. They struggled to make ends meet, and did what they could to survive, and that was all. Angelos saw no shame in that. As for Elena, she definitely was not what his father said and he hated hearing him talk about the woman he loved like that.

"I love her, father. She is the woman I want to be with."

"Pah! Love! What is love? You do not marry for love. You marry for money, title or breeding, but love? There is no such thing as love, you stupid, idiotic boy."

For the first time in his life, Angelos stood up to Loukas. He knew he was taking a big risk, but he was a man now, and Elena and his unborn child meant so much more to him than anything his father could ever say or do.

"There is such a thing as love! I see it every day, father. Everywhere you look on this island there is love. I love her, father, and nothing you can do or say will change the way I feel."

The anger rose in Loukas. How dare his son talk to him that way! He was a useless, pathetic idiot who deserved to be thrown from the house with nothing more than the shirt on his back. His mother had spoiled him too much when he was a child. When she was supposed to be looking after the boy, she had allowed him to go running all over the island fraternising with the lowest of the low. It was time for a change. Loukas would take the boy in hand, and make him realise that he was a Sarkis. He would work hard from now on, find a suitable girl to marry so that he would become the man Loukas wanted him to be, the man that would continue the Sarkis line and take over the family business when Loukas was no longer able.

He thought again about what Stelios had said. Maria Makris. She was the answer to all his prayers. It was time to think about setting that up.

"You will never see Elena Petrakis again. Is that clear, Angelos?"

Angelos was scared. He may be a grown man, but Loukas was his father and he still lived under his roof, and while he did so, he needed to live by his rules. Angelos could never afford to move out, and there was nowhere to go even if he did. He knew he had betrayed Loukas and his Greek honour. He knew Loukas was furious and would do all he could to stop him from seeing Elena, but he loved her. She was the love of his life. He did not want to live without her. Angelos sat with his head in his hands, his life in free-fall, spinning out of control and he had no idea how to stop it.

He looked up at his father, daring to speak. "She means too much to me, father."

Fast and cat-like, Loukas struck Angelos full blow across the face before gripping him about the throat. Angelos tasted blood, and watched as Pigi shrank back, whimpering, not daring to intervene. She feared for her son, but she feared Loukas more.

Loukas's eyes bored into his son's. "You will never see that whore again. If she wants to keep the bastard, let her, but you will have no part of it. This family will have no part of it! Do you understand me, Angelos?"

Shaking from fear and gasping for breath,

Angelos could only agree.

"Yes, father."

Loukas threw his son to the floor and stormed from the room, a fog of anger swirling around him. Angelos remained where he was. He knew his father's word was law. He may be twenty-two years old but, until he left the home, his father ruled his life. He had no choice but to agree.

His beautiful Elena.

She was now lost to him and she did not even know it yet.

~

Loukas ensured that Angelos never strayed far from his sight. He was proud of his business and all he had achieved in life and expected his son to follow in his footsteps. Angelos was forced to work every single day, leaving him no time to get away and see Elena or his other friends. Working in the groves was backbreaking and Angelos hated it. He started early, finished late and came home filthy. Just when he thought he would get a chance to sit and relax, his father had him doing odd jobs around the house, or learning how to look after the books, order stock and administer payment to the farm labourers. Angelos was exhausted and he cried himself to sleep at night, dreaming of the woman he had loved and lost, and the child he would never know.

A few weeks later, Loukas went to Zakynthos Town on business, leaving Angelos in his mother's care. Free of his father for a few hours, Angelos wandered down to the beach. Pigi had pleaded with him not to disobey his father's orders, but Angelos no longer cared. He was desperate to see Elena. At the very least, he needed to see her one last time to explain. He owed her that much. He knew leaving the house was wrong and, if Loukas found out, he would more than likely be thrashed to within an inch of his life. But he only thought of Elena.

As Angelos walked along the sand, watching the water roll back and forth, he finally saw her, hunched near the water's edge, throwing pebbles into the blue waters. She looked so unhappy. More than that, she looked tired, lost and so very alone.

Continuing his betrayal against his father, Angelos hunkered down next to her. He knew he had hurt her deeply. She had lost her sparkle and there were dark circles beneath her eyes.

"You never came. Where were you?" she whispered as tears fell from her eyes, landing in small splashes upon her arms.

Angelos felt awful. He did not know what to do or say to make it right. He did not know how to justify himself. How did he explain that his father hated her and forbade him to ever see her again? He was taking a risk at that very moment, but he could not leave now. He had to try and explain, even if his words hurt her.

"My family, they are proud people, Elena," Angelos began, gently taking hold of her hand, finally sitting on the sand. "They have lived on this island for generations. They own land and money, one of the few families who do. My father..." The words caught in his throat and he found it hard to continue. He stared out at the waves seeking a solution, but none came. Sighing, he dug deeply, searching for the right thing to say. "My father expects certain things from his son, Elena. He expects him to live right. He expects him to carry on family tradition and he expects him to marry the right person."

She looked up at him, her normally bright green eyes dull and lifeless. "He does not think I am good enough for you."

All Angelos could do was shake his head. He felt ashamed. He loved her more than life itself, and yet here he was tearing her to pieces.

"Angelos. Look at me. What did he say?"

He looked up at her, and knew he had to be honest, however much it hurt. So he told her everything.

"He thinks I am a whore and a peasant? Well it makes a change from gypsy, I guess." She laughed loudly, her eyes momentarily sparkling, as her old fire and determination stirred. "Well if it is a peasant he wants, a peasant he will get!" She rose to her feet. "Come on."

Angelos jumped to his feet, his heart in his

mouth. He took hold of her arm, in an attempt to stop her. The last thing he wanted was another confrontation with his father.

"Where are you going?"

"To see your father, of course." She shook him free and marched off along the beach, as fast as her pregnant body would allow. Resigned, Angelos followed.

Loukas appeared at the door before Angelos even got close to the house. He had returned early to find his son gone and his wife whimpering in the corner, not knowing where Angelos was. Anger swirled about him like early morning mist snaking around trees. He strode forcefully towards them with a face like thunder.

"You. IN!" Loukas spat at his son. Angelos was reluctant, he did not want to leave his father alone with Elena. There was no telling what the man would do.

"I said get in the house!" Loukas bellowed, grabbing his son's arm, and pushing him roughly towards the door. Fury flashed in his father's eyes, and Angelos realised he had never seen him this angry before. It petrified him.

"I will not tell you again, boy," the elder man snarled.

Reluctantly, Angelos obeyed and ran to huddle in the doorway with his mother, watching as the scene unfolded.

"Whores are not welcome on my land. Stay away from my son!"

"I am not a whore, Sir. My name is Elena, but you already know that. I love your son very much. We are having a baby. Your grandchild. You should be very happy for us." She was defiant, and stood her ground with her hands on her hips, staring Loukas down. Angelos had never seen anyone stand up to his father before and he loved her even more for it. He continued to watch as his father stepped forward, almost nose-to-nose with her. "Your bastard is no grandchild of mine. I have heard all about your many dalliances. God knows what kind of disease Angelos has caught from you."

"Your information is wrong, Loukas Sarkis. That story was made up by a lecherous man who likes to fuck young girls instead of his wife!"

"Gypsy language and lies. I expect nothing more from your kind! You will ask nothing more of my son or of this family. You are dead to us, peasant. Now get out of my sight!" With a forceful shove, he pushed Elena backwards and she fell hard, landing on the ground with a thud. Angelos cried out for her. He wanted to run to her, embrace her, but knew it was more than his life was worth. Loukas marched up to his son and dragged him inside where punishment awaited him. Angelos had no choice but to leave his one true love and their unborn child floundering in the dust, bruised, humiliated and brokenhearted.

CHAPTER ELEVEN

Zakynthos, Greece, 1940

Angelos's life carried on, but he felt as though time were standing still. He rose each day, had breakfast and climbed into the cart to make his way to wherever he was needed on the estate, and worked until he could barely stand. He hated working for his father. Loukas treated him worse than the locals, but he never argued back, since he was too scared. Angelos had learned his lesson. As Elena had been picking herself up and dusting herself off after the confrontation, Loukas had punished his son severely. In a blind rage, Loukas had used his fists and his boot and by the time he had finished, Angelos was a weeping bloodied mess on the floor. His mother had spent more than an hour bathing his cuts and trying to clean him up.

Once Loukas had calmed down, he returned and informed Angelos that he would not leave his father's side for the foreseeable future. Angelos never had a chance to go and find Elena even if he wanted to. He did hear from one of the farm labourers that she was well and suffered no ill affects from Loukas's rough treatment. While that brought him relief, he missed her so much. He wanted to see her beautiful eyes, to hold her, kiss her, hear her sing, but it was impossible. Their relationship was dead and he would never see her again.

The war in Europe was gaining pace and islanders feared it was only a matter of time before they were invaded. The only person who was not scared was Loukas. The thought of war thrilled him. He had lived through the Great War and he was of the opinion that war made a man of you and showed you the true meaning of life. Angelos disagreed with him, although he never actually voiced his disagreement. He thought war was callous and hurtful. Thousands of people had their world turned upside down and were being dictated to by a man with a frightening vision. A vision that came at a price, and that price was death, destruction and tyranny. Every day, Angelos prayed for the war to end but his prayers remained unanswered.

Days turned into weeks, weeks into months and Angelos's repetitive days became akin to boredom. He hated the estate, hated his father's vision of what he, Angelos, should be, and hated having to toil on the land every day with nothing else to do in his life. Elena had become a thing of the past, and he missed her. As each day passed, his memory of her faded slightly and his hatred of his father grew a little more. He felt like a prisoner in his own home. If it were not for the thought of the war scaring him so much, he would have joined up and gone to fight, but he did not. That would be running away and he knew it would hurt Elena too much, and that was the last thing he wanted to do.

One day a young boy arrived at the house: Elena's younger brother. He hammered loudly on the door and asked for Angelos. Loukas had already left for the day and Angelos had been instructed to remain with his mother and help her out with some odd jobs round the house. Glancing nervously at Pigi, the boy pulled at Angelos's arm.

"You have to come quick, Angelos. Elena needs you. The baby is coming!"

Angelos did not know what to do for the best. His mother was shaking her head furiously, trying to dissuade him from betraying Loukas again. Angelos did not want to disobey his mother, nor did he want to leave her to his father's mercy, but Elena was giving birth to his child. She needed him.

“I am sorry, Mother, but I have to go.”

Turning his back on her, he followed Georgios Petrakis to their village in the mountains. At the small house with pots of brightly coloured bougainvillea sitting outside, Angelos waited for what seemed an eternity. He heard the painful screams of the woman he loved more than life itself, and prayed that mother and baby would come through the ordeal unscathed and healthy. Angelos paced for hours. He was desperate to go inside and see her, but the house was too small and cramped and her parents would not allow it. As the darkness crept in and stars began to appear overhead, an uneasy silence fell, punctuated moments later by a healthy caterwauling. Angelos felt tears of relief fall from his eyes. His baby was born.

A while later, he felt a hand on his shoulder. “Angelos. You may come in now.”

He followed Elena’s father into the shabby, small house and into the room where Elena lay, looking exhausted. Her face was red and covered in sweat from her exertion. In her arms lay a small snuffling bundle. As Angelos approached and sat on the bed, he smiled. He had missed Elena so very much, and despite her lengthy ordeal, she looked more beautiful than ever.

“We have a daughter, Angelos,” she whispered, a contented smile passing across her face.

"A daughter?" he gasped in awe.

"Yes. Look, she is beautiful."

Angelos leaned in and gazed at the small child they had created, half his, half Elena's and perfect in every way. She was a pretty little thing, just like her mother, and he sat on the edge of the bed and cried tears of joy.

"What will you call her?" he asked a few minutes later, once the emotion subsided.

"I like Athena. She is the Greek goddess of wisdom, courage and inspiration."

"Athena. I like that very much."

"I am glad. I think it suits her."

"Me, too."

Angelos and Elena sat in silence, comfortable in each other's presence, all the hurt and anguish suffered at the hands of Loukas behind them. There in that room, in that small fraction of time, they were a family, bound to each other for all eternity, but their happiness was short-lived. As Angelos cradled his daughter in his arms, raised voices and a scuffle came from outside. The sounds grew louder and suddenly, without warning, Loukas burst into the room followed by Elena's father. Hurriedly, Angelos passed Athena back to her mother so that he could face his father. It did not matter what Loukas did to him now. His daughter had been born happy and healthy and that was all that mattered.

"I am sorry, Angelos," Elena's father said.

"Do not apologise for me, Petrakis," Loukas

said. "You do not learn, do you Angelos."

Loukas grabbed his son's arm and dragged him from the room. All Elena's mother could do was comfort her daughter as the men departed. Outside, under the velvety blackness of night, Loukas hissed and spat at Angelos like an angry cat. He called him ungrateful, spoilt, a liar and untrustworthy. Angelos had no words; he no longer cared what his father thought. He just let Loukas yell, replacing harsh words with the pleasant memories of Elena and his pretty daughter to circle his brain. Loukas continued yelling as they made their way home, but Angelos did not hear him. He had brought life into the world, a gorgeous baby girl, and he was so very proud of that.

~

Loukas Sarkis's plan had been set in motion. He realised the relationship between his son and the peasant was just too strong. Even without the child, he had seen the bond between them. It was unlike any he had ever seen before. Since the arrival of the child, it did not matter what he did, his son remained happy and content. Loukas gave up trying to scare him or beat him. Angelos just took it, letting the bruises and cuts heal, while carrying on as normal.

Loukas needed to get rid of the girl and the child. Needed them out of his life. The easy solution would have been to send his son to fight, but he refused to send his only son and only heir to be cut down in his prime. Angelos was too valuable to the continuation of the family and the business.

In Zakynthos Town, he had met with the town officials a few times and remembered the conversation with Stelios Makris about his daughter, Maria. Loukas had been frank talking to Stelios. He was honest about the peasant and child, yet Stelios did not bat an eyelid. Many on the island had already heard, since they made it their business to know Loukas's business. His family had lived on the island for the longest, and was one of the richest.

Stelios was very aware that his daughter was no prize catch, and he had been worried what he was going to do about marrying her off. When Loukas suggested a match with his own son, all his dreams came true. His daughter Maria becoming a Sarkis was beyond his wildest dreams. He knew the Sarkis boy would never truly love his daughter the way some lowly fisherman may have, but it was not about love. It was about the marrying together of two important families and, as far as Stelios was concerned, he was very happy to accept Loukas's offer.

Loukas and Stelios shook on it and agreed that Maria would become Angelos's wife later that year. Loukas was overjoyed. Once the pair was introduced, the incident with the peasant and her bastard child would be behind them and the Sarkis name would be fully restored. He was very happy with his plan. One way or another he would split Angelos and Elena up for good, even if it killed him.

~

As summer turned to autumn, the war still raged. From a distance, Angelos watched his daughter grow and Georgios did his best to keep Angelos informed on her progress, but Loukas kept an even closer eye on his son than before. Angelos felt stifled, like he was drowning, and wished his father would back off and let him live his life the way he wanted. He again considered signing up to the army, but knew in his heart of hearts that he could not bear to be parted from Elena and Athena, despite not seeing them.

Harvest arrived again and everyone pulled together. The olives fell from the trees in droves and were packed up ready to be sold on. Angelos's body ached from all the hard work, but it gave him time to think and enjoy being outside.

One day as he was directing some of the local workers, he lifted his head as though he knew someone was watching him. He heard Athena gurgle before he saw them and he ran to the boundary wall to greet them.

"You are taking a huge risk coming here," he said, smiling at Elena. She was looking so much healthier than the last time he saw her. Her hair was shiny and tied back under her favourite scarf. Her eyes sparkled, the deep green taking his breath away, and her face had colour. He was pleased to see it.

"I saw Loukas leave just now and I overheard him say he would not be back for a few hours. I thought we could spend some time together?" Her eyes twinkled mischievously.

Angelos groaned, wanting nothing more than to spend a few hours with Elena and his daughter. But if Loukas found out, he would be in so much trouble. Harvest was the busiest time of the year.

"If you do not want to, Angelos, then fine. We will see you another time, when it is more convenient to you and your damn family!" Elena snapped. She turned and began to walk away.

"Wait! Give me two minutes." Angelos ran back into the groves and Elena smiled to herself. True to his word, Angelos appeared a few minutes later.

"I can give you one hour Elena, but no more."

"I will settle for that."

They walked away from the groves, taking the rough pathway down the hill, away from people, the road and the chance of being caught. They both knew they were playing a dangerous game but neither cared. They were still too much in love.

Sitting under a tree overlooking their favourite bay, they lay Athena on a blanket between them. Angelos held Elena's hand and told her how much he missed her and how sorry he was for everything that had happened. Elena responded by leaning in and kissing him lightly on the lips. Hungry and desperate to hold her once more, Angelos refused to let her go and kissed her passionately.

"I love you, Angelos Sarkis."

"I love you too, both of you," he said as he stroked his daughter's face. She was the spitting image of her mother and Angelos was glad. It meant that she would grow into a very beautiful woman.

"How are you, Angelos?"

"Me? I am okay."

"Honestly? I know he treats you badly. Why do you not leave home?"

"I have nowhere to go Elena."

"You could come and live with us."

Angelos laughed. "There is no way I could live with you, Elena! There is not enough room for your family as it is, even less now that Athena has been born."

Elena looked disappointed, and Angelos kissed her gently on the cheek. "I would give anything to be with you both as a proper family, but I have no way of supporting us. I need to stay at home for now. We will be together soon, Elena. I promise, but let me do it properly."

Elena was resigned. "Okay. Does he still beat

you, Angelos?"

"Why do you want to know?" Angelos was ashamed. He was twenty-two years old and yet he let his father rule him with a rod of iron and thrash him senseless when the mood took him. Angelos really wished he could escape his poor existence, but Greek tradition was too strong. He had been brought up to live under his father's roof, in the way his father chose. He was a Sarkis and his rightful place was living with his parents, learning the family business so that he could one day inherit it and run it.

"Not so much anymore," he lied.

"That is good. I worry about you."

All too soon, their hour was up and they bade each other goodbye. Angelos was insistent that Elena take the long way around, in case his father suddenly reappeared. Sneaking back into the groves, he was thankful that his disappearance was not noticed and he carried on with his work as normal.

~

Angelos awoke to a lot of noise in the house. It was a Sunday and it should have been a day for them to rest. Groaning, he rose from bed and pulled back the thin drape that covered the window.

"Ah my son, you are awake."

Angelos turned to see Pigi standing in the

doorway with a smile on her face. He rarely saw her smile and it made him happy.

“Morning, Mother. What is all the noise about?”

“They are getting ready for the celebrations, Angelos. It is going to be such a happy day.”

“It is? What is happening today?”

“Your wedding, my son.” She laid some trousers, a shirt and a jacket of his father’s on his bed. “Get yourself ready, she will be here in an hour!”

Standing alone, Angelos pinched himself. Was he dreaming? Had his father finally caved in? He must have! Filled with excitement, Angelos washed himself and changed into the suit. It was a little long in the legs but it did not matter. He was getting married! His father had finally given in and realised how much he loved Elena.

His mother appeared with a tray of food and set it on the side.

“You must eat; you have a long day ahead of you. My son is getting married! You make me so very happy, Angelos.”

Angelos sat and ate as his mother fussed around him. When he finished the last dregs of coffee, she took the tray and instructed him to finish getting ready.

Sitting on the bed, Angelos let his mind wander. What would Elena be wearing? Would she have flowers in her hair? Would Athena, their daughter, be there too? The excitement built in him and he was barely able to contain himself.

The door opened again and Pigi smiled.

"It is time."

Grinning from ear to ear, Angelos walked downstairs and out into the bright sunshine. Loukas had arranged for the ceremony to take place at the house. At first, Angelos could only see a throng of people, his guests. His father stepped up to him and motioned for Pigi to go sit. She kissed Angelos before obeying her husband.

As they walked forward, the priest came into view. Standing at the front was a woman Angelos had never seen before. She was wearing a pretty dress and held a bouquet of flowers.

"Who is that?" he whispered to Loukas.

"Maria Makris, your wife-to-be. Now smile. It is supposed to be a happy day," Loukas whispered menacingly.

CHAPTER TWELVE

Bristol, England, 2001

Staring out of the window, Kate watched as the skies of Bristol turned a miserable slate grey. Heavy rain-filled clouds scudded overhead, spilling their load, soaking everything in sight. The pavement and road glistened, slick with water, and gutters filled becoming mini rivers. It had been a miserable spring and she hoped summer would bring better weather.

"So Kate, what are your thoughts?"

Turning her attention back to the meeting, Kate took in the eager faces around the table. Remembering that she was the boss, she swung back into work mode. "I completely agree, a new campaign would be good idea. The company is doing well but it's always good to offer something new that will give us an edge. Let's get started on it this week, and we'll meet again next week to go through ideas. Right, then. Meeting over, let's get back to work."

Everyone stood, and shuffled from the room, talking amongst themselves.

"Are you okay, Kate?" her assistant asked, while tidying up the mess left by the others.

"Yes Ashleigh. Sorry, I've a lot on my mind."

"Is it still okay for me to leave early tonight?"

"Of course. Why don't you go now," Kate said, smiling. As a boss, she was extremely fair and accommodating to her staff.

"Thanks!" Ashleigh skipped from the room in a whirl of excitement, as Kate sank back into the chair. She took a minute to survey her kingdom. It was only a small one, but it was hers. She had left Cornwall nine years ago. Left her parents, the house she grew up in, and the job that she loved, to start afresh. She wanted to try and get some perspective, to try and work out what to do with her life. She had joined the Tourist Information team in Bristol, and worked her way up through the ranks, saving every spare penny she could.Two years ago she came up with the idea for her company, *Fisher Events,* and she rented a small office in the centre of town. It was an instant success. They offered both high and low end tours of the city as well as catering for company parties in exclusive and unusual venues. She enjoyed it, and it kept both her body and mind active, but the rest of her life was sadly lacking. Since her disastrous break-up with Jase, she had all but steered clear of men. She had convinced herself that work took up too much time anyway. She tried to visit her parents whenever she could, but felt as though something was missing.

She had very few friends and had not seen Fletch for a decade now. He still managed to creep into her thoughts though and she still wondered where he was and what he was doing. She missed him terribly. She wished she could spend just an hour with him, to tell him how much she missed him. But she knew that would never happen. He was gone from her life.

Sighing, she played with the dolphin pendant hanging around her neck and watched her staff go about their work. Each one had that excited look about them. It was Friday and in a few hours' time, they would leave the office for two days of mirth, merriment and quality time with their loved ones.

She would be going home to a quiet, empty house and dinner for one.

She wished she could just click her fingers and get the weekend over in one fell swoop. Tomorrow was her thirty-first birthday. Ten years since her life had been ripped apart, and she was absolutely dreading it.

"Kate. Phone call for you!" She was brought

back to earth with a bump.

Sighing, she left her worries in the meeting room and went to deal with her client.

~

Fletch looked out across Fistral Beach. The Headland Hotel towered behind him and the wide sweeping golden sands and crashing blue ocean stretched before him. He had so many good memories of this place, but they were clouded by the final argument with Kate ten years ago. He had not seen her for so long and missed her a lot. At the time, he thought they would be friends forever. He had loved her so much but never got the chance to tell her. Now, from what he heard on the grapevine, she was a successful businesswoman. She owned her own company and rarely came home, and had well and truly moved on. He, on the other hand, was just a surf bum who had spent years searching for something to replace Kate. But he never found it.

He hated Kate's birth mother for what she had done to her all those years ago. She took the love of his life from him and it hurt deeply. Fletch had tried to get over Kate. He had left, gone to America, bummed around on the beaches in California, taught surf lessons, drunk beer, kissed pretty girls, most of the time more than kissed, but all the time his heart ached for Kate Fisher.

He had come home this weekend, the

weekend of her birthday, in the hopes of seeing her. Mr. and Mrs. Fisher had greeted him with open arms, but sadly there was no Kate. She had stayed in Bristol, choosing to celebrate her birthday alone.

Here he was, a stranger in his own town, completely lost, completely heartbroken.

There was nobody to see and nothing to do. Not even the surf was inviting.

His heart was heavy and he knew he should not have bothered coming back.

~

Kate awoke late. It was her birthday. She was thirty-one years old. Sitting up, she reached for the glass of water she kept on her bedside table, and drank deeply. She wondered what to do for the day. She had no friends or boyfriend to spend the day with, and all of her work colleagues had plans. She could go into town and walk around the shops, but she hated the weekend crowds of Broadmead shopping centre. Sighing, she lifted the remote and clicked the standby button, making the TV spring to life. She flicked through the channels and stopped on the news channel. Moments later, the doorbell rang, disturbing her peace. She wondered if she should just ignore it, but then it could be something important. Sighing again, she padded downstairs and opened the front door.

"Happy birthday, love!" her mother exclaimed, enveloping her in a warm hug.

"Happy birthday, Kate," her father repeated, minus the hug.

This was all she needed. Parental concern.

"Come in, make yourselves at home," she said as she guided them into the living room. "I'll just shower and change." Kate disappeared upstairs. She should have known they would not let her spend her birthday alone. She loved her parents and knew they were only trying to help, but this was not what she wanted today. She wanted to be on her own and allow the day to pass by quietly. She wanted it to be over quickly and with as little fuss as possible. She knew that was now out of her hands. Twenty minutes later, she was sitting in the living room pouring cups of tea.

"So how have you been?" her mother asked.

"Fine. Busy with work," Kate replied quietly.

"That's good. We thought you might have come home for your birthday," her father said.

"Sorry, I thought I had to work this weekend."

There was silence.

"We miss you. We hardly see you nowadays."

"I know, Mum," Kate sighed. She had expected this as soon as she had opened the door. "But my job keeps me so busy."

"I know dear, but as boss, surely you could let

someone else take over occasionally?"

Kate had no answer. She knew she was deliberately staying away, but could not admit it. Her parents would be hurt if they found out.

"Anyway, we wanted to give you this," her mother passed her an envelope.

Kate smiled weakly as she reached out and took it. Slowly she opened it and pulled out the birthday card. Both parents had written their own messages of love and celebration and it warmed her heart. She hugged them both.

"Thank you. I love you both, too," she said as she placed the card on the mantelpiece. It was the only one to grace it. It was sad, really, for someone of her age. She sat back down next to her parents.

"We also have this for you," her father said, passing her another envelope.

"What is it?"

"Open it."

She did as her father instructed and out fell Athena's birthday card and the bank passbook. Kate gasped in shock. She never expected to see them again.

"I thought these had ended up in landfill!"

"No dear. You weren't thinking straight and I thought you might want them one day. I have checked and the bank on the passbook is here in Bristol. We are staying for the weekend whether you like it or not and are going to the bank first thing on Monday. Your father has already made an appointment."

"But..."

"No buts, Kate. Enough is enough!"

~

Kate reluctantly put her parents up for the weekend. They took her out for a meal for her birthday and made her leave the house with them on the Sunday so that they could go for a long walk along the docks. As cross as Kate was for them turning up unannounced, she enjoyed spending time with them. She had missed them more than she thought she would.

Monday morning rolled around quickly and, after calling Ashleigh to tell her she would be late in, she grabbed her coat and bag and unenthusiastically followed her parents to her car. After parking up, they walked the short distance to the bank, where Kate and her parents were shown into the bank manager's office.

Sitting with a parent on either side of her, Kate felt trapped and nervous. This was not how she wanted to spend her Monday morning; she had too much work to do. She brought herself back to the present. Her mother was explaining the situation to the bank manager, who nodded politely.

"It is nice to meet you, Mr. and Mrs. Fisher and, of course, you Kate. I am aware of your situation; Hobsens Solicitors had already briefed me. I did not expect to have to wait ten years for you to visit us, though," he laughed, trying his best to lighten the tense mood.

Kate squirmed uncomfortably, not knowing what to say.

"Kate just needed time to come to terms with everything," Margaret said while laying a comforting hand on her daughter's arm.

"Right well, shall we get down to business? I will need proof of ID for you, Kate."

"I don't have any."

"Here you are." Margaret opened a familiar brown envelope and passed a fading birth certificate and some other papers across the table. Kate was shocked; she had never seen her birth certificate before.

"Thank you, Mrs. Fisher." He studied the documents for a moment. "It all seems to be in order, and you have the passbook, too?"

"Yes," she handed the old book to him.

"I won't be a moment."

He hurried from the room, leaving the Fishers sitting in silence. The passing seconds felt like hours and it was unbearable. Kate wondered what she had done in a previous life to suffer so much turmoil.

The door opened and the bank manager returned. "We have updated the passbook for you, and I am pleased to say with the interest added you have inherited a tidy little sum of money. Let me know if you would like to withdraw anything today or if you want to transfer any funds to another account."

Kate stared at the figure on the pages before her. The number of zeros shocked her. She could do so much with it, but at that moment she had no idea what. Athena had left her a nice little nest egg that would make her very comfortable indeed. "Thank you. I think I will leave it for now."

"That is fine. We are here if you need anything. All we have to do now is pop down to the vault, and then you can get on and enjoy the rest of your day."

"The vault? What's in the vault?"

"Your safety deposit box."

Kate was shocked. "I have a safety deposit box?"

"Athena did, but now that she is no longer here, it is yours. The will stated that it be left to you. So you now own the contents."

"What is in it?"

The bank manager chuckled. "That I can't tell you. Safety deposit boxes are the property of the renter, so not even I have the privilege of knowing the contents. Would you follow me, please?"

He led them from the room and through a door marked 'private'. Blindly, and in a confused state, Kate followed him through the never-ending corridors. They stopped in an ante-room.

"Only Kate can go in. You will have to wait here, Mr. and Mrs. Fisher."

Kate spun her head around to look at them, but they merely nodded in support. Breathing deeply for courage, she followed the bank manager into the room. The walls were lined with little metal boxes, all of them numbered. He put the key into number 176, pulled the box from its slot, and placed it on the table in the centre of the room.

"All you do now is lift the lid. If you want to take anything away with you, just let me know. I will need a signature from you."

The door shut behind him and Kate was alone. Shaking, she sat and took a deep breath, then slowly lifted the lid, and surveyed the contents. There was an envelope with a solitary name written on the front in a foreign hand, a blue velvet pouch tied at the top and a small black jewellery box. Opening the box first, she gasped. Inside was an exquisite silver and emerald ring, weighty and gleaming in the harsh electric light. Lifting it from the box, she slipped it onto her finger and was surprised to see it fit her perfectly. She quickly removed it, placed it back in the jewellery box and closed the lid.

She picked up the envelope and opened it, pulling out the contents. It was a faded yellowing page, containing a mass of words in a language she did not understand. It was frustrating not to be able to read it and she wondered what it said. After sliding it back into the envelope, she lifted the velvet bag. Opening it, she tipped the contents onto the table. It was a necklace; a tarnished silver chain from which a silver locket hung. The front was engraved with an ornate letter E, and on the rear was more of the same script as the letter. Kate fiddled with the clasp and managed to open it. One side of the locket contained a photograph of a woman, a very beautiful woman. On the other side was a man.

She sat back not knowing what to do next. She had two choices, put everything back and leave them to bask in the annals of time, forgotten. Or, take them with her and try and work out what they were.

Ten years ago, she had decided that Athena did not matter and that her parents were the most important thing in the world to her, but what if she really was meant to find out about her past? What if that was really her purpose in life? She groaned. The last thing she wanted to do was upset her parents, but then, they had set the wheels in motion by keeping Athena's card and bank book, and bringing her here today. What if they wanted her to do it? Kate sat and stared at the monotonous wall of safety deposit boxes, hoping and wishing an answer would show itself, but nothing came. She knew she had to make the decision, so she got up and paced back and forth a bit before finally opening the door. The bank manager stepped forward, smiling.

"All finished?"

"Yes."

He followed her back into the room, closing the door behind them. "I would like to take some items away with me. Can I leave the bank passbook behind though?"

"The deposit box is yours, Miss Fisher. You may take or leave whatever you like."

"Okay," she said as she lifted the three items and put them in her bag, replacing them with the passbook. She closed the lid and nodded at the bank manager.

He placed a logbook on the table, showing her where to sign and date, before sliding her deposit box back where it belonged and locking it.

"This key now belongs to you. You are able to access the box whenever you want."

Kate took the key from him, safely put it in the zip pocket of her bag, and thanked him for all of his help.

Outside the bank, Kate and her parents wandered back towards the car. Once inside, Kate sat for a moment, still trying to take everything in.

"Are you okay, love?" Margaret asked.

"Yes. It's just a lot to get my head around."

"I know, but it will get easier with time. You just have to try and do what is right."

The Fishers persuaded Kate to take the rest of the day off so that they could take her to lunch and spend some more time with her before they went home. Later that afternoon, they sat in Kate's living room drinking tea and chatting.

"Before we go, you should have this." Margaret pulled Kate's birth certificate out of her bag and passed it to her.

"Thanks." Kate opened it, and briefly scanned the page, it was weird seeing her name written as Katerina. She had been called Kate for so many years, that Katerina felt strange to her. After placing it on the table, Kate rummaged in her bag, and showed her parents the items she had removed from the safety deposit box.

Margaret studied the letter in the envelope. "Do you know, this writing looks a little bit like Greek to me."

"Really?" Kate said.

"I think this ring is an emerald," Brian said as he studied it. "Have you seen the writing on the band?"

"No." Kate leaned forward and looked more closely. "*To my wife Athena.* This must have been my mother's wedding ring!"

Kate was learning so much in such a short space of time, and it was beginning to overwhelm her. She placed the ring back in its box and set it on the side, turning her attention to her mother. Margaret was trying to open the locket, but she couldn't figure out the clasp.

"Let me." Kate took it from her and released it, letting the two halves swing open.

"My god, Kate! That could be you."

"What could?"

"This woman. Look at her, she looks just like you."

"Is it Athena? You met her didn't you?"

"Yes we did, briefly. She looks similar to Athena, but I don't think it's her. The picture looks too old."

"I wonder who it is."

"I've no idea, but I'm sure you will work it out. We really should be going now, my love, or it will take us forever to get home."

Kate threw the locket, envelope and ring box into a nearby drawer and slammed it shut, before showing her parents to the door. She hugged them tightly, promising to speak to them soon.

"Oh, I've left my cardigan in the living room. See your father to the car, dear."

Margaret disappeared and Kate obliged, walking outside with her dad. Moments later, Margaret reappeared with her cardigan. Kate hugged them again before waving goodbye. Shutting the front door, she walked into her living room, turned on the TV and settled down for an evening of lone entertainment.

CHAPTER THIRTEEN

Bristol, England, 2001

The twinkling lights of Bristol city centre danced, and revellers drunkenly walked arm in arm across the road without any thought for the busy traffic. Kate walked past the Hippodrome Theatre, where the pantomime was showing, a sure sign that Christmas in Bristol had officially begun, despite it only being the beginning of December.

She pulled her coat tightly around her and picked up speed. The weather was getting colder and snow was forecast. She hoped she could get home, pack her case and get to Cornwall before it rolled in.

It had been almost nine months since she had seen her parents. Nine months since her birthday and nine months since visiting the bank. She had gone back to work the next day, pushing the weekend and what she had learned about Athena to the back of her mind. Life continued as normal, and nothing changed. The Fishers were still her parents and Athena was still dead. All she wanted to do was get on and live her life.

Running up the car park stairs, she reached her level, located her car and climbed in. It would only take ten minutes to get to her house, another ten to change and grab her case, and then she would be on her way south to Cornwall and her parents. She was looking forward to seeing them. Work had been busy and, although she loved her job, she was very tired and needed a break. Yes, a few days in Cornwall was just what she needed.

~

Kate opened the front door and paused a moment to listen to the familiar sounds of her mother clattering around in the kitchen and her father laughing at something on the TV. With a smile, she closed the door, threw her bag and coat over the banister and propped her case against the wall.

“Kate! You made good time,” Margaret hugged her daughter tightly. “Brian, come sit, dinner’s almost ready.”

“Kate,” her father said, patting her arm and smiling. “It’s nice to have you here again.”

"Thank you, Dad. I'm glad to be here."

~

Margaret and Brian were up early the following morning, pottering about the house, anxiously waiting for Kate to rise. At just gone ten am, she finally padded down the stairs.

"Sorry I'm awake so late. I haven't slept that well in ages," she yawned as she sat at the table.

"That's okay. Tea?" Margaret held out the old brown teapot that she still insisted on using.

Kate nodded, trying her best to stifle another yawn. Margaret poured a cup of hot brown liquid, and added a dash of milk to it before sitting opposite her daughter.

"We wanted to talk to you, Kate," her mother began.

Kate looked at her parents, a feeling of déjà vu flooding back.

"What about?"

"Your mother and I have spoken to someone on your behalf about these."

Brian dropped the locket and envelope on the table in front of her.

Kate was shocked. "How did you get them?"

Margaret smiled at her daughter. "I'm sorry Kate but I took them when you weren't looking. I knew the moment you put them in that drawer you would bury your head in the sand and forget about them, and go back into your shell and continue on as normal. I got the letter translated for you and asked them to tell me what was engraved on the back of the locket."

"You had no right! Bloody hell, Mum, why, for once, can't you just leave things alone!" Kate stood and turned to leave the room.

"Kate Fisher, sit down! How dare you talk to your mother that way!"

Kate knew that tone. Her father did not use it often, but when he did she knew he was angry. She turned and lowered herself back into the chair.

"Sorry, Mum."

"It's okay. But I think this thing with Athena has been getting to you, Kate. You haven't been the same since we told you about your adoption. You've shut yourself off from everyone who cares about you: us, Fletcher, your friends. It's not healthy, and we can't bear to see the happy, outgoing girl we love so much, living like a hermit! Running away doesn't help Kate, it just makes things worse and we worry about you all the time. You aren't the Kate we know and love any more, and we want to help. Until you do something about it, you will always feel this way and it's not doing you any good."

Kate shrugged. She really did not care. As far as she was concerned, Athena was dead to her, but if her parents felt the need to assuage their own guilt by using Athena then so be it, let them try.

As for Fletch, she just could not go there again.

"Fine. What does it say?"

Margaret smiled and passed a piece of paper to her. "Here is the translated letter."

Kate began to read.

My darling Athena,

My darling daughter. If you are reading this it means that you escaped from the island without me and I was left behind. As I write this letter, what I have to do fills me with dread. I do not know who I can trust. Even now, I write in haste by candlelight fearful of what is to come. You my darling daughter brought such light to my life and you made it complete. As complete as it could ever have been, and I loved you with all of my heart.

One day you will want to know about your family and I hope that your saviour will tell you. You were born during such a terrible time, the world was at war and we were all scared of what the future would hold. My future was already a mess, and I could not let you be a part of it.

I was always doomed. Sometimes I wish that the Sarkis family, the olive groves and Xigia Beach never existed. They just remind me of everything I have lost.

Always remember me Athena, for I fear for my future.

Your loving mother
Elena Petrakis

Kate had not expected the letter to be so sad. Quickly she scan read it again, but realised it still did not tell her much about Athena and her family.

"What is the point of this, Mum?"

Margaret held up the locket and showed Kate the back of it. "This inscription says *I love you Elena*. I think the picture of the woman inside may be her."

"But how can that possibly help?" Kate was frustrated. The whole thing was starting to really piss her off.

"Your father and I have being doing some digging. We have found only one Ionian island with a Xigia Beach, and an olive producing family called Sarkis. It is called Zakynthos."

Kate considered the information for a moment. "It's not much to go on, though."

"True, but it's better than nothing," Margaret said.

"So what do you expect me to do?"

"Nothing. It's all been taken care of," Brian said.

"What does that mean?"

"This is your Christmas present. Open it."

Kate tore at the envelope and out fluttered a travel agent voucher.

"What's this for?" she asked, shocked.

Her father spoke, his tone laced with love and concern.

"You work too hard, Kate. It's time you had a

holiday and time you sorted your life out. You can't go on like this."

"I..." she began.

"No Kate. This has gone on long enough. The voucher is valid for six months, and the only condition is that you use it to go to Zakynthos. You will go for two weeks, and you will do what your birth mother, Athena, asked. Your mother and I have talked about it at length and we agree. Until you face this head on, deal with it and get over it, you will never be able to move on with your life. Yes, you have a business, a very successful one and we are so proud of you, but you have nothing else. You have no friends, no boyfriend, no life outside of work and it has to stop! We can't keep worrying about you. Enough is enough!"

It was the longest speech her father had ever made and it shocked her. He hardly ever raised his voice but today he had been stern and authoritative.

"And if I say no?"

"It's your choice. You're an adult, and we can't force you to do anything, but we won't put up with it anymore, Kate. You're miserable, you're wasting your life, you need to stop worrying about the past and about hurting us, and start living your life. We love you and we know you love us too, but you need to come to terms with your past, otherwise you will end up spending the rest of your life as a virtual hermit wondering what might have been."

Tears blurred Kate's eyes. She knew they were right. She had tried to pretend that the news from ten years ago had not affected her, but it had. It affected her deeply. She had spent a decade wondering if there was more to her family history. She had lost Fletch because of it, she had left home because of it, and she had almost become estranged from her parents because of it. Her mother's voice interrupted her thoughts.

"Your father is right. You need to do this, Kate," she said softly. Kate looked at her parent's kind faces and knew they were right. She needed to go. It had taken over the last decade of her life, eating away at her, blackening her very soul. It was time she faced it head on.

"I just don't know where to start. How do I look for people who may not even exist?"

"You'll work it out."

"And if I don't?"

"Then at least you'll know you tried. It's better to have tried, than spend the rest of your life wondering," her mother said with finality.

Sitting back in the chair, she knew what she had to do. She had to go to Greece, to try and find out about her birth family. Only then would she really know who she was and where she came from, and be able to start living her life.

CHAPTER FOURTEEN

Zakynthos, Greece, 1941

A new year arrived bringing with it much change. The situation in Europe had become dire. France had been invaded six months earlier and the might of the German Army continued to creep ever closer, swallowing whole countries in its wake. The Germans had come to Italy's aid and, by the end of 1940, Germany and Italy stood shoulder-to-shoulder as allies, a worrisome development for the rest of the world. Many stories were broadcast across the airwaves and it seemed that the Germans were ruthless in their campaign against the rest of Europe. They blitzed England, destroying entire communities and razing cities to the ground. They caused death and destruction everywhere they went and dictated their newfound way of life to those countries now in their grip. It was a sad state of affairs and, however hard countries fought against them, the Germans it seemed were always a step ahead.

Angelos hated listening to the news. It was filled with sadness, death and destruction. He did not really understand any of it and the whole thing perplexed him greatly. He had asked many people he knew why the Germans were doing these things, but no one really seemed to know. Politics had never been a strong point, and so all he knew was that people were suffering and countries had been invaded with no way of defending their rights. It upset him greatly, and he dreaded it happening to their peaceful paradise. Despite his reservations, he was as desperate as everyone else to know the latest information. Living on the island was like living in an hourglass, and every new invasion made the islanders feel as though they were living on borrowed time. Life carried on, but the threat of the ever-enveloping war was becoming too much to bear.

Angelos was still working for his father but he now lived in a small house on his father's land with his new wife, Maria. His wedding day was still a complete blur; he could not believe his father had tricked him so cruelly. He had stumbled towards his wife to be, praying that he was suffering from a nightmare, but he failed to wake and had been forced to stand and accept the girl for the remainder of his life. She was the polar opposite to Elena. Where Elena was willowy and beautiful, Maria was plump and plain. Elena had sparkling eyes and shining hair; Maria's were lifeless and dull. Elena was outspoken, brave and filled with life; Maria was quiet, shy and boring.

The wedding party had lasted all day; his father and Stelios showing off like preening peacocks to all their guests, proud of their alliance. Angelos had felt sick, and had nothing but hatred in his heart for his father. Later that evening, Loukas and Stelios had walked Angelos and his wife to their new house, bidding them good evening with much merriment. As the sound of their laughter faded in the distance, Angelos knew with dread that he was forced to give himself, completely to a woman he did not know and would never love the way he loved Elena. What was he supposed to do? Silently, Maria had crept into their bedroom and he knew that as a new husband he had a duty to perform. With a heavy heart he closed the bedroom door behind him, and joined his new wife in bed.

~

Elena left Athena with her parents. As much as she loved her daughter, she felt trapped in the house. She had not seen Angelos in nearly three months, and was at a loss to know what he had been doing and why he had not been to see her. It was unlike him and she missed his company.

She knew that creeping down to the olive grove was a risk, but it was the only sure way of finding him. She waited all day, impatiently pacing up and down, unable to concentrate on anything for long. Finally, twilight arrived and she slipped out of the house knowing that the cover of late winter light would better serve both of them.

Peeking over the wall, she saw him cutting up old and storm-damaged trees into logs that would go into store to be used for firewood. She glanced around looking for Loukas, but was relieved to find that it was just the two of them. She opened her mouth, allowing the melodic notes he had always loved to wash over him.

Angelos lifted his head instantly and they locked eyes. His heart melted, but his head refused to let him move. He was married now; Elena was his past and he was to have nothing more to do with her. He knew that he should turn and leave, but as much as his head tried to win out, it was his heart that eventually made him do its bidding. Stepping forward, he slowly walked towards her. Nothing about her had changed, she was still as beautiful as ever, and he wondered why life had so cruelly taken her from him.

"My Angelos. Where have you been, why have you not come to see us? Your daughter misses you, and so do I."

Angelos climbed the wall and pulled her away from the groves. After crossing the track, they disappeared into the small woodland that ran alongside the groves.

"Elena, I..." he was lost for words.

"What is it? Is it your father?" She reached forward and took his hands in hers, bringing them to her cheek and then kissing them. The feel of cold metal against her face made her take a step back. Lifting his right hand, her heart plummeted.

"What is this?" she whispered.

"I am so sorry, Elena. My father forced me. I had no choice."

"You are married?" She was so shocked she could barely get the words out.

Angelos watched her crumple before him. Before she could flee, he folded her in his arms and held her tightly.

"I love you Elena, I love you so much."

She fought against him, her Angelos, the man she loved. She pushed him back, and he fell into a tree. "If you love me, then why marry someone else? Who is she anyway?"

"Maria Makris."

Elena felt as though she had been punched in the stomach. "The daughter of Stelios Makris?"

Angelos just nodded.

"Your father hates me that much?"

Angelos shrugged, not knowing what to say.

Leaning against a tree, Elena slid to the ground. "I always knew your father and Stelios disliked me, but to do this. Oh Angelos, how could you let them?"

He sat next to her, trying to explain. "My father threatened me, Elena; there was nothing I could do. He tricked me. He and Stelios planned the whole thing. By the time I realised what was happening, I was in the middle of the ceremony. There was nothing I could do."

"Do you love her?"

"No. I do not love her."

"Do you kiss her and make love to her like you did with me?"

Angelos wanted the earth to swallow him. "She is my wife. There are certain things I must do."

Elena felt sick. The thought of Angelos touching another woman the way he used to touch her made her distraught. She buried her head in her knees and cried.

"Do not cry."

"What am I supposed to do, Angelos? You are married to someone else now and you no longer love me or want me. And what about our daughter?"

"I *do* still love you Elena. I love you with every fibre of my being, and Athena will always be my daughter. I will always be there for her, for both of you, if need be."

"But we can never be together."

"Yes we can, Elena."

"How? It is impossible."

Angelos could no longer bear it. He leaned forward and kissed her, running his fingers through her hair, and Elena feverishly kissed him back. Lying her on the ground Angelos did what they both wanted, he made love to her there on the woodland floor, naked skin moving softly against naked skin. All that mattered was here and now and the two of them. He did not care that he was breaking his marriage vows, or that his wife would be wondering where he was. The only woman that mattered to him was Elena, now and always.

~

Loukas stared at Angelos. He wondered what was wrong with the boy. He had everything he could ever need and yet he walked about like a sullen teenager. He had hoped that the marriage and responsibility of being a husband would change his son, but Angelos was worse than ever. Loukas and Stelios were desperate to become grandfathers but the wait was becoming long. It angered Loukas that Angelos had managed to drop a bastard so quickly with a peasant, but when it came to nice girl like Maria, they were still childless. Loukas wondered why that was. He should make it his business to find out. Maybe Pigi could have a word with Maria to see if everything was okay? If this marriage failed,

Loukas would end up looking a fool, and he would not be made to look a fool by anyone, especially his son.

Leaving his house, Loukas climbed into his cart, and flicked the reins at the donkey, instructing it to make its usual journey. He did not have time to worry about his son now. There was too much work to be done.

~

Sitting in the café, Angelos drank coffee while listening to the latest radio report. Spring had arrived and the island was blossoming. News about the war, however, was grave. The British had come to Greece's aid and fought bravely, doing all they could to help, but it was futile. The Germans finally invaded and mainland Greece was now under the Axis occupation of the Germans, Italians and Bulgarians. Angelos suddenly realised that his prediction of a short war had been very wrong. The entire world was fighting hard with each other and no one knew where it would end or who would eventually win. It was a frightening and sobering thought.

After downing his coffee, he stepped out of the café and climbed onto his bicycle. He cycled to Elena's house in the mountains. He needed to see her and Athena, needed to feel real, needed to feel alive and there was only one person who could make him feel like that.

Elena Petrakis.

His marriage to Maria was awful. He tried his best to be a good husband, but he hated the sight of her and could not bear being in the same room as her. He did feel sorry for her. It was not her fault. She was as much a pawn in this whole mess as he was, but it did not change how he felt. Elena was the only woman for him.

Elena's mother opened the door and nodded curtly to Angelos. She had learned not to question the pair's relationship. As far as she was concerned, they were free to do as they chose, so she turned a blind eye to the lovers just as long as Loukas Sarkis stayed away.

"Elena!"

"Mama," came the distant voice. A moment later she appeared wiping her hands on her skirt.

"Angelos? Is everything okay?"

"Yes. I just needed to see you."

She stared for a moment and saw a mix of confusion and fire in his eyes.

"Mama. Can you look after Athena? I will be back soon. I promise."

Her mother nodded before disappearing into the house. Elena closed the door behind her and stepped out onto the street, taking Angelos's hand in hers.

"Will you tell me what is wrong?" she asked as they walked towards the small woodland near the village.

"I just needed to see you. I was listening to

the news and it was all so terrible. The war is doing so many horrible things to so many people, Elena, and I hate it. You and Athena are so precious to me and I needed to come and see you and tell you that."

"Thank you."

"I also wanted to give you this,"

They stopped under the canopy of trees and he handed her a small gift. She smiled, took it from him, and carefully opened it. It was the first and only present he had ever given her and it was beautiful. She lifted it from the packaging to take a better look, and the silver locket glinted in the light. The front was engraved with an ornate E and he motioned for her to turn it over.

"It says *I love you Elena*."

"Oh Angelos it is beautiful, but I cannot accept it."

"Why?"

"You know why."

"Open it," he instructed.

Sighing, she fiddled with the catch and it popped open. Inside was a grainy photograph of him. "I thought you could add a picture of you, and then we would always be together."

Despite knowing she should not accept it, Elena relented. Maybe one day she could give it to her daughter and Athena would always carry her parents close to her heart.

"Thank you, Angelos. It is beautiful."

"You will keep it?"

"Yes. I will keep it."

Angelos threaded it about her neck and secured the clasp.

Hand-in-hand, they strolled through the fragrant, pine-scented trees. It was not too cold for the time of year and they enjoyed the walk. It was so quiet, as though they were the only two people inhabiting the island. In a dense part of the wood, Angelos stopped, took Elena in his arms and held her tightly, smelling her hair, kissing her neck and her lips. He wanted her in a way he had never wanted anyone before. He slid his hands down her arms, gently lifting her skirt, feeling the softness of her legs.

"Angelos. We must not do this. Remember what happened last time."

"I no longer care, Elena. I want you. I always have and always will. Please, be mine."

"No, Angelos. I will not do that anymore. Not unless you leave Maria and marry me!" She pushed him away.

Angelos swore and looked at her as the tears formed in his eyes. He was in an impossible situation. He loved Elena very much, but knew he could never leave Maria and marry her, at least not while his father lived. They were doomed. But it did not stop him wanting her.

"Please, Elena?"

"No, Angelos!"

They stared at each other, neither of them

backing down. Things had reached an impasse. Neither would ever be able to have what they really wanted. There was too much that stood in the way.

"I will always love you, Elena. You know I will."

She looked at him, blinking away the tears. She knew she was about to lose him forever, and did not know how to stop it. He was the love of her life and she would never love anyone the way she loved him.

She pulled herself together and finally found her strength.

"Never come to my house again, Angelos. Stay away from me, do you hear?"

Turning, she blindly ran through the trees, tears falling from her eyes, deep choking sobs hindering her, but she did not stop until she reached the village. For a moment, she paused to see if he was behind her, but there was no sign of him. It was in that moment she knew he was lost to her. Angelos always came after her. Even after the worst of arguments, he had always followed to make amends. This time it was different. This time they had parted ways and there was no turning back.

In that moment, Elena finally knew what it was like to feel truly alone.

CHAPTER FIFTEEN

Zakynthos, Greece, 1941

It was a warm April morning, the sun was still rising, and there were few clouds in the sky. Angelos walked towards the beach, a place he still loved. Sometimes he liked to get up early and just go and sit on the sand to mull over life. It was the only place he could escape to, the only place he felt truly alone. He had left Maria fast asleep in bed. She would no doubt rise and discover him gone, but he no longer cared what she thought.

Nearing the coast, he turned onto the path that would take him down to his favourite spot. It was then that he saw them. Three small airplanes. As they flew over the neighbouring island of Kefalonia the airplanes suddenly released a clutch of small black dots. From a distance, Angelos strained to make them out. As the planes moved away, small semi-circular canopies began to appear one by one, above the dots.

Parachutists.

His blood ran cold and fear froze his heart. Kefalonia was being invaded.

His trip to the beach was forgotten. Fleeing to the café, he yelled at anyone who would listen. Slowly the news began to spread and Zakynthians gathered in small groups on clifftops, beaches and country lanes discussing what Angelos had seen, fearing what was to come next. The sky was clear again and no other parachutists could be seen, and they began to breathe a little easier, until a handful of seaplanes appeared on the horizon once again heading towards Kefalonia. The onlookers thought of their fellow Ionians and what they were going through. They wondered if the invading army had been kind or if they had taken everyone prisoner. Panic and worry washed through the island like a high spring tide and they feared for what would come next.

They did not have to wait long.

As the sky turned a brilliant blue on the first day of May, Angelos woke, uneasy and unable to sleep. He got up and walked to the café, surveying the horizon. He heard the noise before he saw them, coming from the north. Two seaplanes. After landing off the Zakynthian coast, they deposited their passengers onto the Greek shore. Angelos ran to the closest vantage point, hid behind a tree and spied on the invaders. A small group of Italian soldiers, decked out in grey uniforms, were standing on the shore, where two seaplanes were moored. The seaplanes were swiftly followed by a flotilla of boats that easily traversed the calm turquoise waters.

Many islanders, disturbed by the sound of the airplanes, came to see what was going on. They warily gathered to watch the incomers. There was little they could do to stop them and the occupation of Zakynthos was swift and authoritative.

That day, island life changed forever.

~

By the summer of 1941, Greece had been fully invaded, and Greeks were forced to live under the Axis of Occupation rule. Islanders tried to go about life as normal, but things had changed. They no longer had the freedom to do what they wanted, when they wanted. The Italians watched their every move, and took over town halls and businesses. Curfews were put into place and movement was restricted. Food became scarce and Zakynthians began to feel like prisoners in their own home. Even if they wanted to escape, they could not. It was impossible.

Angelos still went to the café, but things were

different there, too. They were no longer allowed to listen to the radio or talk of Greece's allies. On this visit, Angelos was nursing a cup of coffee, keeping his head down and avoiding eye contact with the four Italian soldiers who sat opposite. They were loud and uncouth, and liked to push the locals around; he did not want to become the object of their latest game.

The door flung open and Angelos glanced up. His heart soared as Elena walked up to the counter. It had been so long since he last saw her. She was as beautiful as ever, and he missed her, but the café was too public a place for him to talk to her. The soldiers turned their attention to her and slowly, like a pack of lions seeking out prey, they gathered around her, preening and showing off. She had nowhere to go and turned her back to the bar. She was left with no choice but to use her feminine charms to escape their attention. She caught Angelos's eye, giving him the faintest nod as she ran, but he did not dare acknowledge her or go after her. He did not want to be taken away by the soldiers.

One of the Italians whispered to the others and left, following in Elena's footsteps. A couple of fishermen entered the café and Angelos took his chance to sneak out, running quietly to try and catch up with Elena. He saw her, walking quickly, desperately trying to get away from the Italian, but the soldier was too quick and he caught hold of her arm, forcing her to stop. Angelos, still following, ducked behind a wall. He was so close to them that he held his breath, fearing they would hear him. He was surprised to hear the man speak in Greek.

"You are a very pretty girl. I am Captain Pietro Cipriani."

"Hello, Captain," Elena said, taking in the man. He was tall and muscular. His hair was almost as black as raven wings with eyes almost as dark. She felt like they bored into her and she had nowhere to hide.

"Captain is so formal. You may call me Pietro."

"Hello Pietro."

"I feel at a disadvantage. You know my name, but alas, I do not know yours." The Italian was smooth, but there was an edge to his voice that warned Elena that she should do as he asked.

"Elena. My name is Elena."

Behind the wall, Angelos silently chuckled. He knew her well enough to envision the defiant look on her face. He had heard the same tone in her voice the night she stood up to his father.

"Elena. A very pretty name for a very pretty girl. Are you married, Elena?"

"What is it to you?"

Angelos feared the soldier's response, but the Italian just laughed.

"I like your bravado. Strong women are my favourite kind. Maybe you and I can come to some arrangement, *piccolina*." Pietro smiled.

Sitting as still as he could, Angelos could hear the lasciviousness in the soldier's voice. He wanted to yell at him to get away from her and never to speak to her again, but he was a coward and stayed where he was, hidden and silent.

"I do not like men like you. You are the enemy, and I spit on the enemy."

Pietro laughed again. "Such a fiery temper, Elena. You should watch yourself. Your tongue will get you into trouble one day. You need to understand that we are your captors and you must do what we say."

"Never!"

"Never say never. Ciao, bella." Moments later, Angelos heard footsteps retreating so he poked his head over the wall. Elena was staring after the man in shock. Quickly, he grabbed her and pulled her down behind the wall where he cradled her in his arms, allowing her to cry and let the hurt, anger and confusion out.

A while later as they walked back up the hill, Angelos finally spoke.

"You must be careful, Elena. I do not trust the Italians. You are so headstrong and I fear they will hurt you if you say or do the wrong thing."

"Oh Angelos. You worry too much. It will be okay." She looked at him for a moment, and he noticed she was wearing the locket. It pleased him and he was glad they were talking again after the way things had been left.

"How is married life, Angelos?"

"Boring."

"Do you love her yet?"

"No," he sighed. "I wish I could find love for her, but I just do not feel that way about her. Let us not talk about it again, Elena. It pains me too much."

"Okay."

They fell silent once more. It seemed that with the arrival of the Italians, the island had changed. Fewer birds seemed to fly and the trees and plants had lost their sweet fragrant blossom. Even the sea seemed to have lost its bright shimmer. At the fork in the road they stood awkwardly for a few moments, neither wanting to say goodbye, but both knowing they must. Making it easy for him, Elena smiled and turned without saying a word, and walked on up to the mountains. Resigned, Angelos walked down the lane to Maria, his wife.

~

Pietro sat overlooking the square in Zakynthos Town. He had been on the island for a month now and already it felt like home. He had always been a nomad, choosing to live life wherever it took him. He had no family, a wife he hated and could not stand to be around, and no children, so signing up for the war had been an easy decision. Some of his old friends had ended up in the back of beyond, but he was lucky. He ended up on an island paradise, with beautiful sunshine, pretty girls and a quiet and obedient population. So far, the Germans were happy with the way the Italians were running things and it made life easier. It meant they could do what they wanted with their time, as long as order remained and they showed the islanders that they were the ones in charge. So far it seemed to be working.

Today he had a meeting planned with some of the previous town officials and some local business owners. Pietro hoped it would go well, but you could never tell, especially with Greeks. Many people thought Italians had fiery tempers, but they evidently had not met any Greeks. They were just as bad! Pietro's mind wandered back to the pretty little *piccolina,* Elena. He had hoped to see her again, but sadly he had not caught a glimpse of her after that first meeting. If he were to live on the island for the foreseeable future, a pretty girl like her would suit him very well.

Pietro's thoughts were interrupted when his comrade beckoned him inside. It was time for them to turn their heads to politics.

Loukas and Stelios looked up to see two swarthy Italians enter the room. They had agreed for everyone's sake to keep the meeting low key. The Italians sat opposite; one pulled out a cigarette and lit it before speaking.

"So you must be Loukas Sarkis and Stelios Makris. We have heard much about you. I am Captain Pietro Cipriani."

Loukas and Stelios merely nodded.

Pietro continued, "As you are aware this island is now governed by us, everything that happens now goes through us. The people obey our rules. If we decide that things are to be done differently, then the islanders accept this and will not answer back. If we come across trouble makers, we will deal with them accordingly."

Loukas raised his hand and asked, "Exactly how will troublemakers be dealt with?"

"That is for us to decide at the time, but I have heard that your old castle at Bohali, has some excellent cells." The Italian laughed at his own joke, before getting back to the point. "You need not worry about such trivial things. What we need from you is for you to help the islanders understand that they have no choice but to follow the rules and obey us. Can you do that?"

Loukas and Stelios nodded once more.

"Any questions, gentlemen?"

Loukas and Stelios shook their heads.

"I have one, if I may," Pietro said. "Do you know of a girl called Elena? She is a pretty little thing. Long hair, no shoes, scruffy clothes. I need to speak with her."

Loukas nodded. He could tell that the Captain's question was of a personal nature and he would be more than happy to let his enemy take the gypsy in hand. “Yes, Elena Petrakis. She lives up in the mountains, near to Exo Hora. I can get a local to take you there. Has she done something wrong?”

“No. I just need to talk to her. Your offer of help is welcome. Thank you.”

Pietro stood and left the Greeks sitting in uncomfortable silence. Loukas and Stelios had hoped to govern the island one day, working their way up to mayor and deputy, but the war had snatched it from under them. The only thing they could do was side with their enemy in the hope of recognition further down the line. They both knew it was a dangerous game, but play it they must.

~

It was a beautiful sunny day and Elena was out picking flowers. She enjoyed walking through the fields, watching the wildlife and feeling part of nature. She just wished the world was not at war. Her island did not feel right, now that the enemy had landed. Everywhere she looked, she saw grey uniforms, jeeps, guns and planes. It broke her heart to think they were now prisoners of a madman’s army. The future she had feared so much was upon them and she had no idea how it would all end.

As she went to cross the road, a jeep approached. She stood still and fiddled with the flowers in her basket, waiting for it to pass. It was unusual to see the Italians this far up in the mountains. The jeep began to slow and her pulse quickened. With a screech that sent up a cloud of dust, it stopped a few feet away from her and a soldier jumped down. Lowering her eyes, she concentrated on the field opposite and walked quickly across the road; anything to get away from her enemy.

"Wait!"

She heard the voice, but carried on walking.

"Elena Petrakis! I command you to stop!"

She whirled around to face the man. How did he know who she was? "You command me? Who are you to command me!"

She dropped the basket and was glaring, hands on hips. As the man came closer, she realised there was something familiar about him.

"I am sorry. I did not mean to make you drop your flowers. Here, let me." Bending down, he turned over the basket and scooped up the stems, carefully placing them back where they belonged. Standing, he handed the basket back to her.

"Who are you?"

"Do you not remember me, Elena? I remember you. We met at the café the other day."

Elena studied him, and then she remembered. He was the Italian soldier she had run into the last time she saw Angelos.

"Ah yes. I am sorry; I do not recall your name."

"It is Pietro."

"Your Greek is very good, Pietro."

"Thank you."

"Why are you here?" She felt uncomfortable, and wondered if she had done something wrong. "Am I in trouble?"

He laughed, "No. I just could not get you out of my mind and wanted to see you again."

His response floored her. "But..." For the first time in her life she was speechless.

"Has my feisty *piccolina* nothing to say?"

"I do not understand."

Pietro guided her to a fallen log by the road and motioned for her to sit. "You are a very pretty woman, Elena, a pretty woman with great spirit. I would like to get to know you better."

"I do not fraternise with the enemy of Greece!" she replied, suddenly finding her voice again. How dare he talk to her like this.

"I can understand why you would feel that way, but I assure you I am merely here to help keep the peace. I like you Elena. Please say you will think about it."

She glared at him, arms crossed. "Never!"

"Okay. I know when I am beaten," he shrugged and stood, dusting down his trousers. "It was nice to see you again, *piccolina*."

He began to walk away, but stopped and walked back towards her. "There is one more thing." He pulled her up from the log and, before she knew what was happening, he threw his arms around her, and his lips were on hers, hungrily kissing her. Her brain told her it was not right, he was her enemy, this should not be happening. Her body kicked in and with every instinct she fought him off, pushing him away. She wiped her mouth with the back of her hand and took a step back.

Laughing, Pietro shook his head. “You are a very brave woman indeed. You will see me again soon.” Turning, he left her alone in the field feeling ashamed and confused.

CHAPTER SIXTEEN

Bristol, England, 2002

Kate sat at her desk staring at the ever-growing pile of paperwork. She was due to leave work in three hours but still had not finished everything she needed to do. Mild panic rose within her. She was nervous enough about leaving the company for two weeks as it was, but if she did not get this paperwork done she would not be going at all and could lose her best client in the process.

Her staff had been shocked at the announcement. Kate Fisher taking a holiday? It was unheard of! But they had quickly learned the news was true. She would be gone for two weeks and she was leaving them all in charge. As six pm arrived, Ashleigh bundled Kate into her coat, and pushed her out of the door. In return Ashleigh was met with stern words and a promise to make sure their best client was top priority.

Kate was perturbed. It was as though she had just left a newborn baby with a bunch of teenagers, and she was not sure she had made the right decision. But she had to trust them. The following day she would be on a plane travelling to Greece and work would be out of her hands.

~

Excitement buzzed through Kate as she ran around the house gathering her belongings. A few minutes later she was in a taxi on the way to Bristol Airport. It had been so long since she had had a holiday and, although she had reservations about the real reason she was going, she had to admit that she was excited to be getting away.

Why had she not done this sooner? She could not wait to leave the UK and visit somewhere new. A bit of sunshine would not go amiss either. It had been a long cold winter, and she was looking forward to feeling the warmth in her bones, and the sun on her skin.

The flight was quicker than she expected and she spent most of it staring out of the window as they passed over Europe. As the aircraft began its descent, she absorbed the view. The sea was a mix of bright turquoise and deeper blues. The land was earthy and scrubby and shot through with deep greens, brown rocks and sandy beaches. Zakynthos did not look very big, but it did not bother her. She was just excited about being somewhere different, experiencing a new culture and getting away from England.

Finally the plane touched down with a small bump and a screech of tyres before coming to a halt. The warm air kissed her skin as she stepped from the plane onto the tarmac. She smiled. It was great to feel the warm Mediterranean sun upon her face, and she knew in that moment that she had made the right decision to come here. Following the other passengers into the small terminal, she easily passed through customs and collected her case and stepped out into the bright sunshine to find a taxi.

She gave the driver the address of her hotel, and then settled back to enjoy the journey. Despite similarities, the scenery was very different to the UK. Once they had left the environs of the airport, the roads turned into country lanes. There were no pavements to speak of, just grass verges, shrubland and trees. Every now and then a house or shop appeared at the side of the road, interspersed with the rich soil and lush greenery that seemed to be everywhere. The air flowing through the open window was warm and the sun shone brightly, bathing everything in a comfortable glow. Occasionally, Kate caught glimpses of the sea, shimmering brightly in the distance, and just the sight of it relaxed her. It was not long before they were driving down a narrow road edged with olive groves and dotted through with grass and bright wild flowers. Turning a corner, they arrived at the hotel on the north east coast of the island near Kypseli. After paying and thanking the driver, she dragged her case along the path and into reception.

"Welcome!" A pretty woman looked up from the desk, greeting her with perfect English.

"Hi. I didn't expect you to be English," Kate said.

The woman laughed. "I get that a lot. I'm Michelle. I come over every year to work for the season. There are lots of English people here who do the same."

"I'm Kate Fisher. It's nice to meet you."

"Likewise," Michelle said scanning the computer. "Kate Fisher, we have you down for a two week stay. Why don't I show you your room?"

Kate nodded and followed Michelle up the stairs and along a light and airy whitewashed corridor. Stepping into the hotel room that would be her home for the next few weeks, she was pleasantly surprised. There was a small kitchenette, a spacious living room, a bathroom and a bedroom. Michelle explained where everything was and then left her to get settled.

Opening the double doors in the bedroom, Kate stepped out onto a wrap-around balcony that could be accessed by almost every room. The view was incredible. To the left, the rough, green terrain of the island was dotted through with the occasional building, eventually rising to hilly peaks. To the right was an expanse of sea that seemed to go on forever. Dependent on the light, the sea's colour shifted from brilliant turquoise to deep cobalt blue. It was difficult to gauge where sea ended and sky began, but small wispy clouds occasionally passed overhead, disrupting what was otherwise a perfect bright and sunny late spring day. In the distance she could see the faint outline of land, and she was not sure if it was another island or mainland Greece.

Settling back on one of the patio chairs, she pulled out a book and decided to relax for a bit before unpacking her case.

~

With her sunglasses on and a bottle of water in her hand, Kate headed towards the main road. It was quiet and very peaceful. Long grass and wild flowers grew at the side of the road, and the sun shone brightly as she walked. The road was dusty and winding and eventually she came to a decision point: turn left or right? She chose right, and eventually found herself on a long pebble-covered beach. It was nice to be near water again. She had missed the coast so much since moving to Bristol. Sitting down on the warm pebbles, she watched as small waves washed back and forth with a swishing noise. They lifted smaller pebbles, rolling and pushing them slowly along the beach; constantly moving, constantly changing.

Unlike her.

Her parents were right. She was stuck in her comfortable job and had just stopped, seemingly going nowhere. She had no friends and no one to share her life with. How had it come down to this?

She wondered where Fletch was and what he was doing. They had spent so many hours sitting together on a beach, talking while growing up. She had lost track of the number of early mornings that she had run down to watch him flick and turn his board, riding the waves until eventually he lost the battle and plunged into the sea.

She felt a surge of sadness go through her. She wished they had both swallowed their pride and made up after their argument. She really missed him. Funny, handsome Fletch, her best friend in the whole world. She picked up a large pebble, and angrily flung it into the waves, venting her frustration. They had both been so stubborn and pig-headed and were now both adrift, lost to each other. It had been too long and there was no going back now. She wished, there in that very moment, that she could turn back the clock, wipe the slate clean, go back and change history, but she knew that could never happen.

Great heaving sobs racked her body, and she pulled her legs up, hugging her knees, allowing all of the pent up emotion to spill from her body. Finally, alone on a beach in a foreign country, Kate began let go and relax for the first time in years.

~

The sea shimmered like glass in the early morning sunlight. It was quiet and peaceful, and Kate felt like she had been transported to heaven. In the distance, a boat passed, leaving a line of white froth in its wake. She breathed deeply, a mixture of smells enveloping her that were a pleasant change to the fuggy smell of the city.

"Beautiful isn't it," Michelle said, as she set a pot of tea on the table along with two bowls containing food.

"It is. I was surprised when I got here. You always see pictures of Greece and they are of little harbours filled with boats, whitewashed buildings with blue domed roofs or ancient ruins on clifftops. Zakynthos seems very different. It's not like I imagined at all."

"You know why, don't you?"

"Why?"

"Because it's so much better!" Michelle said. Kate laughed as Michelle walked back inside. Pulling the bowls towards her, she dipped her spoon in one. The sweet taste of fruit salad was a welcome change from her usual boring breakfast cereal. Once finished, she lifted the other bowl and savoured the creamy yet slightly bitter thick white contents. The traditional Greek yogurt was delicious, and nothing like the sort you bought in the supermarket back home. It was so much better, and something she could definitely get used to.

The boat she had been watching finally disappeared behind the headland, leaving a sparkling expanse of blue in its wake, and she sighed. Coming here was definitely the right thing to do. She had come to the island with a purpose, but that purpose was loose and not thought out. She realised then that she had no plan. How was she supposed to even start finding out about her family? She had little to go on. How did she go about discovering a past that had been hidden, a past that was so far removed from her own life that it was almost as if she was never supposed to discover it?

Michelle appeared next her, breaking her train of thought.

"Is there anything else I can get you?" she asked as she cleared away the dirty dishes.

"No, thank you." But after a slight pause, added, "Actually there is something you can help me with."

"Of course," Michelle said as she sat opposite, relieved to be able take the weight off her feet even if it was for a few minutes.

“Is there an easy way of getting around the island?”

“Yes, if you can drive. I can recommend a car hire place, and I can drop you down there if it would help?”

“Thanks. That would be great.”

Michelle could see something else was bothering the girl. She had no idea whether it was grief or a wayward boyfriend, but something was definitely off.

“Is everything okay, Kate?”

“Yes. I just have a lot on my mind.”

“Want to share?”

“You don’t need to hear my woes. But thank you for the offer.”

Feeling slightly disappointed, Michelle shrugged and stood, leaving Kate to finish her cup of tea.

~

Having changed her clothes, Kate bounced down the stairs to reception. She was looking forward to getting out and seeing the island. Michelle was behind the reception desk surrounded by paperwork, looking a bit stressed.

“Is the offer of helping me sort out a hire car still there?”

“Of course. I’ll just get the owner to watch the desk for me.”

“Thank you.”

At the car hire company in Tsilivi, Michelle handled everything for Kate. She was glad Michelle was there as she understood no Greek at all, and even though the owner spoke English, he was difficult to understand. Once they had settled on the best car, the owner handed Kate a set of keys, a map of the island and ran through a brief set of driving rules for Greece. Michelle kindly translated everything before leaving Kate to it and racing back to the hotel.

Kate decided to drive across the island to see what she could find. Leaving Tsilivi, she followed the sporadically placed road signs towards Zakynthos Town. She had learned that the Italians re-named it Zante Town during the war, but most locals still called it by its original name, Zakynthos Town. After a few false starts and wrong turns, it was not long before she reached it and found herself near the busy harbour absorbing the many sights and sounds of the town. Tall palm trees surrounded a large paved square. The harbour was wide and sweeping, and was filled with boats, which bobbed on the gentle movement of water. A salty smell came from the turquoise waters and tingled as it hit her nose. She marveled at the many buildings including the large Venetian church tower that reminded her of St. Mark's Square. The town was busy and crowded, cafés and roadside shops enticed locals and tourists with the smell of heavenly food and myriad gifts. She could not find anywhere to park, so continued on, promising herself that she would return another day. Reaching the end of the harbour, she followed the signs to Laganas. The lads in the office had mentioned it, telling her she should definitely go there.

Kate turned off the main road, and it was not long before she was in the heart of Laganas strip. She found a parking space and pulled in. Getting out of the car she stretched and caught sight of the sea in the distance. After locking the car, she walked down the strip towards it. Both sides of the road were lined with a multitude of shops, cafés, restaurants and nightclubs. She was not really sure what to make of it, but decided to reserve judgment until she had seen it properly. Abruptly, the road ended at a small concrete car park and Kate found herself looking at a large sweeping beach, lined with yet more bars and restaurants. She strolled along the busy shoreline taking in the sights and sounds. She could understand why the lads had recommended it. It was wall-to-wall bars and lots of pretty girls. Just their sort of holiday. It was not really Kate's thing, but she appreciated it for what it was.

She wandered into one of the bars, took a seat at an empty table, and ordered a drink. Gazing out across the sea, her brain went into overdrive again. How was she going to find out about her family? She did not speak Greek, could barely get around the island and had no idea who to talk to about getting started. It felt like an uphill battle already and she had barely begun. An hour later she was still none the wiser, and she was beginning to get a headache. The waiter came over to ask if she wanted another drink but she politely declined. She left the bar, and walked back to her car.

Taking the main road north, she passed Zakynthos Town and the turn off to her apartment. Carrying on northwards, it was not long before she reached Alykes. Rather than stopping, she drove through until she reached a small inlet with an island sitting in the middle of the bay. She sat in her parked car for a minute, looking at her map, and worked out that she had arrived at Agios Nikolaos. She got out of the car and walked to the small brick wall, sat on it and looked out at the calm turquoise waters. A handful of people were on the beach, a few boats were moored in the natural curving harbour, but other than that, it was relatively quiet. At the edge of the beach was a small covered restaurant, so she walked over to it and took a seat all the while marveling at the sea as its waves gently lapped at the restaurant's edge. She realised she was starving so she took a seat and ordered lunch. Watching the water lap back and forth, she thought of Fletch again. He would have loved it here. She really did miss him, and wished he was here; he would have helped her make sense of everything. She sipped her water and shook thoughts of him from her mind. It was time to forget about him, enjoy the tranquility of the place and wait for her food to arrive.

It was not long before she was back in the car studying the map once more. The owner of the restaurant had recommended she visit the shipwreck. Driving through ever narrowing lanes that wound slowly upwards, through dusty scrubby gorse-lined roads, she found herself driving blind. Signposts were almost non-existent and she wondered how anyone ever found their way around the island. It was with more luck than judgment that she finally reached her destination.

Steep white cliffs appeared before her as she stepped from the car. They descended sharply to a deep blue sea. Waves crashed at the base of the cliffs, frothy and white. Walking the path to the edge of the cliff, she reached a small stone wall and a viewing platform with a metal rail that hung out over the cliff. It looked precarious and she hated heights, but she swallowed her fears and slowly stepped along it until she reached the end. Staring straight down, she was shocked. Directly below lay an arc of cliffs, in which hid a sheltered beach. Lying at the centre of the beach was a rusted, listing ship. She stared in awe, taking in the beautiful view. She had not been on Zakynthos long but she had already fallen in love with the place.

A noisy group of tourists appeared behind her, and there was not enough room for all of them on the viewing platform so she stepped back on to firm land to let them have a look. Instead of leaving, she sat on the wall and stared out across the brilliant blue sea edged with striking white cliffs, trying to make sense of her life and everything that had happened.

CHAPTER SEVENTEEN

Zakynthos, Greece, 1942

The remainder of 1941 passed in relative calm. Even though they hated them, islanders grew used to the presence of Italian soldiers. They were allowed to go about their business with minimal disruption, but life was hard and everyone was well aware that they were prisoners, and that their life was not their own. As the year came to a close, they were harshly reminded of a war that was still very much close to home.

A British submarine, passing through the narrow waters between Zakynthos and Kefalonia, hit an Italian mine. It killed almost everyone on board, and shook the islanders to their core. Death and destruction had landed right on the island's doorstep. War was here to stay and they were nothing more than pawns in the game.

When Elena heard about the loss of the submarine, she went and sat on the cliffs at the north of the island, staring out at the death-tainted waters. She felt the loss deeply. She hated that an evil monster was controlling the world. Things had to change. Life could not continue like this. Too many people were dying, but she knew she was just one small person in a very big world and there was little she could do to help.

The next day, while walking through Zakynthos Town with Athena, she thought about it again and wondered if there was something that she could do, but she knew it was pointless. What could one woman possibly do to help, when entire armies and country leaders were failing so dismally? Slowly she meandered the back streets, keeping a firm hold of her daughter's hand. Athena was now walking, but still had to be carried sometimes. Elena was determined to let her daughter have as much freedom as possible and was relieved when she no longer needed to push her round in her pram. She stared into half empty shops. With little to no stock, hardly any of them opened now. Even if they had, most of the islanders did not have the money to buy anything anyway. She continued to walk, taking in life as it now was, changed and uncertain. Up ahead, a group of men hid in the shadow of a doorway, watching her, their backs against the wall, and their faces etched with a furtive look. She knew they were up to no good.

"What are you doing?"

"Nothing, girl. Move on. You will draw attention to us."

"Only if you are doing something wrong."

"I said move on!" the voice hissed back.

Shrugging, Elena carried on along the road and turned the corner, disappearing from sight. She stopped and stood silently on the next road patiently waiting. She was relieved that Athena was remaining quiet. A moment later she cautiously peeked back around the corner. The men had stepped away from the wall. Two of them were looking up and down the street, as if keeping watch, as another reached into a doorway and pulled out a can and a brush. Dipping the brush into the can, he sloshed it around before removing it. It was now coated with bright red paint that gleamed on the end of the bristles. Elena watched in fascination as he streaked the wall, as though writing, but she could not see what. Minutes later the men scattered in all directions leaving the street quiet and still.

Intrigue welled within her and she walked back down the road to take a closer look. The paint was not dry, but the writing was very clear.

RESIST.

The word was powerful and yet Elena was unsure why the men had chosen it or what they meant by it. She did not wait around to find out. Heading back down towards the harbour, she quickened her pace, and made her way safely and unseen.

The word stuck with her for the rest of the day and stirred something in her; as much as she tried, she just could not get it out of her head. She had managed to get a lift to town and home again in a neigbour's donkey and cart. Lifting Athena down, she thanked the man. As he went on his way, she grabbed hold of her tired daughter's hand, turned into a lane near the olive groves and stopped. Angelos was ahead, walking hand in hand with his wife Maria. She missed him dreadfully but knew that there would never be anything more between them than friendship, if that. Seeing him again made her heart sink. She hated the thought of him being with another woman; a woman who was dowdy, timid and unbecoming.

The awkward moment arrived all too soon. Like a rabbit caught in headlights, it was Angelos who finally spoke first.

"Elena."

"Angelos." She turned to his wife and said, "You must be Maria, it is lovely to meet you."

"Yes, and you," Maria said quietly, glancing at Athena.

Silence fell between them, and no one knew what to say next. It was Elena who broke the tension.

"I must be going. It has been a long day. Athena is hungry. Good-day, Angelos, Maria." She nodded and walked past them, head held high as she did, but despite her bravery she felt nothing but sadness.

Angelos watched her go. He continued to live a miserable existence since marrying Maria. He worked all the hours under the sun, as his father and Stelios became more and more affiliated with the Italians. The two elder Greek men spent many hours in town on 'official' business, but it did not fool Angelos. He knew they had chosen sides and that the Sarkis and Makris families were firmly aligned with the enemy. Angelos knew they had only done it out of self-preservation, but it shamed him greatly. With his father always being at the Italians' beck and call, it was left to Angelos to pick up the slack and make sure that the Sarkis business and home continued to run smoothly.

His relationship with Maria had not fared much better. She was clingy and needy and hated being left on her own. He knew that seeing Elena and his child would not help the situation. Angelos wished his wife would find something to occupy herself, but she had no personal skills and never went out unless he was with her. Instead she chose stay at home all day, cleaning and tidying the house when it was clean and tidy enough already.

Angelos still yearned for Elena. He hated the

life he had been dealt and wished he could change it somehow, but it was impossible. He was stuck. This was his lot and he just had to get used to it.

"Do you still love her, Angelos?" Maria's voice interrupted his thoughts.

"What?"

"I said do you still love her?"

"No. Of course not."

She knew he was lying, she saw the look on both of their faces upon meeting. They were two people who were still very much in love with each other and, in that moment, Maria knew that it would always be so. But how could she tell her husband that she knew he was a liar? She could not, so she chose to stay quiet. She hated her father for marrying her off like this, for submitting her to a life of hell, with a man who did not care for her. She wished things were different, but they were not. So, like many other women, she would just have to make the best of a bad lot.

~

The night was pitch black with only the smallest sliver of moon occasionally peeking from behind scurrying clouds. The three men moved silently, keeping to the woods and fields, hugging walls, hedges and trees; anything that would give them the cover they greatly needed to keep out of sight of the Italian army. They need not have worried, since most of the Italians were asleep or in their favourite bars drinking. They had become a bored and lazy army that preferred the pleasures of life to fighting a war.

As the men reached the edge of the wood, they saw the old hut, nestled in amongst the ancient trees and bushes. Hiding behind a large tree, they waited for the signal: two short man-made owl hoots. They ran from their hiding places and entered the small wooden hut. Once the door was shut, they seated themselves around the table in silence. A lone candle burned at the centre of the table, throwing ghostly illuminations about the room.

"Thank you for coming. We will be known as 'the resistance'. If you need to address me, you will call me Dionysis. We all know what is happening in Europe. We all know about the war, and we all know that we are prisoners of the Axis powers," Dionysis spoke plainly. "While our island is under Italian rule, our lives are not our own. They lead us to believe that Hitler's way is best, that we should all follow him and bow down to him, but we must not. We are Greek, this is our home and no one can ever take it away from us or tell us how to live."

The men around the table nodded in hearty agreement.

"We will do everything we can to show our oppressors that they will not win and that we will fight them every way we can. I cannot tell you how, but I have received word from the mainland that the resistance movement there is strong and fighting back. Greeks are standing up for what they believe in and refusing to obey their German dictators. We must do the same. We will graffiti, we will hand out leaflets, we will carry weapons for our protection and we will smuggle food and medicine to those who need it most. We will go up against the Italians whenever we can. I have smuggled a small radio out here so that we can listen to the latest news from our allies. I need you all to be strong and carry out any tasks you are given. It will be dangerous, and there will be times when your life will be in peril, but we will succeed."

The men nodded again.

"I also need you to recruit, but be careful who you trust. I have learned that the Italians are lining the pockets of Loukas Sarkis and Stelios Makris. Neither man can be trusted, nor can their families. It is disappointing, but war brings out the worst in people. Do not let them hear of what we are doing or we will fail. That is all for now. Here are the handbills I have printed." Dionysis handed them a stack of individual papers, each printed with a single word: RESIST. "They are simple," he continued. "*Resist* we will and *resist* we must."

The men nodded, and stuffed the handbills under their shirts so they were hidden to the outside world. The men knew that getting caught with these simple papers would be risky. Dionysis slowly opened the hut door and released the men one by one, watching them slink into the shadows, disappearing as swiftly as they had arrived. Alone once more, Dionysis sat at the table and turned on the small transistor radio, in the hopes of catching some useful information. Already the war was beginning to wear him down, but he could not stop now. Too many people were depending on him.

~

Elena left Athena home with her mother and went to the nearest village for supplies. Her wicker basket was hung over her arm and she whistled as she walked, her bare feet kicking up the dust on the road. Zakynthos's winter had finally departed and she was enjoying watching the flowers and trees bloom. Birds were flying again and the sea was a calm crystal blue. As she enjoyed the beauty of the morning, she heard the dull rumbling of a vehicle behind her. Turning, she saw an Italian truck heading towards her. Quickly she ran behind a hedge to hide, praying it would pass quickly. As it neared she heard it slow, and her heart thudded. Moments later an Italian soldier appeared next to her.

"Why do you run and hide?" he demanded.

Elena lifted her head to look at him, and was shocked to see Pietro.

"Elena?" he reached out his hand to help her

to her feet.

"Thank you. I am sorry, but I do not trust your men. I heard a terrible story the other day. A girl was walking home and she was not quick enough to hide and your men, they forced themselves on her and did unspeakable things to her."

"They were not my men, *piccolina*. I would never allow that. I am sorry that you do not trust us. We only have your best interests at heart."

"Our best interests?" Elena could only laugh. "You keep us here like caged animals, prisoners on our own island, with so many rules. People are starving and barely have enough food to feed their children, they have no medicine when they need it, and yet your army eats well and drink the bars dry. That is not best interests, that is enslavement!"

She stormed along the hedge back to the road. Pietro ran to catch up with her.

"Let me help you, Elena. Let me protect you."

She whirled around to face him, seething with a thundercloud of hatred. "Protect me! You could never protect me, Pietro, and I refuse to live by the rules of your uniform, or anyone's for that matter."

Pietro sighed. She was a feisty one, and he knew that she could get him into so much trouble if he let her, but he could not help it. He wanted her in his life. "My darling, beautiful, strong,

Elena, you have captured my heart, and I mourn every day that I do not see you. Be mine." He ran his hand down her cheek to the nape of her neck. His eyes, locked with hers, never wavered for a moment and he pulled her to him.

Elena felt like she was caught in a spell. Her brain was telling her to run, but her legs refused and she was unable to move. For the second time, the enemy's lips found hers and for the second time she surrendered unwillingly. Moments later, her head won out and she pushed him away and glared at him in defiance.

"Do not ever touch me again!"

This time Pietro allowed her to storm off. He would break her down. It may take some time, but she would be his eventually. He would make damn sure of it one way or another.

~

Sitting in the square with her parents, Elena bounced Athena on her knee. The child was growing fast now, not only was she walking she had begun to talk. It was rare that Elena got to relax with her family and daughter; there was always something that needed doing in the house. Today was a public holiday and many islanders were enjoying a day away from normal life. The Italians constantly walked at the edge of their lives, but they chose to ignore the soldiers and enjoy their day. A young boy weaved his way through the chairs, quietly begging for food scraps, but most people shooed him away before he even had a chance to ask. Elena caught his eye and motioned to him. He wandered over and smiled broadly.

"Here have this," Elena said, holding out a small piece of baklava. She had really been looking forward to eating it when she got home, but his need was greater than hers.

The boy grinned and thanked her and, in a swift movement that barely caught the eye, he swiped the sweet cake and deposited a folded piece of paper into her hand before running into the crowd.

Confused, Elena dropped her hands to her lap. Cautiously she looked about, but no one was watching her so she slowly opened the piece of paper. It had one word on it, *RESIST*. Panicked, she re-folded it and placed it in her dress pocket. Unnerved, she checked around to see if anyone had seen her read it but the celebrations continued as normal.

"Are you okay?" her mother asked.

"Yes, but I think I have a headache coming."

"Leave Athena with us, and go and get some rest."

"Okay." It was the chance she needed. She left the village and walked back towards her house. Before she reached it, she felt a tug at her arm and an icy cold shiver travelled the length of her body. Slowly she turned, expecting the worst, but it was only the grinning boy from the square. He placed his finger to his lips and beckoned for her to follow him. Unsure of what to do, she checked left and right, but the street was empty. They were completely alone. The boy beckoned again, so she gave in and followed. Walking silently up the long deserted street, they eventually reached a small church.

The boy opened the door and gently pushed her inside. The door closed softly behind her and she found herself alone. Nervously she stepped forward and walked along the chilly stone floor. Everything in the building felt cold to the touch and the church was dark and gloomy. As she reached the front, she saw a man sitting in the shadows, praying. A whisper came from him that she could barely hear.

"Sit behind me, Elena, and pretend you are worshipping."

Elena did as instructed. She could not see the man's face, but knew he was Greek by the clothes he was wearing and his thick accented voice.

"You took our propaganda. I am impressed. I knew you would after seeing you in Zakynthos Town. You watched us from the street corner before going back to see what we had written. You are a brave woman. I have heard how you stood up to Loukas Sarkis over the years. We need someone like you."

"Someone like me? Why?"

"You are a woman. You are brave and you know a lot about the Sarkis family from your affair with Loukas's son. You are very valuable to our cause."

"Your cause? What is your cause?"

"We cannot discuss that here. It is too dangerous. Meet one of my men where the road splits between Anafonitria and Volimes, at midnight tonight. He will know you. Now you must leave."

"But I..."

"Go! I will answer all your questions tonight."

Elena obeyed him and ran from the church as quickly as she could. The sunlight was bright and she blinked repeatedly as her eyes adjusted to the light. Her heart was pounding and she had no idea what had just happened. She ran home as quickly as she could. Once there, she lay on her bed and replayed the conversation over and over in her head. They said they needed her, but for what purpose she had no idea. All she could do was meet them and see what happened.

~

Elena had eventually drifted off to sleep. When she awoke it was dark. Slipping from bed, she padded through the small house to the kitchen, where she poured a glass of water and ate a hunk of bread dipped in olive oil. She glanced at the small clock, which read eleven pm. One hour. She sat and drummed her fingers on the table. Should she do as the man asked? Should she go and meet his colleague? What if it was all an elaborate trap by the Italians? What if Loukas Sarkis wanted her out of the way once and for all, and had created some evil scheme to have her arrested or killed? Her brain went into overdrive, and she gave herself a good talking to. The only way she would know was by meeting the man and finding out what he wanted. To hell with it all, she would go and deal with the consequences later.

Elena grabbed her shawl, made sure Athena was fast asleep, then sneaked from the house and ran along the lane to a break in the hedge. She knew the island so well that getting to her location unseen was easy. She traversed fields and back roads, with only a hint of moon to guide her way. She felt the thrill of being out during curfew and the excitement of being free to roam flooded through her.

Just a few minutes before midnight, she arrived at the meeting point. There was no one there, so she remained hidden in the undergrowth watching, listening. A few moments later, she saw a man run across the road and hide under a small tree. He was definitely Greek. She looked around to make sure they were truly alone and ran across to meet him.

"Hello. I am Elena."

"Shush." The man pushed her down and they

sat in silence for a few minutes. Satisfied that they were alone, he pulled her noiselessly along behind him. Elena kept pace with the man whose long legs took the fields in great strides. It was not long before they arrived at a small wood. They crept stealthily through it using the thick trees as cover. Soon a small wooden hut appeared and they stopped again. Elena heard two owl hoots and then they quickly moved from behind the trees and towards the hut. Moments later, under the dead of night, they were inside sitting at a table. Every seat was filled and Elena noticed that she was the only woman. She should have been scared but she was not. She felt like this was where she was meant to be. Four men surrounded her at the table and they were silent for a few moments, until finally one of them spoke. Elena recognised his voice instantly. The man from the church.

"Welcome to our group."

"What is this?" she asked.

"I will explain. We are a resistance movement. We are small, but we have all agreed to resist those who oppress us. We are subtle and sleight of hand with what we do, but our message is spreading and we hope that many more will join us soon. You are a trusted part of our group now; you will be very useful in our cause. You must never talk to anyone about us, you must take care not to get caught, and you will address me as Dionysis. Do you understand?"

"Yes," she nodded. She was being asked, as a woman, to help fight the invaders. She felt very proud. Finally she could be herself, do what was right and follow her heart.

"Wait a minute…did you say your name is Dionysis?" Elena asked.

"Yes. It is the name I have chosen to give myself for this purpose." The man grinned. "I think you understand the significance?"

"Yes I do. You have named yourself after the patron saint of Zakynthos. It is very clever and patriotic."

"I thought so." The smile left his face and he placed his hands on the table. "Now we must get down to business. I have heard grave news via a contact on the mainland. The Germans have begun killing Jewish people. It is said they have death camps and in these camps they exterminate the Jews by gassing them. We will have to make sure that we protect our own Jewish population. They are part of us, and an important part of this island and its community. We need to step up our campaign. I need you," he pointed at two of the men, "to graffiti all over the island. Do not get caught and if you do, remember do not give us up. It is time to let our voices be heard."

He studied Elena for a moment before speaking. "For you, I have important work. You must find out from Angelos Sarkis what his father is up to. He and Stelios Makris spend far too much time with the Italians. We need to know what they are doing." He then concluded, "That is all. Here are some more handbills, keep handing them out."

With that, they all stood, and then one-by-one the men left the hut vanishing into the night. Elena found herself alone with Dionysis. He shut the door and motioned to the seat she had just vacated.

"I have one more thing I need you to do, but only you and I can know about it. I understand that you are already on first name terms with an Italian officer? A Captain Cipriani?"

Elena was shocked, "How do you know that?"

"It is okay. One thing you will learn about me, Elena, is that I know a lot of things. I am everywhere and yet nowhere. I see things on this island that most people will never learn of. You have been very good at resisting the captain's advances so far, which is one of the many reasons why I know I can trust you. But from now on, this is what I need you to do."

Elena listened carefully to the plan Dionysis laid before her. She took it all in, every single word, her brain absorbing exactly what was expected of her. It shocked her. It sickened her, but she understood and realised that this was her destiny and, from that moment, she knew her life would never be the same again.

CHAPTER EIGHTEEN

Zakynthos, Greece, 1942

Elena awoke to the slow rumbling of thunder. It was still some way off, but growing closer with every reverberation. The summer had been hot and humid, and the current storm was one of many they had endured. As lightning flashed, it highlighted the silhouette of the man who was fast asleep next to her. She had been lying in his bed for just over a month now, but only one other person knew.

She had hated herself the moment she started on this path. She was fraternising with the enemy and if people found out, she would be treated worse than Loukas Sarkis ever treated her. Wrapping a blanket around her, she padded downstairs and out into the dark night. The moon perched in the sky above, bathing the world in a bright silver glow. She looked up for stars but they were barely visible. Clouds were beginning to gather on the horizon, growing bigger and darker. The storm was getting closer. The earth beneath her feet felt damp and she could smell rain on the air. She jumped as another flash of lightning lit up the sky, illuminating the hills around her. It would not be long before the storm was directly overhead, rattling the island.

She took a seat on a log, and continued to watch the approaching storm as she thought back to that night in the woods, sitting in the hut listening to Dionysis. She had been shocked and horrified at what he had asked of her. She had been trembling and unable to speak as he explained what he wanted her to do.

"I know this will be very hard for you Elena, but you must accept Captain Cipriani's advances. We have a war to fight, and to have someone on the inside, someone like you who can get us information, will help our cause greatly. It will help us fight the enemy. Your personal sacrifice is needed, Elena. There is no one else I can I ask."

Elena had felt numb. Dionysis was asking her to sleep with the enemy. She desperately wanted to help the war effort in any way that she could, but giving herself to the Italian would be like selling her body. The thought revolted her. There had to be some other way. She would do anything but that. She had pleaded with Dionysis not to force her, but in the end she knew it was the only thing she could do. She had no choice but to agree.

She had carried her secret with her for weeks now, all the while helping with passing handbills to villagers, standing watch while others marked walls with *RESIST* and smuggling much needed food up to the poorest families in the hills. She was honoured to be doing what she was doing. She was helping to fight against their oppressors and it made her proud, but at the same time her heart was heavy at having to prostitute herself for the cause. She knew it was something she would have to live with for the rest of her life, and it was a burden she would have to bear alone.

She had been to see Angelos, waiting until he was alone in one of his father's olive groves. She had crept up behind him and placed her hands over his eyes. He knew who it was before she even released them. Smiling, she realised how much she still loved him and wished that things were very different, but they were not.

"What are you doing here?" He seemed baffled at her arrival.

"I have missed you."

"You still wear the locket," he said, brushing his fingers against her sternum.

"Of course I do, and I always will."

"How is Athena?"

"Beautiful. She is talkative too even at her young age. She is sweet and a little feisty."

"Just like her mother then." They walked along the olive grove, to find their favourite tree, its boughs large and plentiful.

"You remember this tree, Angelos?"

He knew they were on dangerous ground. "Yes, of course." Angelos paused a moment then asked, "Why are you here, Elena?"

"I have already answered that. To see you."

"Why? I never see you anymore. We live separate lives now."

"I know and that needs to change. We are older Angelos, and things are different now for our island. We need our friends."

Resigned, Angelos sat under the tree, and leaned against its large trunk. Elena followed his lead and leaned against him.

"Is your father not working today?"

"No. He is in town and Maria..." He paused a moment, then continued, "Maria has gone out with my mother."

There was a heavy silence that fell between them, the air thick with unasked questions. Elena was the one who finally broke it.

"I heard your father does business with the Italians now."

"I do not know."

"Oh come on, Angelos. You help him run the business; surely you know what is going on?"

"Why do you want to know?" he asked suspiciously.

"Just interested. I heard some gossip, and I wondered if it were true. I would hate to see you caught up in it."

He sighed and admitted, "Yes. I have heard him talking about it to Mother. They, him and Stelios, are working with some Italian captain called Cipriani. I do not know what they are doing exactly, but I do know that whatever it is, they are helping to protect the rich families and businesses on the island. Life is very different for us. We seem to be able to come and go as we please, and our food rations are bigger than others, too."

"Pah. I knew your father was a dog who would only do the devil's work," she spat.

"Elena!"

She sighed, "I know. I know. Do not talk about your father that way. But does it not make you mad, Angelos? Some of the poor families in the villages are finding it very hard. The Italians harass them daily. Food is scarce, what little they do have has to be hidden in pots buried in the ground so that the Italians do not steal it. Medicine is almost non-existent and we are ruled over by men who do not even know why they are here anymore. This war is a fool's errand, and people like your father and Stelios do just as they please!"

Angelos did not want to have this argument any longer. He stood and brushed down his trousers before helping Elena to her feet.

"I should get back to work," he huffed and walked away, leaving her where she stood, feeling empty and alone. She knew what she had done was very wrong. She had used him to get information, she had made Angelos believe she cared about him again, and it broke her heart. If this was war, then she would rather die now than continue the suffering.

Another flash of lightning brought Elena out of her daydream and back to the present. Shifting on the uncomfortable log, she pulled the blanket tighter around her. Pietro was still stretched out on the bed asleep where she had left him. She liked the depths of night. It was a time when she was able to creep from his bed and sit in silence, alone with her own thoughts, with no one to tell her what she should or should not be doing.

Her shame was ever present and never left her. She hated what she was doing, and wished that she could just walk away, but somehow, she found herself drawn to Pietro. It was not that she was in love with him, she barely even liked him, but there was something about him that fascinated her, and she felt powerless whenever she was with him, as though she was under a spell, unable to resist. Another flash of lightning lit up the sky, swiftly followed by a ground-shaking rumble of thunder. The storm was almost overhead now and tiny drops of rain began to fall. She felt a hand on her shoulder and it made her jump. Pietro sat next to her and pulled her closer.

"*Piccolina*. What are you doing out here?" She closed her eyes as he wrapped his arms around her.

"I am watching the storm."

"Come back inside, you will get cold," he said as he kissed her neck, making her shudder. Despite hating him, the merest touch from his lips or hands always sent her into a spiral. She tried to think straight but she could not. If she never had to see him again, she would be happy, but she was stuck with him. She was in too deeply, and knew she would never be able to escape. She hated Dionysis for forcing her to do this, but deep down she knew it was for the greater good. War, it seemed, brought out the worst in people.

"Do you not want to watch the storm?" she asked.

"Once you have seen one, you have seen them all. I would rather make love to you."

"You Italians, you are never sated."

Giving her no choice, he unfurled his arms. He stood and lifted her up in one swift movement and carried her inside. Laying her on the bed, he pulled the blanket away, threw it to the floor, and climbed onto the bed next to her. Elena closed her eyes and prayed for it to be over swiftly.

~

A few days later Elena and Dionysis were sitting in the hut. The others had been given their orders and moved on.

"Tell me what you have learned," Dionysis said.

"Angelos is reluctant to talk about his father, but he did tell me that the island's rich families are getting preferential treatment from the Italians."

"And the Italian. What have you learned from him?"

Elena shifted uncomfortably in her seat. Her gaze met his and she thought back to when it had all started.

She had been walking up in the hills, along the west coast, completely unaware that Pietro was following her. Sitting up high overlooking the sea, she had been staring down at the crystal waters daydreaming. A crackle of foot on branch startled her and she looked up to see the Italian grinning.

"You followed me!"

"Yes *piccolina,* I did."

"Why?"

"Because last time we met, you told me about your fear of what some officers from my army do, and I thought you may need some protection. It was also a nice day for a walk."

"I do not need protecting!"

"Okay. But I am here anyway, so maybe you

will allow me to spend a little time with you?"

Elena laughed. She could not help it. Despite his uniform and the fact that he was the enemy, he made her smile. "Well as you say, now you are here, you may as well sit," she said and patted the ground next to her.

Pietro sat, pulled out a cigarette and lit it. The bitter aroma wafted around her and she breathed it in. It was enticing. It struck her how very different to Angelos he was.

"So what do you and your army do all day on our island?"

He shrugged. "Many things. We keep the peace, report back to the Germans, we eat, we sleep, we laugh and we drink."

"You sound like a terrible army."

He laughed, "I think you are probably right."

They were silent for a moment, when Pietro asked, "And what is it you do all day, Elena?"

"Not much. I look after my daughter, I help my parents, and I run errands. The rest of the time my life is my own and I do as I please."

"I have heard this."

"You have?" His response shocked her.

"Yes. Sadly some on the island do not favour you. They call you names, not pleasant names, I am sorry to say, and they say that you are nothing more than a peasant."

He was surprised when she laughed. "It is good to know that Loukas Sarkis has still not changed his opinion of me. You would think he would find a new word. Peasant is becoming boring now."

"You know about this?" Pietro was surprised.

"Yes. Loukas Sarkis has always hated me. It is because of him that his son Angelos and I never married and why my daughter is a bastard!"

"Oh. I did not know. Do you still love this man, Angelos?"

She hesitated for a brief moment. "No. I no longer love him. He is no longer part of my life. He is married and has his own life now." She hated lying, but knew it was for the best.

"That is good. I would not want to share you with anyone."

"You what?"

He laughed, "I am no romantic Elena, but you must have guessed by now that I like you a lot. We could be good together. If the war ended tomorrow and I had to go home to Italy, I would ask you to come with me."

"But you are..."

"I know. I am the hated enemy, you cannot be seen fraternising with me. So let us not tell anyone. Let us keep it as our little secret."

She looked at him, taking in his dark eyes and hair, and his tanned face and nodded. She thought of her family, of Athena growing up in a peaceful world, of her parents and brother, their finally being safe. Having food on the table rather than scrabbling around for morsels. She made her choice. Leaning in, she ran her fingers through his hair, and grinned. "I like secrets, and I think you would be a fun one, Pietro."

Pietro did not speak; he pulled her to him and kissed her longingly. As Elena kissed him back, she closed her eyes, knowing that everything she did was for the sake of her island and her family. It was the only choice she could make. From then on, Pietro shared so much with her. He told her about his meetings with the Sarkis and Makris men, he shared the latest information from the Germans and she learned more about how his army worked and how they operated on the island. She fed all of this back to Dionysis and he listened with patience and understanding.

"You have done well, Elena. Whenever you hear anything significant, you need to tell me. There are many people in our network now. They can get a message to me if you are unable to get away."

"Yes, Dionysis."

"One last thing before you go. You will need this." To her surprise he laid a handgun on the table before her, and she shuddered with the thought of it being near her.

"You want me to have a gun?"

"Yes."

"But, why?"

"What you are doing is very dangerous, Elena. I cannot guarantee your safety. You may need this to protect yourself in the future."

"Are things going to get that bad?"

"That I cannot answer. None of us really know what is around the corner."

She lifted the gun feeling the weight of it. "I do not even know how to use it."

"You will. When the time comes you will."

A while later, Elena left the hut and ran through the woods in the darkness. She stopped to catch her breath by a tree and sank to the ground. She looked at the gun in her hand and, for the first time she really began to question her actions. She had aligned herself with the island's resistance, a highly dangerous thing to do. She was putting her entire family at risk. God only knew what the Italians would do if they caught her, but she was fairly sure that they would make her family pay, too. She could not bear the thought of them being imprisoned or being sent off to concentration camps.

Over the last few weeks she had done some questionable things to gain information. The worst was lying to Angelos and sleeping with an Italian officer. She was being pulled in so many directions and it made her head spin. What kind of person was she becoming? For the first time in her life she really hated herself. If that was case, how could anyone else really love her?

Elena sat under a canopy of trees in the dead of night as questions and accusations about herself swam around her head. Hugging her knees to her chest and rocking slightly, she cried her heart out. Sobbing loudly, not caring if anyone heard her. Once she finished, she stood and held the gun tightly. She had to remember that she was doing this for Athena. She was doing this so that her daughter and all the other children on the island had a future, a future without fear and oppression. She had to carry on. She was in too deeply and the end game was too important.

~

Loukas shoveled food into his mouth and looked around the table at his family: his pathetic wife, his useless son and his miserable daughter-in-law. Of all people, Maria was the one he respected the most. He knew she was aware of Angelos's past with the gypsy and yet she was determined to keep her husband by any means necessary and he admired her for that. Even better she had announced a few days earlier that she was expecting their first child. You would have thought Angelos would be happier, but he had sulked ever since.

"I have to go into town for another meeting tomorrow. I think you should come with me, Angelos."

His son looked up. "Me? Why?"

"Because I said so. Does there need to be any other reason?"

Angelos shook his head and went back to

eating his dinner. A day with his father was not what he had planned.

~

The following morning Angelos followed his father up the steps into the town council building in Zakynthos Town. He was glad to be indoors. Winter had settled in and the island was becoming cooler and the skies bleaker. Wearily, he sat in a chair next to his father and waited for the meeting to start. It was not long before Stelios arrived and the two men stood tall, flaunting their power. Angelos was bored of it. The last week had been hell. Maria had announced that she was going to have a baby, and it brought his past with Elena flooding back. Loukas was already telling everyone how excited he was about the birth of his first grandchild. It made Angelos mad, he already had a child, but as far as his family was concerned she did not exist, Loukas it seemed, had conveniently wiped Athena from his memory. Now Angelos had been dragged into town to meet with the island's enemies. It made him feel uncomfortable. He already knew that some of the islanders had not taken well to Loukas and Stelios's fraternisation, despite reaping some of the benefits.

Angelos looked up and the door swung open. Two officers entered and took a seat at the table opposite. Angelos eyed one of them, with a look of fleeting familiarity. He was sure he had seen him somewhere before.

"Gentlemen. It is good to see you again." Pietro smiled, pouring himself a coffee.

"Captain, may I introduce my son Angelos."

Angelos nodded, his brain working overtime; he was sure he recognised the man.

"Good morning, Angelos, I am Captain Pietro Cipriani. It is good to finally meet you. I have heard a lot about you."

"You have?" Angelos wondered what his father had been saying, so he turned to him but Loukas merely shrugged.

Pietro laughed, "I am sorry, I did not mean to confuse you. I meant that I have heard a lot about you from Elena." His eyes glinted mischievously as he watched both the Sarkis men squirm at the mention of her name. "Elena Petrakis is a very beautiful woman who has a lot to say about the Sarkis family. I think she is especially fond of you though, Angelos."

"There is nothing between my son and that gypsy," Loukas spat.

"There may not be now, especially as I have heard that she has another man sharing her bed, but I do think she still loves your son. Do you still love her, Angelos?" The question hung uncomfortably in the air and Pietro's eyes, no longer mischievous but angry, bore into Angelos's.

"Enough of this ridiculous charade!" the other

Italian bellowed. "We are here to discuss business like men, not the virtues of women like schoolboys!"

The room fell silent, and they all looked at Pietro waiting for him to speak again.

"Angelos. I need to ask if you know who is distributing these." Pietro placed a resistance handbill on the table and slid it slowly across to the Greeks' side. Angelos had never seen it before, but Loukas had. He remembered the small boy in the market square trying to pass him one. Loukas racked his brain for the boys name but it did not come.

"No. What are they?" Angelos asked.

"Some kind of resistance pamphlet. They are everywhere on the mainland and we have been lucky so far that the Greeks on this island have behaved well and lived alongside us obeying our rules. But it seems, some have now joined this resistance movement and want to defy us and the Germans."

Pietro lit a cigarette and pulled deeply on it before releasing a pall of grey smoke.

"If it were just the leaflets, that would be one thing, but it is not. They daub walls with red paint. It is becoming more and more common. If this carries on they will disobey us, steal from us, attack us and people will get hurt. I chose you, Loukas and Stelios, because of your positions on the island. I hope I was not wrong in that choice.

You must do everything to infiltrate these people and find out who they are. It is not acceptable, and they must be found and punished."

Loukas and Stelios only nodded. Pietro stood, indicating that the meeting was now at an end. Placing his hat on his head, he straightened his jacket and grinned widely. "It has been a pleasure, gentlemen. It was good to meet you, Angelos. I shall give Elena your love, but I doubt that she will care as her affections now lie elsewhere."

Filled with rage, Angelos sprang to his feet. How dare the Italian talk to him like that! But it was too late. Captain Cipriani was already out of sight, his fading footsteps the only the thing to remind them that he had been in the room.

"What do we do now, Loukas?" Stelios asked. He had never been sure about his position in this working relationship, and the captain's words worried him. They were, first and foremost, Greek. The Italians were their enemy, the invaders. Whatever the captain said, the Italians were still in charge and would be for the foreseeable future. Stelios was nervous and knew that Loukas was out for glory, however it came.

"We do as they ask. These peasants need to know how lucky they are to still be alive."

Stelios glanced at Angelos and caught his eye; he could see the anger on the boy's face. He knew that the boy could cause problems for them, but it was not his place to say anything. Angelos was Loukas's son, not his, despite his daughter being married to him.

"Father..."

Loukas rounded on Angelos. "Not one word from you. You have already said and done enough. Just because I brought you here does not mean that you are entitled to an opinion."

Turning to Stelios his tone lightened. "Stelios, my friend. We have been given something special, we have been accepted by the Italians. I do not agree with everything they or the Germans do, but we are safer staying on side with them, than choosing another path. If that means turning in a few farm labourers for a bit of graffiti and leaflet printing, then so be it."

Loukas stood and pushed back his chair. "Give my best to your wife. Come for dinner in a few days, it would be good to see you up at the house again. We can celebrate the news about our grandchild! Angelos come, we are leaving."

Angelos stood and followed his father from the room, shrugging as he passed Stelios. He had little choice but to obey his father, but he had a feeling that they had just agreed to walk into the lion's den. Things would not end well.

~

It was New Years Eve and the clock was ticking ever closer to midnight, but no one in the resistance cared for celebrations. They were huddled together in their new meeting place, awaiting orders. A routine Italian patrol had discovered the hut a few months before so they had abandoned it. Luckily no one had been caught, but Dionysis had no choice but to change the meeting place. It had been too risky to use the hut again. He had decided that the caves up in the mountains were the best place for them to meet. They were difficult to get to, and only the islanders knew of their existence.

Once orders had been given and information shared, the resistance sneaked away into the night. A few stars glinted overhead shining brightly in the depths of winter, but the moon was waning, a mere sliver of light on the horizon. Islanders were woken by the sound of distant engines, and rushed from their beds in time to see fighter planes overhead. Fear of being bombed gripped them and they ran for cover, but the night was silent save for the sound of engines and machine gun fire. Elena was leaving the cave when she saw the airplane get hit. It tumbled in the sky, smoke belching from its frame before finally crashing into the sea. From the corner of her eye, she caught sight of a parachute, and it looked like the pilot was safe. Carefully watching its descent, she calculated where it landed before running back to the cave.

Dionysis turned, gun in hand, the moment he heard the twig snap. Confusion passed over his face. He did not expect to see Elena again that evening.

"Dionysis. You must come. A plane has crashed near Kampi, and someone has parachuted to land."

"You just saw this?"

"Yes."

"We must go and investigate, but we must use caution, Elena. It could be the enemy, and the Italians may also be searching for the man."

"Pah! The Italians will all be drunk in their beds by now, or asleep with their women. They will not care."

"We must still use caution. You must do as I say."

"Yes, Dionysis."

The pair crept from the cave, and Elena gave directions, explaining to Dionysis what she had seen and where she thought the man had fallen. For hours they searched, but failed to find him.

"I do not understand. I saw him fall."

"You may have, but these are trained soldiers, and they know how to hide themselves. He will be long gone now."

Trudging back under the shadowy cover of trees, they heard a sound, like an animal in pain. Dionysis motioned for Elena to stay quiet and follow his movements. Slowly, under cover of tree and rock, they crept carefully towards the sound. Elena's heart beat loudly in her chest, and she felt the adrenalin rush through her body. What if the man they were seeking was a German pilot? What would Dionysis do? Would she finally be forced to use her gun on the stranger, or would they simply take him prisoner? She did not have long to wait for an answer. In a naturally carved ravine, shaded by large trees and bushes, lay the body of an airman. Edging closer, they saw he was unarmed and worryingly still. Dionysis instructed Elena to keep lookout, before creeping into the ravine to check the man. As soon as he reached the injured man, Dionysis could see that his uniform was English; he was an ally not an enemy. Dionysis breathed easier and motioned for Elena. Once she was by his side, they set about checking the man for injuries.

"I think he may have broken his leg. Get me some strong tree branches and I will try to splint it. The sun will be rising in an hour; we need to get him out of here. I think the caves will be best for now."

Elena did as instructed. Dionysis carefully shook the man conscious and explained who they were and where he was, but the airman just stared blankly at them before drifting unconsciousness again. Elena returned with two fallen tree branches she had found in the undergrowth. They strapped his leg as best they could before helping the man to his feet. Between them, Elena and Dionysis helped the airman through the woods and up to the caves. It was hard going. The man was tall and difficult to move with a splinted leg and his being unconscious made him feel like a dead weight, but eventually they managed to get him to the caves just as the light began to change, signaling the start of another dawn. In the cave, they settled him on the rough floor and threw an old blanket over him to keep him warm.

"Stay here with him, Elena. I will return in an hour."

She watched Dionysis disappear into the woods before sitting next to the airman. All she could do was anxiously wait for him to return.

CHAPTER NINETEEN

Zakynthos, Greece, 2002

The plane landed on the dusty tarmac with a thud and a screech. As it came to an abrupt halt, passengers pinged open their seatbelts and clamoured to be the first from their seat. They dragged their hand luggage from overhead lockers and from under seats, before the *remove seatbelt* signs were even turned off, ignoring the glares from the cabin crew. A few minutes later, the doors opened and Fletch found himself walking down metal steps to the tarmac below. The sun was hot and bright and he pulled his sunglasses down to cover his eyes.

As much as he liked his mates, Shane and Jase, he was already wishing he had not joined them for Shane's stag week. Most people went on stag weekends, but Shane decided he wanted a whole week with his mates on a Greek island, where they could party, drink and no doubt, where Shane and Jase were concerned, sleep with as many pretty girls as possible. The invite had surprised Fletch. He had not seen them for so long, and he did not really feel like they were friends anymore, but Shane insisted he be there.

After returning to Cornwall last year, he had made the decision to stay, rather than running back to California. There was nothing there for him anymore and he had had all the fun he could. Running away had not done him any good at all, and he had only delayed the inevitable. He should have stayed all those years ago and fought for Kate, but he had not. Being back in Cornwall was comforting and familiar. Everywhere he went he saw Kate, remembered things about her, and felt like he was near her, but he was not. She had run away as well, to Bristol, and even though he felt like driving up to see her, he had hesitated. More than hesitated. They had been apart too long, and too much time had passed. And anyway, if she had wanted to talk to him she would have done so already. Her parents would have mentioned that he was back and she would have come to him. Would she not?

But she had not, and that told Fletch everything he needed to know. Too much time had passed, they were no longer friends and nothing would ever be the same again.

When Shane had mentioned his stag week, at a chance meeting in the local pub, Fletch had agreed to go straightaway. He thought another trip abroad might do him good. It would be something to help take his mind off Kate. She still sneaked into his brain, still left her mark on him and despite everything he tried, he just could not stop thinking about her. Yes, coming to Greece was the best idea.

Behind him, Shane and Jase, already drunk from consuming too much beer on the plane, were chatting up two pretty blonde girls. Fletch sighed. Now that he wondered if it really was the best idea after all. It was going to be a very long week, but it was too late now. He just had to try and make the best of it.

~

Kate sat back and watched as the boat skimmed over the tranquil turquoise seas heading to Navagio Beach. She was looking forward to seeing the shipwreck up close after viewing it from above. Staring up at large, steep white cliffs, topped with deep lush greenery, she marveled at the geography of the island. The farther out they went, the deeper the colour of the sea became. Every now and again, the boat rocked with the gentle swell of ocean waves, but as they rounded the headland they became a little rougher, making her grip the side of the boat.

It was not long before they entered the chasm between the high overbearing cliffs of Navagio Beach.

“Shipwreck Cove!” the boat owner Christos shouted, as he manoeuvred the vessel onto the shore. He anchored it to the sand with a thick rope then helped Kate and the rest of the tourists onto the beach. The group dispersed in different directions, each with their own plan for the day. Kate just stood and stared. It was one of the most isolated places she had ever been. If Christos suddenly abandoned them, there would be no way of leaving the cove. The cliffs were steep, foreboding and impossible to climb. Between the cliffs was a large expanse of rough golden sand and the shipwreck lay at its centre.

Kate walked up the beach to investigate the ship first. It was a huge mass of rusting, creaking metal. It had definitely seen better days and, after its fateful demise, it had been left to a slow death courtesy of the harsh coastal elements. Walking around it, Kate saw how it leaned precariously and was surprised it had not already toppled over. After exploring a bit more, she laid out a towel on the sand, put up an umbrella loaned to her by Michelle, and lay down. Rummaging in her bag, she pulled out a book, flipped down her sunglasses and began to read.

~

Fletch looked out of his apartment window. He had always been an early riser; the call of the sea was strong, and dragged him from his bed most days. The sun was still rising and the vibrant blue sky was slowly removing the orange bleed of a new day. He could hear Shane and Jase snoring. It had been a late night and they had trawled the bars and clubs in Laganas. He had stood in a corner, filled with boredom, watching as the lads drank the night away, danced and chatted up as many girls as possible. Fletch felt sorry for Shane's fiancée Jackie; she seemed to be totally oblivious to his wayward behaviour. Fletch did not understand why people bothered getting married if they had no intention of staying faithful. He would never have done that to one of his girlfriends.

His mind wandered back to Kate again. He wondered where she was and what she was doing. Probably sitting in her smart office in Bristol, running her little empire. He wondered if she had finally met someone, if she was now married, if she had children. He wanted to ask her parents but felt awkward. He did not know what to say. Selfishly, he hoped she had not and that she was still single. If she were single, there was still hope. Fletch knew he loved her, and that he never would stop loving her. He would never love anyone the way he loved Kate. He missed her and wanted her back. He just wished that he could tell her how he felt.

Grabbing his room key, he snuck out of the apartment. He wove his way around scattered sunloungers and stopped at the edge of the swimming pool. Shedding his clothes until he stood in his swimming trunks, he closed his eyes, breathed deeply and dived in, slicing his way through the cool, crisp water. He loved being in the water. If he could not go surfing, swimming was the next best thing. He wanted to see some of the island, but the lads were not really up for it. All they wanted to do was drink and lie in the sun during the day. It was going to be a tedious week, and he was not sure how much longer his patience would last.

~

Kate sat up and reached for a drink. It was hot on Navagio Beach, a veritable suntrap. The cliffs did a good job of blocking most breezes. She looked out across the shimmering water and realised that she really was in paradise. She was glad she had come to Zakynthos; she had definitely needed a holiday. The Athena situation had not gone away, neither had her unending feelings for Fletch, but at that moment she had no idea how to deal with either. How could she even begin to find out about her past when she had little information to go on? As for Fletch, how could she tell him she loved him, and would do until her dying day, if she did not even know where he was?

Fleetingly, the old feelings of confusion that she had carried for years reappeared. She knew that until she dealt with them, they would always be there and would always rule her life. Somehow she had to try and find a way forward. She needed a friend; someone who could help and she knew exactly who that friend was.

Standing, she waded into the sea and cooled herself off, allowing the plan to formulate in her mind. It was time to put a stop to all of this nonsense and get on with her life and, in order to do that, she had to find out about her family. Yes, as soon as she got back to her hotel she would put her plan into action and ensure it succeeded.

~

Angelos felt the age in his bones. His body was stiff and he found it difficult to walk far nowadays. Sitting in the square under the shade of a tree, he sipped a coffee. His doctor told him he should cut back on it, but Angelos ignored the man. He loved the taste too much and would not give it up for anyone. His life had been a long one, fraught and filled with heartache and disappointment. Every day he thought about the past; it was always with him and never left his side. When he woke in the mornings he would remember some snippet from that time, something that brought tears to his eyes. But his mind was beginning to fade; as he aged, things had become muddled. He could cope with his body failing, but not his mind. Some days were clear and if you asked him a question he could have answered it with complete certainty. Other days, he waded through fog, only to be left with random images that cluttered his brain and made no sense at all. There was always one constant and she remained forever. Her face, her touch and her smell were imprinted upon his brain as though she were the very essence of him. She was the one thing he could not forget about, nor would he want to.

A gust of breeze, that seemed to come from nowhere, passed across him, and it was then that he knew. Something was coming, something that would change his life, what little remained of it, forever. The island was about to give up her secrets.

~

Kate's mind worked overtime on the drive back to her hotel. When she arrived, she quickly changed and jumped into the pool. Pumping her way through the cool, chlorinated waters, Kate begged her brain to shut down and relax just for a little while. She did not stop until her muscles ached and lungs screamed. Turning onto her back, she gazed up at an almost cloudless blue sky. She could be anywhere in the world, anywhere at all.

"Are you having fun?"

Hearing the voice Kate flipped over. Michelle was sitting on a sunlounger.

"Hi. How's your day been?" Kate asked, swimming to the pool edge.

"Oh the usual. You okay? I thought we were going to have to stop you for a minute there. I was exhausted just watching you!"

Kate laughed. She climbed from the pool and towelled herself down. "I had a few things running round my head and I always find exercise helps my brain sort itself out."

"I see. Do you want a drink?"

"Yes, please. I'd love some water." Kate settled herself on one of the sunloungers and stared out across the sea. Michelle went inside, returning a few minutes later. She placed the drink next to her.

"Holler if you want anything else."

"Thanks." Kate drank deeply. "Actually do you have a few minutes? I'd really like your opinion on something."

"Of course," Michelle said as she sat next to her. "How can I help?"

Kate was not quite sure how to begin. She mulled it over for a moment before deciding to start at the beginning.

"My life is a mess, Michelle. I know you are here to work and are probably very busy, but I really need your help. I don't know who else I can talk to." She paused long enough to see that she had not scared Michelle away, then continued. "Ten years ago I found out I was adopted. We think that my mother was Greek. I only know her name, Athena. There was mention of a Sarkis family, and Elena Petrakis and the Ionian Islands, but not much else. We think the families may have lived here on Zakynthos, but I have no idea how to find out. I'm so confused. I never knew my real mother and, even though I love my adoptive parents dearly, I feel that part of me is missing. I don't know who I really am or where I belong." She stopped to take a sip of water and realised it was the first time she had been honest with herself since finding out about her adoption. "Is there any way you can help? Do you know anyone who can point me in the right direction?"

Michelle was shocked. She knew Kate had been hiding something, she could always tell, but she had not been expecting this. She had expected to hear about a girl who had run out on her wedding, or about a vicious break-up with her boyfriend, but not an ancestral tragedy. She thought hard for a moment. She could see the girl was hurting; it showed in her eyes. Michelle was at a loss, but if there was anything she could do to help, then she would try.

"I will do what I can, Kate. You will have to be patient though. This is Greece, things are not always easy or straightforward and the wheels turn slowly, sometimes very slowly. Let me ask around and I will see what I can find out for you."

"Thank you, Michelle. I really appreciate it."

Michelle patted Kate on the hand and gave her an understanding smile before standing up and walking back inside. Kate took another sip of water before lying back and closing her eyes. It was not long before she drifted off to sleep in the sun, her subconscious weaving an erratic dream of cliffs, crystal seas and a woman resembling her dead mother who was always just out of reach.

~

As the three men walked the strip at Laganas, they passed numerous bars and clubs. Each had loud music that punctured the night with heavy bass-laden sounds. Fletch had spent the day with Shane and Jase draped over sunloungers at the apartment. Fletch had eventually lost himself in a good book, blocking out the drunken laughter coming from his friends. Despite waking with hangovers, Shane and Jase spent the day by the pool with a couple of bottles of beer. They had already picked up and discarded two girls from Birmingham, much to Fletch's disgust, and the three were now heading into the clubs for a long evening of further drunken madness. Fletch lagged behind as the others talked football. He was debating turning round and heading back to the apartment for a peaceful night or, even better, flying home, but he knew Shane would be furious if he did. So he chose to bite the bullet and pretend he was enjoying himself.

Jase stopped and turned to playfully punch Fletch on the arm. "Fletch, mate! Come on! Get over it, whatever it is." He caught Fletch in a playful headlock and ruffled his hair, something Fletch really hated. He pushed Jase away and planted a fake smile on his face.

"Sorry lads."

"What the bloody hell's up with you anyway?" Shane asked. He was getting fed up with Fletch's miserable attitude and wished he had not bothered inviting him.

"Nothing," Fletch protested. "Come on; let me buy you lads a beer." Eager to please, Fletch stepped into the nearest bar.

"That's more like it!"

Four bars and countless pints later, Fletch came out of the bathroom of the latest beach bar to find Shane and Jase sitting in chairs on the veranda. A young blond was running her fingers through Jase's hair. A young redhead was busy kissing Shane. *They really don't waste any time, do they*, Fletch thought.

"Fletch, mate, sorry we couldn't find a girl for you," Jase said drunkenly, running his fingers up and down the blonde girl's legs.

"You're okay, Jase. I'm not bothered."

"That's right. You're saving yourself for Miss

Right, aren't you?"

Shane broke away from the redhead and looked across at Jase, shaking his head in warning. They were all very drunk and he could see where this was heading. Jase had always had a problem with Fletch, and he knew that it would not take much for him to wind Fletch up.

"What's that supposed to mean?" Fletch asked.

"Let's face it. When was the last time you had a girlfriend, or even shagged someone?" Jase taunted. "Or are you secretly gay? That's it, you're gay aren't you!"

The two girls sniggered, clearly enjoying the show.

Shane stood, tipping his girl to the floor, where she landed with a thud and a surprised yelp. He placed himself between Fletch and Jase.

"Lads. I think you should shut up now." Shane knew where this was heading.

"No, it's okay, Shane. If Jase has something to say let him say it. We're all grown-ups."

"You waited too long, Fletch. She'll never be yours, you know. Never."

"Jase," Shane warned.

"Kate moved on years ago. She waited till you had gone Fletch and then found someone else. It didn't take her long."

"You're wrong, Jase."

"Am I?" he sneered. "Maybe you should ask me how I know?"

Jase pushed the blonde from his lap and now stood face to face with Fletch. Leaning in, he whispered loudly in Fletch's ear, "It's a shame you never told Kate how you feel, you missed out. She really is great in bed."

Fletch saw red and threw himself at Jase, shoving him away, hard. Jase fell over a chair and landed on the floor with a heavy thump. Shane laid a hand on Fletch's chest to prevent him from doing anything else and held his other hand, palm out, toward Jase. The two girls ran off not wanting to get involved.

"Lads. Let's not have a brawl. We don't want to get arrested."

Fletch stared at his so-called friends. Shane was right. Jase wasn't worth it. None of it was. Turning on his heels, he fled the bar.

For the first time in his life, Fletch cried. The tears were for Kate, the woman he had lost and the woman he would never see again. Hearing that Jase had some kind of relationship with her made him feel sick. Why had she done it? What on earth had she been thinking? Everyone in the surf community knew how unreliable and unfaithful Jase was as a boyfriend. He hoped that Kate had been the lucky one and that Jase had treated her well, but it was obvious that he was still up to his old tricks. He really hoped Jase had not hurt Kate. If he had Fletch would not be responsible for his actions.

CHAPTER TWENTY

Zakynthos, Greece, 2002

Kate and Michelle drove across the island in Michelle's car, listening to the local English speaking radio station. They were heading to the south of Zakynthos.

"Are you going to tell me where we are going?" Kate asked, watching the vibrant greens and muted browns of vegetation and olive trees pass by.

"No. You'll have to wait. It's a surprise."

Kate groaned, "I hate surprises."

"I promise that this will be a good one."

"Can we get something to eat soon? I'm starving."

"Yes. Soon."

It was hours since she had had breakfast, and the sun was directly overhead and the day was hot. Kate wondered what Michelle had up her sleeve. She hoped it was something to do with her mother, but there was no point in pushing her. She suspected Michelle would only tell her when she was ready to do so.

Pulling up at a restaurant, Michelle parked. They climbed out of the car and walked inside. Tables and chairs were dotted around the large open space, with a bar at one end. Michelle weaved her way through the tables, motioning for Kate to follow, stopping briefly at the bar to order some food. It was then that Kate noticed an elderly man sitting alone at a table. A walking stick was propped against the wall and a cup of coffee rested on the table's surface.

Michelle went to him and gently placed a hand on his arm and he greeted her in Greek, his eyes shining. She smiled and responded. Kate watched the animated discussion in fascination. She did not understand a word they were saying, but it seemed as though they knew each other well. Michelle turned in Kate's direction and beckoned her over. Kate stepped up to the table and nodded to the man.

"Kate. This is Nikolaos. Nikolaos, this is Kate."

The old man regarded her. Shakily he stood and took her face in his hands, studying her carefully. Kate thought it a strange greeting but let the man continue. Suddenly, he slowly spoke in English.

"I would never have dreamed it possible, and yet here you are. It is true what they say. What the island loses will, in time, return to her."

Bemused, Kate just smiled. She had absolutely no idea what Nikolaos was talking about. He released her face and motioned for the two women to sit. Once settled, Michelle ordered some more coffee for Nikolaos, and then allowed the man to speak.

"I have lived on the island all of my life. I have known many people, some have gone, lost to time, others still remain. I have seen and heard many things, Kate, and most of them would shock you. I understand you are asking about a family called Sarkis and a woman called Elena Petrakis?"

"Yes."

"And you say that your mother was called Athena?"

"Yes. Do you know them?"

Nikolaos frowned for a moment. "What you must understand, Kate, is that some things are too painful. Some things can never be discussed." He closed his eyes for a moment, before remembering where he was and whom he was with. He sighed. "Yes. I knew the Sarkis family. My full name is Nikolaos Makris. My father, Stelios, and Loukas Sarkis were great friends. My sister Maria married Loukas's son, Angelos. You could say we are family."

Kate leaned back and her eyes widened. She had been holding her breath and released it slowly. The Sarkis family *did* exist. Was Maria her grandmother? If so, did that make Nikolaos her relative too? And what of Elena Petrakis? Her mind whirled with a thousand possibilities.

"I see you have already begun to try and work it out, Kate. But you will never come up with the right answer yourself. The situation is more complicated than you could ever dream and it is not something I can tell you." He paused long enough for Kate to think he had said everything he had to offer. But then, Nikolaos suddenly resumed. "There is only one person on this island who could ever tell you what you want to know, but I am not sure they would be willing or able. I am sorry Kate but I cannot help you any further. Thank you for the coffee." He slowly stood, using the table and stick for support, and carefully walked around the other tables towards the exit. Kate was shocked. It could not end there, it just could not. She had come so close. She ran over to Nikolaos and gently placed her hand on his arm.

"Please Mr. Makris. I beg you. Help me! I need to know who my family was," she pleaded with a wavering voice. "I am lost. I am so alone. I don't know who I am and I need to know. I *must* know." She was crying now, sobbing wholeheartedly, unable to stop. Michelle rushed to her side and hugged her tightly.

Nikolaos pondered for a moment. He knew he should do the right thing, but would he be forgiven for it? He looked at Kate again and saw the hurt and anguish and realised she was right; she had a right to know. “If you go to Exo Hora, you will find Angelos Sarkis. He lives there with his daughter Sophia and her husband. Treat him gently, though. He has been through so much and his mind is not what it was. It is best not to tell him I told you where to find him. In time you will understand why.”

Turning, Nikolaos left the restaurant. Kate and Michelle sat back down, and Kate tried to calm herself. Their food arrived and she tried her best to force it down.

“So, what now?” Michelle asked.

“I suppose I should go to Exo Hora. Do you know where that is?”

“Yes. I’ve only been once. It’s up in the mountains. I think you should heed Nikolaos’s warning though, Kate. This island hasn’t always been peaceful and the older generation has been left with many scars that haven’t healed and probably never will. I know you want to find your family, but you need to consider them, too. Take some time to think about this. It’s not just you involved.”

“I know,” she sighed. Despite being desperate to learn about her family, the last thing she wanted to do was hurt others in the process. She had a difficult choice to make.

~

After his row with Jase, Fletch stormed back to their apartment. Thank god he had his own room and did not have to share with the lads. He spent the night awake, staring at the ceiling, mulling everything over. He knew that it was all his own fault. If he had not argued with Kate and run away to California, they would still have been friends and she would not have ended up in the arms of that womaniser. He was angry with Jase for taking advantage of her, especially after everything she had been through. Had Jase known about her adoption, he wondered? Kate had never liked to share her problems with anyone other than him. And what of Kate? Why had she felt the need to turn to Jase? Had she been that desperate, or had Jase just been a convenient substitute?

His mind tumbled and crashed like tides in a spring storm and as the clock struck five am, he finally gave up. He changed into his swimming trunks, quietly left the apartment and padded to the pool. The sun was beginning to creep over the horizon as he dived in. Powering through the water, he swam length after length, desperate to rid his brain of everything. By the time his lungs and limbs began to scream from overexertion, the sun had fully risen.

He finally stopped and leaned on the edge of

the pool, letting his hard, deep breathing settle into a more normal rhythm. His mind was clearer, but he was still angry with Jase, and knew he would need to talk to him to clear the air. Pulling himself out of the pool, he looked up to see a worse for wear Shane staggering home.

Shane stopped in his tracks, then walked over, pulled up a sunlounger and took a seat next to Fletch.

"I'm sorry, mate. I should've told you."

"I don't have a problem with you, Shane, and it wasn't your place to tell me."

"But still, you liked Kate. Jase should've left well alone, but you know what he's like."

"What happened?"

"You really want to know?"

"Yes."

"They went out for about eight months, he taught her to surf and she hung out with us."

"Hang on. He taught her to surf? She hates all of that. I tried for so long to get her to surf."

"I know, mate. I don't know what happened, but after you left, she was different. Her and Jase clicked and they were a great couple. I know you aren't going to like hearing it, but they were."

"So if they were so great, what happened?"

"Jase happened. His ex-girlfriend turned up, and instead of dealing with it, he acted like a complete shit and Kate stormed off."

"So they broke up."

"Of sorts."

"What aren't you telling me?"

"Kate came back that night. I think she forgot her bag when she first stormed off. She noticed Jase was missing and went to find him. She caught him and his ex at it."

"Stupid bastard," Fletch spat.

"Trust me. He knows what an idiot he was, and he paid for it. He genuinely did care about her, but she refused to have anything to do with him again. She moved to Bristol and Jase never saw his ex again."

"Serves him right."

"Why did you never tell her, Fletch?"

"Tell her what?"

"Oh come on. It is so obvious. The two of you are made for each other. I've never seen a couple more in love than the pair of you. Where did it all go wrong?"

"I've no idea. I was going to tell her, but every time I tried something would come up and it just wasn't the right time."

"And now?"

"And now there's no going back."

They fell silent.

"Shane, can I suggest something?"

"What?"

"If you love Jackie, don't cheat on her. She's a nice girl and she doesn't deserve it."

"I know. But I feel like I'm getting old, and getting married means the death of so much."

Fletch laughed, “If that’s how you feel, maybe you shouldn’t be getting married!”

Fletch stood and left Shane to ponder that thought. He was glad he knew what happened. He wished he had told Kate how he felt all those years ago. Maybe things would have been different. So now he had a choice: he could either get on with his life and forget about her once and for all, or swallow his pride and go to Bristol when he got back. It was not that far from Cornwall and maybe he could salvage something from all this mess.

~

Kate slept well that night. She had expected to spend the night tossing and turning, thinking about Nikolaos Makris and Angelos Sarkis, instead she had slept soundly. While sitting on the hotel patio eating breakfast the following morning, she thought back to the previous day. She had not expected to find anyone to help her, let alone get such positive news so early on. She had only been on the island a few days and yet she felt more relaxed than she had in years. She even felt happy. She never thought she would be able to say that again.

Michelle was right, though. She needed to think carefully about how to handle visiting Angelos. He would be an old man now, and she did not want to upset him or his family. Until she worked out what to do, she would just enjoy her holiday and do some more exploring. She had waited ten years to find out who her family were, a few more days would not hurt.

CHAPTER TWENTY-ONE

Zakynthos, Greece, 1943

It took Dionysis almost three hours to return to the cave. By the time he arrived, Elena was frantic. Every noise she heard, be it the breath of the wind, the distant crash of the waves or rustle of an animal in the woods, made her jump. She kept the gun in her hand, not wanting to hold it but finding some kind of comfort in the fact that she had a way of protecting herself if she needed to. As the hours passed and Dionysis did not show, she began to expect the worst. Relief flooded through her as he finally stepped into the cave, looking tired and drawn.

"How is he?"

"Okay," she reported. "He has been sleeping

for most of the time. I think he is in a lot of pain."

"I have something that will help him."

Dionysis threw the bag he was carrying to the ground and began to pull out the contents. There were clothes, another blanket, and a small collection of containers filled with water, food and medicine.

"First, we need to remove his uniform. You will have to cut his trousers off, and when you have done that, put them in the bag. They will have to be burned so that there is no evidence of him being here. You must also let me see any personal items you find."

Elena nodded and set about undressing the man. He was heavy and she found it difficult to move him, but eventually after much perseverance and a little help from Dionysis, the man's uniform was discarded and his top half had been re-dressed. Elena stepped back to allow Dionysis to treat the man's leg. It was in a bad way, and there was little he could do other than clean and dress the wound, and strap the leg in the hope that it would be okay. It was too risky to bring a doctor to see him. In the meantime, Elena went through the man's uniform to check for any personal items. There was nothing at all, not even any papers to say who he was. She then rummaged through the bag and found some medicine that would help the man with the pain. As Dionysis pulled a blanket over the man's lower half, Elena gently shook him to try to rouse him. Eventually the man opened his eyes and, with a start, tried to sit up, fearful as to where he was and who the strangers were.

It was Dionysis who spoke first. “I am Dionysis. You are English?”

The man nodded, “Yes. I am a pilot in the Royal Air Force. Where am I? The last thing I remember was being hit by enemy fire.”

Dionysis was surprised to learn that the man spoke Greek. “Zakynthos, a small island, just off mainland Greece. You have been very lucky. Other than a broken leg and a few cuts and bruises, you seem to be okay.”

The man nodded. He seemed wary. “Who is she? Your wife?”

Dionysis laughed. “No. She is a friend, but do not worry, she can be trusted.”

“Does she have a name?”

Dionysis shook his head in Elena’s direction. Even though they were allies, passing her real name to the man was too dangerous.

Elena ignored the look, and took the man’s hand in hers. “My name is Elena. We will look after you, but for now you need to take this medicine. It will help with the pain in your leg. It is too dangerous to take you to a doctor and we just have to do what we can to help you heal.”

The man nodded, and did as instructed. She then passed him a flagon of water and some bread and olives, which he accepted gratefully.

"I need to leave now," Dionysis announced, then motioned to Elena. "I need to talk to you."

Just inside the mouth of the cave, they huddled in the shadows, whispering.

"I need to go and find out if anyone knows about the plane coming down. We need to work out how we are going to keep him and hide him from the Italians. You must stay here and look after him. Do you have your gun?"

"Yes. When will you return?"

"When I can. If I am not back by nightfall, you know things have gone wrong and it will be down to you, Elena."

With those final words, Dionysis slunk away and she was left alone to watch over the Englishman.

~

Pietro leaned against the doorframe of the small house he lived in, smoking a cigarette and gazing at another beautiful day. He had not slept at all; he had paced up and down most of the night filled with worry. Elena had said she would come to him, but she never arrived. He wondered what it was that kept her from him. Maybe her daughter was ill, or she had been caught during curfew and been marched straight back home again? Whatever it was, it did not improve his already fractious mood. Pietro was bored of the war, and missed Italy, especially his beautiful house, with the rolling well-tended garden. He missed his friends, his local bar and his favourite restaurant.

The only thing he did not miss was his wife, the woman he married when he was too young, who had turned his life into a living nightmare. War had come as a relief. Handed an opportunity to run away from her, he had grasped it with both hands, but now that he was here, he missed everything about home, except for her. The only thing he loved about being on the Greek island was Elena. She brightened his day but, deep down, he worried that he loved her more than she did him. He saw how Angelos Sarkis had reacted when Pietro mentioned her. It was obvious that the man was still in love with her, and who could blame him?

Throwing the spent cigarette to the floor, he ground it down with his heel to make sure it was out before slamming the door behind him and walking to the café to get a coffee. He would go to find Elena later, but until then he needed sustenance before reporting for duty.

~

Angelos hated what he was doing. At his father's insistence he had been spying on neighbours and friends for months now, and he felt like a traitor. When his father first told him what was expected, he was shocked. How could Loukas even consider siding with the enemy?

They had stood in the kitchen for an hour arguing about it, with his mother and Maria anxiously looking on. Loukas had been furious and demanded Angelos do what he was told. Angelos would have gladly taken a beating, but he was not prepared for the gun. His father, who had always been a vicious man, was now carrying a weapon, given to him by the people who governed them. It had made Angelos sick to his stomach. To have your own father align with the enemy and turn a gun on you was more than Angelos could bear.

Reluctantly he had given in; he took his father's orders, and reported back just enough to make his father happy. He took the handbills when they were offered, and told his father, giving a loose enough description so that the offender could have been half of the men on the island. He watched from corners as men painted bright red letters on walls and buildings, and gave the same loose descriptions. He pretended however not to notice when people stole food to give to those more deserving living in poverty in the mountains and villages. He could not bear to think of families like Elena's starving. He wished he were the one leafleting, daubing graffiti and stealing food. He desperately wanted to, but could not. He was a traitor and he knew that if the locals ever found out, he would be ostracised or, worse, put to death as an example. Angelos hated his life, and wondered what he had done to deserve all of this.

None of it was fair. Not fair at all.

~

Elena kissed her mother on the cheek.

"Where have you been?"

"Nowhere."

"You must have been somewhere. You know I love you Elena, but your daughter will not raise herself. You cannot go running about the island at all hours of the day and night. You are older now, you are a mother, and you have responsibilities."

Elena slumped into the chair. "I know Mama, but the war has changed things. We must all do things that take us away from our lives, things that are hard to do, but that in the end will give us all a better life."

"What do you mean by that, Elena?"

"Nothing, Mama."

"Sometimes the life we want is not the life we receive, my child. You must stay and look after Athena now. Your father is out, and I must go to buy food."

Sulking in the chair, Elena watched as her mother left, putting her in charge of her daughter. Athena giggled upon seeing her mother and held out her arms. Elena's heart melted and she smiled. She did love her daughter, but things had become so complicated. Pushing all thoughts from her mind, she concentrated on one thing. Athena. Reaching down, she picked her up, and held her small frame tightly, kissing the top of her head. This was the most important thing right now, holding her daughter and telling her that she loved her.

~

Angelos managed to escape from the house. He had felt stifled. If his father was not getting on top of him, it was his wife. All he wanted was to be alone. His father had gone to see the Italians, and Angelos was not needed this time. He took the opportunity while it presented itself and wandered down the lane to his favourite wood. He had not been there in such a long time. Stepping under the boughs, he noticed it was not as dense as normal. The trees had shed most of their leaves in preparation for the winter ahead. Light peeked through and cast eerie shadows. The crackling of a branch behind him made him whirl around. These days he was frightened of being followed.

"Elena. What are you doing here?"

"I wanted to talk to you."

Angelos gave a hollow laugh. "Why me? There is nothing left between us, and you are the whore of an Italian soldier now."

His words hit hard, as if he reached forward and punched her in the stomach, taking the wind out of her. He sounded just like his father. How did he know about Pietro? As if reading her mind, he spoke.

"I was not sure until now. He never actually came out and admitted it, but the implication was there. You yourself just admitted it. How could you, Elena? He is the enemy!"

"I..." she shook her head. The wood was quiet, calm and still, wrapping itself around them, making them feel as though they were the only people left on earth.

"The war has made fools of us all, Angelos."

"It has. I wish things were different."

She knew what he meant. She thought back to that day, sitting on the wall, watching him walk towards her. She wished she had just let him walk on by, but she had not. Now they sat on opposite sides of the fence.

"Can I trust you, Angelos?"

"Why do you ask?"

"I need your advice."

"I am not sure that I am the right person to ask," he admitted as he motioned for her to sit next to him. She tilted her head, considering for a moment before joining him. It was dangerous to get too close to him. Her heart could not take it.

"I am not the person I was before, Elena. My father is working with the Italians. He and Stelios report to Captain Cipriani every week. They have forced me to work for them and I hate it." He hung his head in shame.

"Oh, Angelos," she said, her voice tinged with sadness, and then she gave in and sat next to him, holding him tightly. "Your father has made your life impossible for you."

Angelos only nodded; he no longer knew what to say.

"What do they make you do, Angelos? Tell me."

"I am forced to spy for the Italians. I am forced to tell them everything I see and hear. I am forced to turn on my friends, my neighbours and people I have known all my life. I told him no, I told him I did not want to do it and do you know what he did to me, Elena?"

She barely dared to whisper the words, "He beat you? Please do not tell me that he beat Maria?"

"No, thankfully, but it was worse. He held a gun to my head, Elena. He threatened me, in front of my pregnant wife. He told me if I did not do as he asked, he would shoot me like a dog in the street and leave me to die. He told me if I did not do it, I would be a traitor to the great Axis powers. How could he do that, Elena, to his own son?"

"Oh Angelos, my poor Angelos," she moaned, and rocked him back and forth allowing him to cry. Her mind was drawn back to his fleeting words. *My pregnant wife*. It still hurt to think that he now belonged to someone else. They sat for what seemed an age. Elena now knew what she had to do, if only to protect Angelos. She had to go and see Dionysis. She had to continue the good work. She had to put a stop to men like

Loukas and Stelios, evil men who did not deserve all they had. She had to make sure that the resistance protected Angelos.

Sitting back, Angelos wiped his face and smiled. Reaching forward, he lifted the silver locket. "You still wear it."

"Of course I do. You may be married and I may... I will always love you, Angelos Sarkis, even if we can never be together."

"And I you. Are you happy, Elena?"

"What is happy? We are at war, we are prisoners on the island we so lovingly call home, we have lost our way and our morals. Those who are supposed to love us do not, and I do not see a future for any of us. How can I be happy?"

"You must be careful."

"I always am."

"I mean it, Elena. I know you. I know that sooner or later you will join up with the resistance if you have not done so already, and when you do, we are placed on opposite sides. We will be enemies. You have to know how much the Italians, my father and Stelios hate the resistance. They will do anything to see them fail. They will stop at nothing, including making them prisoners…even killing them."

"You have nothing to worry about, Angelos. You said it yourself, I am the whore of an Italian soldier. I am protected and I have nothing to fear."

Angelos groaned, "I should never have called you that. I am worse than my father. I am very sorry."

"Your apology is accepted." She stood and brushed down her skirt. "I must go."

"Remember what I said. Whatever side you are on, be careful, Elena Petrakis. The enemy is everywhere and no one can be trusted."

Elena merely gave a wave and disappeared into the trees, leaving Angelos sitting alone.

~

The resistance and the Italian army danced around each other constantly throughout the winter and into early spring. Every few days, Elena went to the caves to sit with the English airman, who was called Richard. She liked talking to him. She learned all about his home, a town called Bristol, in the south of England. It had a harbour, a suspension bridge that spanned the river and large parks. She liked the sound of it. Richard told her how he left behind a girl he liked, called Alice. Richard knew Alice wanted to marry him, but he was not sure if he wanted to marry her.

"Why not?"

"The war changes everything. If the Germans have their way, I may not even have a country to go back to. If that happened, there would be no future at all. I do not want to end up marrying someone and live in hell with her. It would not be living, it would barely be an existence. What about you Elena?"

"What about me?"

"I know that you are resistance. You and Dionysis would not have saved me if you were the enemy. They told us all about the resistance in our training. I think you are very brave. Do you have a husband at home?"

"No. I live with my parents and my brother. I do have a young daughter, but no husband. I suppose you are shocked now, that I have had a child out of marriage."

"Not at all. I assumed your husband had died."

"He did not." For some reason Elena felt comfortable with the Richard, and even though she knew it was a risk, and that Dionysis would be furious, she opened up. She needed a friend, someone who would not judge her and that she could share aspects of her life with. "Before the war started, I fell in love with a Greek man that lives on the island, but he comes from a rich family and I am from a poor one. His father hated me so much. He still hates me. The man I fell in love with loved me just as much as I loved him and we spent many happy days together but it was not to be. I had a child and his family refused to accept my child or me. The man I loved is now married to someone else and I am alone. I spend all of my time fighting for my homeland, and looking after my child. I hate myself so much, Richard. I have done unspeakable things in the name of war, things that I am not proud of. I do not think I will ever be able to forgive myself."

Elena tried so hard not to let her emotions show but a floodgate opened. All the hurt, anger and despair from the last few years crashed over her like waves and she struggled to keep her head above the chaos.

"It cannot be that bad, Elena. Have you killed anyone in cold blood? Have you set off bombs? Have you stolen?"

"No."

"Well then, as far as I can see, you are not a bad person."

She looked up at him and knew she had to be honest.

"It is worse than that, Richard. I am a traitor to my country, to my friends, to my family."

"How? What have you possibly done to make you a traitor?"

"Dionysis has forced me to sleep with an Italian officer, a captain, to get information that will help the resistance."

"And you did?"

"Yes," she whispered.

"People have done worse. May I ask you a question?"

She nodded.

"When you were with the Italian, did you ever tell him anything about the resistance, or betray any of your family or friends?"

"No. Never!"

"Then you have nothing to worry about. All you did was get close to a man to get information for the resistance. Many others have done it, so it does not make you a traitor, but it does make you very brave."

"So I am not a traitor?"

He laughed. "No you are not a traitor."

"I hate it though. I hate the smell of his tobacco. I hate being with him. I hate feeling him touch me. I hate it when he calls me *piccolina*. I do not even know what it means."

"I think it means *little one* in Italian."

"Oh…" They were silent for a few minutes before Elena said, "What should I do, Richard?"

"I think you should do what is right for you, Elena. It seems to me that you have spent your whole life pleasing everyone else and not looking out for yourself. Maybe it is time you thought about *you* for a change. I think you would be much happier if you did."

"But what about the war? I cannot stop helping the resistance now."

"You do not have to. You just choose the bits you want to do. If there are things you do not want to do, tell them. They cannot force you to do things against your will."

"It is that easy?"

"Yes."

They fell silent and Elena thought back over their conversation. Maybe Richard was right.

Maybe it was time to start putting herself first. She no longer wanted to be aligned with Pietro or his Italian army, even though Dionysis told her she was doing it for a good cause. There was only so much she could take. Enough was enough and she wanted out. She wanted her life back, she wanted to feel clean again, and the only way that could happen would be to walk away from Pietro once and for all, and hope that things would be okay.

~

The resistance movement on Zakynthos had grown, but no one knew exactly how many there were. They were highly secretive and planned their campaigns in silence, with only those who were essential to the plan having access to the details. They were stealthy and their attacks, both small and large, hit hard, reminding the Italians that even though they were their captors, the Greeks still valued their freedom and fought for it as much as they possibly could. In turn, the Italians were ill-equipped to cope with the island's terrain and most had no clue of how to find their way about like the locals did. The Italians became increasingly frustrated and began to arrest any local they thought of as conspiring against them.

In the height of summer, the resistance leaders met high in the hills. It was somewhere the Italians rarely went, since they generally stuck to the main town, some of the smaller towns and the coast so that they could look out for Allied invaders. The night was dark and the moon was already shining brightly. Huddled in the caverns under ancient rock, the resistance looked down upon the land they loved, giving their reports. Elena listened intently, taking in every word. Tonight she would have to tell her comrades what she had been up to and she was dreading it. The truth was about to come out.

"Elena." Dionysis's voice brought her back to the present.

"Yes."

"Can you tell us anything?"

"Yes. Last night, when I was with Pietro..."

"Who is Pietro?" one of the men asked, interrupting.

Dionysis held up his hand to quell the voices. "I gave a special assignment to Elena almost a year ago, she will tell you."

"Pietro Cipriani is an Italian captain. I have been lying in his bed for almost a year in order to get information from him..."

"Pah! Loukas Sarkis always said you were a whore, and now we know it!" the man shouted. The others laughed loudly, and the sounds echoed around the cave almost deafening her.

Dionysis slammed his hand on the overturned crate before him. "Quiet! Just because we are in the mountains does not mean we cannot be heard. You have no right to talk to her that way. She is one of us. *I* told her to do this. She was reluctant at first, but eventually she saw the greater good. This is war! We all have to do things we would never have considered before. You have all done things you did not want to. Immoral things. Some of you have stolen, some of you have used your own babies and children to smuggle food, medicine and weapons. One of you has killed, and more of you will likely do the same before this war is over. Do not question Elena because she is a woman and uses her body to get information that may help save your lives one day! As for Sarkis, I will not hear his name spoken here again! That man and all who associate with him are sworn enemies of Greece and will die for their defection."

The cave was quiet and Elena felt her blood run cold. She remembered her conversation with Angelos. He was now her enemy. His death, it seemed, was inevitable. It was a thought that brought her great sadness.

"Now back to business. Elena, please carry on."

"I have been gaining Pietro's trust and he now believes that I love him and am on the side of the Italians. He believes I have lost all interest in anything but him and my daughter. The time I spend with him is precious as it is not always easy to get away, but he has opened up to me. At the moment, the Italians are bored. They do not want to be here, and they all want to go home. They are lazy, they drink a lot and most do as little as they can to get by." She paused and took a deep breath before continuing.

"The relationship between Hitler and Mussolini is strained. I believe a change may be coming but I do not know what kind of change or when, if it happens at all. At present we are lucky, we are allowed to move fairly freely about the island. But the Italians are adding new lookout points on the main roads. They have placed men in the Venetian watchtowers at the north and east of the island. The Italians now have a base in Exo Hora and they are preparing for something big. Pietro seemed worried last night. About what, he would not tell me, but change is definitely on the way."

"You have done well, Elena. That is it for tonight. Please leave silently."

Elena was the last to leave and Dionysis caught her arm.

"Do you love him?"

"Who?"

"That is the question, Elena. I know your history with Angelos. He is the father of your child; you still carry his locket about your neck."

"How do you know about that?"

"Do you think I would not recognise one of my own creations?"

"Oh." Elena ran the chain through her fingers.

"Well?"

"I have always loved Angelos, I think I always will, but he has made a life for himself that does not include me and Athena. His father did his best to keep us apart and succeeded. I know Angelos only does what he does because of Loukas. Did you know that Angelos stood up to Loukas and refused to do his dirty work with the Italians, and Loukas put a gun to his own son's head and threatened to kill him? How could Angelos possibly say no?"

"I did not know that. That knowledge may just have saved Angelos's life."

Elena breathed a sigh of relief. "Really?"

Dionysis gave a small nod.

"Promise me, Dionysis. Promise me that you will do everything you can to protect Angelos. Please do not let him die."

"I promise."

"Thank you."

"And what of the Italian?"

Elena burst into tears. "I hate myself, Dionysis. I hate being with him. I feel like I am betraying everyone: my daughter, my parents, my brother, but mostly myself. I do not want to do it anymore. I cannot do it anymore. I am scared Dionysis. Really scared."

"My dear little one. Life has tested you, has it not? I am sorry for putting you in this position. It was unfair of me, but you must understand that what you do, you do for this island and for all of Greece. There is no one else who can do what you do, Elena. Is it such hardship to continue for a while longer?"

Elena sat and thought about everything; her head was spinning. She was so confused. How had her life ended up like this? Most people she knew on the island had been gifted normal lives: a life worth living, a love that they married, children they cared for and a place to call home. She may have Athena, but the rest of her life was a mess and now she was a pawn in the game of war. She had no one to turn to. Angelos, the man she still loved with all her heart, was no longer part of her life. She was sleeping with the enemy in order to help the resistance, which was such a dangerous thing, and now she was also helping to hide and protect an English airman. Where had it all gone wrong for her?

She sighed and looked out across the darkened island, bathed in the moon's silvery glow. She knew that her path in life had been chosen for her long before she began living it and she was merely a passenger along for the ride. She was in too deeply, and all she could do was what was asked of her. She had to help the resistance, whatever the outcome may be. That was her fate.

"I hate this, Dionysis. But I know that you need me, I know that I have no other choice but to carry on. I will just have to learn to live with myself. It is all I can do."

Elena wiped her eyes, removing a stray tear that threatened to fall. She refused to let Dionysis see her cry. She would leave that for a desolate hour in the depth of night, when she sat alone staring at the starlit sky once again, questioning the choices she had made.

"You are very brave, Elena. We both know that Pietro is our enemy and there will come a time when you will have to choose between your island, your beliefs, and him. I must warn you now that, if he ever finds out what you have been doing, your life will be in peril. There will be little that I can do to protect you. Every member of the resistance knows the ultimate price for their actions is death; it is the same for you, too. You do understand that? I will not force you to carry on if you do not want to. I know I can be persuasive, and I am not lying when I say that we need you, but if you truly refuse to do it, I will not force you. It is your decision, Elena, and yours alone."

"I know." She was very well aware of the risk she was taking. "But as you said Dionysis, you need me, and we are fighting a war. If Greece and this beautiful island need me, then they shall have me."

"As long as you are sure?"

"I am sure."

"Then, it is time you went. Take care of yourself, Elena Petrakis. Your daughter needs her mother."

With these parting words, she slipped into the darkness and cautiously made her way home.

~

Pietro finished the cigarette and threw it to the ground, exhaling the remaining smoke to the elements. He was fed up of the war. They had been on the island for two years now and nothing had changed. The rest of the world was still tearing itself apart and they were no nearer to a resolution. He heard the stories from his superiors about Jews being rounded up and locked up in concentration camps, their belongings seized, their houses and shops burned to the ground. Even those who went into the camps were not safe. They were herded into chambers and gassed until they were dead; innocent men, women and children. And why? All because one man with a twisted version of reality said it must be that way.

That was what made it worse for him, the death of so many women and children. It disgusted him and he no longer believed in the war he had been sent to fight. He wished he could run away, take Elena and her child with him, but traitors and deserters were shot, and where would they go anyway? He could not go to Italy, he still had a wife there, and Germany seemed to have a tight grip on a large part of the world now.

He had not seen Elena for a few days and he hoped that she would come to him tonight. The sky had already begun to darken, the day nearing its end. Sitting on the small veranda he watched as his colleagues walked past.

"Pietro! Come join us!"

"No. I am in no mood to get drunk."

"You have become boring, Captain. You need some ouzo in your belly and a country girl in your bed!"

Pietro waved them along, ignoring their jibes. He could have had them reprimanded, since it was no way for them to talk to a senior officer, but he knew that they were as bored as he. What good would it do to come down hard on them? None at all. Their laughter eventually faded to nothingness, and he sat back lighting another cigarette, enjoying the taste as he inhaled deeply.

As the sun finally dipped over the horizon, the moon rose in tandem and stars began to twinkle. Throwing another spent butt to the ground, he pushed back the chair and went inside to remove his uniform. A noise startled him and he turned his gun ready to defend himself.

"Pietro! It is only me. Why so jumpy?"

Placing it on the side he bounded forward. He lifted Elena in his arms and whirled her around. Smiling, she slid her arms around his neck pulling his head towards hers.

"I have missed you so much," she breathed between tender kisses.

"And I you. I wondered when you would come, I have not seen you for days, and I have missed you so much."

"I know. It is not always easy for me to get

away."

"I am glad you are here, though. I have a surprise. Come." He took hold of her hand and guided her through to the back of the house. In the kitchen he lifted a wicker basket and slid out of the back door, keeping a finger to his lips. Quietly she followed him up the alleyway to the fields that lay beyond the village. Climbing a wall, she giggled as she slid into his arms on the other side.

"Shush. If we get caught we will be in trouble."

"Sorry!" she whispered.

Under the cover of night, they traversed the fields until they found themselves somewhere quiet and safe away from patrolling soldiers. Opening the basket, Pietro pulled out a blanket and threw it on the ground before emptying the contents onto it.

"I have made us a picnic."

"It is wonderful. I am very hungry, too. We just do not seem to have enough food nowadays. Where did you get all of this?" she asked, marvelling at the array of village bread, olives, and other delicious morsels. The sight of it made her mouth water, but she also felt guilty. Some people on the island were starving and barely able to feed themselves, and here she was eating food that could have gone to them, and kept their cupboards stocked for days.

"I am an Italian officer. We live well, even in war."

Too tired and hungry to care, Elena dived in and ate heartily. Once they had finished, they shared some wine and lay back on the blanket to gaze up at the stars.

"I wish it could be like this forever, Pietro."

"Me, too. I am bored of the war. I wish it would all just end."

She turned to face him, "But if it ended, you would go home and I would never see you again."

"You believe that?"

"I do not know." She was not really sure of anything anymore. Dionysis's words continued to roll around her head.

Trust no one.

"I would see you again. I would see you every day, we would no longer be at war, and we could live together wherever we wanted, happy and free," Pietro said.

He ran a finger down her face and across her lips, making them tingle. Leaning forward he kissed her deeply, and Elena allowed him to do what he wanted. She knew that he could no longer resist the urge to be with her and she allowed him to spend the rest of the night making love to the woman he loved under the stars.

CHAPTER TWENTY-TWO

Zakynthos, Greece, 1943

Elena continued to feed information back to the resistance, which kept them strong and ahead of the Italians. She visited the Richard every week and sat and talked with him, sometimes for hours. His wounds had healed and he could now put pressure on his leg and stand, although he still found it difficult to walk. She told him everything about her life, how she was still laying with Pietro, and how her daughter was growing almost daily. In turn he told her more about his life in England and how he missed his family and friends.

Dionysis had been working on an escape plan to try and get the Richard back to his own country, but so far everything they tried had failed. The closest they had come was organising a rescue boat, but two of the resistance were caught on a midnight recce and had been shot dead by Italian soldiers. For weeks, their bodies had lain dead over the top of a barbed wire fence, bloodied and riddled with holes. No one dared move them; they were too scared of getting caught. It was a stark and horrific reminder to the islanders that they were still under the rule of the enemy. Dionysis had made the decision to wait a few months before trying again. It would be safer to all involved to keep hiding Richard rather than attempting another escape so soon.

In turn, Loukas, Stelios and Angelos continued to spy on the locals for the Italians, but by now the Italians were becoming bored, and a wind of change was blowing strong. As summer arrived, news filtered through that the Allies were advancing with some, albeit limited, success. Zakynthians' hopes were raised and they dared to dream of a swift end to the war.

Elena was late arriving to the resistance meeting one night in July. It was almost over by the time she got there and she was breathless and could barely speak. Dionysis could see the terror in her eyes as he passed her something to drink. "What is it?"

"I have just heard from Pietro. Mussolini has been imprisoned. He has been replaced and

Germany is mobilising its troops."

"What does this mean, Dionysis?" one of the men asked.

"It means nothing has changed. For now the Italians remain here, but they may get new orders. We keep doing what we are doing. The Allies are beginning to win the war; it will not be long before they are here."

Filled with reassurance, the men took their orders and disappeared into the night.

Elena remained to have her usual chat with Dionysis.

"I need you to keep a very close eye on Pietro and report everything back to me, Elena, however insignificant. This war is far from over."

"But you just said the Allies are winning the war. I do not understand."

"Elena. The Germans are the real leaders of this war. The Italians are just the hired help. With Mussolini now in prison, it means Germany no longer has a use for Italy. Unless the Allies reach us I fear this war will continue, and the Germans could invade us."

"Oh god."

"I try and speak the truth to you, Elena, as I know you will use it to your advantage. I hope that I am wrong and that we will soon be at peace, but we just do not know what will happen. Go home to your family. Your daughter needs you."

She could only nod. Leaving Dionysis behind, she crept through the darkness, eager to get home as fast as she could to hug Athena tightly.

~

The next two months were the most unsettling of the war so far. The Italians had all but given up, many of them were jaded and fed up and just wanted to go home. They were as worried about the news of Mussolini's imprisonment as the Greeks were. They may have been Germany's allies but many still feared their ruthlessness. Pietro was worried by the news of their great leader's demise. He knew it spelled trouble for the Italians. He hated politics, but was well aware that they were a mere pawn in Germany's giant game. If the Germans came, as they were predicting, he would have to choose a side. He no longer wanted to be associated with a nation that killed innocents in their thousands. Neither did he want to die at their hands for desertion. It was a difficult choice he hoped he would never have to make.

Life for Angelos had become easier. The meetings between his father, Stelios and Captain Cipriani had stopped and he was no longer required to spy upon his fellow citizens. He felt relief, but Loukas was furious at this turn of events. The Italians had promised him the earth and the promises had all been broken. He was no longer inside the trusted circle and he felt unsettled by it. Things changed at home too.

Maria gave birth to a beautiful healthy daughter called Sophia. It reminded Angelos of all he had lost, but the moment he looked into Sophia's eyes he knew that none of it was her fault, and he would always love her, even if he could never truly love her mother.

~

Elena awoke to beautiful burnished autumn sunlight piercing through the curtains. Pietro stirred beside her and she rolled over to lie on top of him. Staring into his eyes, she smiled, leaned in and kissed him. He ran his fingers through her hair and down her back.

"This is a nice way to be woken, Elena. When I am asleep I miss you, when I am working I miss you, when you leave the room…"

"…you miss me!" Elena laughed.

As much as she hated what she was doing, she had become used to Pietro's presence and realised that in some ways the Italians were as much pawns in the German's war as everyone else.

Suddenly the bedroom door banged open, making them jump, and an embarrassed Italian soldier stood there wringing his hands.

"Captain Cipriani, we have company!"

Rolling Elena off him, Pietro jumped from the bed, pulled on his uniform, and ran from the room. The soldier hung back for a moment, eyeing

Elena's nakedness. Reaching to the floor, he lifted her clothes and passed them to her, and lustfully ran a finger down her bare arm.

"You should get dressed and leave, whore."

He fled the room, following in Pietro's wake. Shaking slightly from her encounter, Elena quickly dressed. Peeking through the window she watched the scene before her. Pietro and the young soldier were standing with two men in very recognisable uniforms. Her body went cold and her hands became clammy. Realisation hit her square in the stomach and she ran to the bathroom, vomiting until there was nothing left to come up.

It was the ninth of September and the Germans had landed.

~

Pietro was furious at being disturbed, but as he stepped from the house, placing his cap squarely on his head, he knew the soldier had been right to get him. The sight of two German soldiers made his heart plummet. Why had nobody told him that they were coming? Did this mean that the island would now be under German rule? Glancing back at the house, he saw no sign of Elena. He hoped she would have the sense to get home as quickly as possible. Stepping forward, he greeted the two men and climbed into the waiting vehicle. When everyone was aboard, they set off towards Zakynthos Town. As Pietro stared at the passing trees and houses, he knew it was going to be a long day.

~

After leaving the house, Elena knew what she had to do. Running through fields and past hedges, leaping over fallen branches and crossing small roads and tracks, her feet pounded the ground until finally, breathless and aching, she reached home. Banging through the front door, she tore through the small house yelling for her brother Georgios.

"Elena Petrakis! What is all this noise?" her mother demanded.

Elena ignored her mother and yelled for her brother again.

"What?" he appeared moments later, not happy about being woken.

"Mama, Papa, I need to talk to Georgios alone."

"Whatever you have to say to your brother can be said in front of us," her father said.

"It cannot."

"Yes, it can."

Elena stared for a moment then shrugged. They were her parents, what harm was there?

"Georgios. You need to go to Dionysis. It is urgent. You must avoid the main road and take great care. Tell Dionysis that the Germans are here. We have been invaded and are under

German rule now."

Without another word, Georgios quickly pulled on his shoes and ran from the house. Elena saw the shock on her parents' faces. They both stared at her, unable to speak.

"You cannot tell anyone Mama, Papa. You have to understand no one must ever know. You cannot even talk about it between yourselves."

Her father spoke, "I have questions."

"Only if they are quick. I cannot promise to answer them, but if I can I will."

"You and our son. You are both resistance? You both help the locals, give them food, and medicine and keep the evil that is suffocating our island at bay?"

Elena nodded. She decided that a simple action would be safer than words.

"My daughter. I am so very proud of you." Her father reached for her and hugged her for the first time in her life.

"You cannot and must not tell anyone. If anyone ever asks, you know nothing. You must promise me!"

"We promise," her father said as her mother nodded in agreement.

"I must go. I have work to do."

With that, she swept from the house, leaving her parents in dumbfounded silence. She had no idea where she was heading but one thing she knew was that she needed to see her enemy. She needed to get close to them, to get an idea of who they really were. The island was truly at war now and it was every man and woman for themselves.

~

Angelos and Maria were having lunch under the shade of the veranda with Loukas and Pigi. Sophia lay asleep in her basket. A car trundled along the drive and came to a stop in front of the house and they looked up to see Captain Cipriani stepping from its confines. Loukas stood to greet him.

"Captain, welcome to my home. How can I help you?"

"I am here on business. I would like you to meet Commandant Brandt. He has been appointed Governor of Zakynthos by the Führer himself." He allowed the gravity of the situation to hit home with the family. "The commandant is now in charge of the island of Zakynthos. You are now under German rule. The commandant needs a headquarters and has chosen this house. You will move your family out immediately and your possessions will become the property of the German Army. We will, of course, allow you to take your clothes and a few items of personal sentimentality."

Loukas stood and strode forward. "How dare you! I have helped you for years. You must tell them, Captain Cipriani! Without me you would not have known what half the peasants on the island were getting up to. This is *my* house; it has been passed down through the generations. I will not give it up."

Pietro was unsure of what to say, but the commandant took control. He stepped forward, while removing thick black leather gloves. "I am sorry you feel that way, but you have no choice. The house is ours."

"Over my dead body!" Loukas yelled.

The commandant shrugged, and pulled a Luger from his pocket. "Have it your way." Without hesitation, he pointed it at Loukas's head and pulled the trigger. The lone shot echoed around them and Loukas fell forward, landing with a thud. Pigi screamed as blood oozed from her husband's head staining the soil. Maria stood and reached for baby Sophia, holding her tightly to her chest to protect her from the chaos. Pietro was as sickened as the Sarkis family at the callous murder, but he had to hide his feelings. If he showed any sign of weakness he would likely end up dead, too.

The commandant put away his gun and pulled on his gloves. "You have one hour, then we return. If you are not gone by then we will kill you one by one, until you do as we ask."

Pietro followed the commandant back to the car and climbed in, and seconds later they were disappearing down the drive. Rushing forward,

Angelos knelt next to his father and checked for a pulse, but the glazed dull light in Loukas's eyes already told him he was dead. There was nothing he could do. Behind him, Angelos could hear his mother whimpering and his wife crying as she continued to cradle their child. Standing, he went to comfort them.

"Father is dead. There is nothing more we can do for him." Then with urgency, he continued, "You must listen to me. I need you both to go and get your belongings. Pack up as much as you can. Maria, go to our house, get what you can. We do not have long. I will help Mother."

"Where will we go, Angelos?" Maria asked, shaking.

"The only place we can go, to your father's house."

She nodded and did as her husband asked.

Angelos steered his mother towards the main house. Once inside, he sat her down, and ran around the rooms filling carpetbags and crates. In his father's office he rummaged through the files in the desk. Finally locating the paperwork he was searching for, he stuffed it under his shirt. They may have lost their home for now, but who knew what the future would hold?

With only five minutes to spare, the donkeys were harnessed onto two carts that were loaded with everything they needed. As they passed through the gate onto the lane, the large car pulled alongside.

The commandant smiled up at Angelos.

"I am glad you have seen sense, boy."

The car moved on and the family was left to continue the lonely journey south, no longer the island's richest and most prominent family. Loukas Sarkis was dead. They had lost their homes and most of their possessions, and they had no one to turn to except for Stelios. Angelos hoped and prayed that his wife's father would take them in or they would be forced to sleep in the street like peasants. The irony did not escape Angelos.

~

Elena ran through the lanes and fields trying her best to avoid the Germans that now seemed to be everywhere. She had been out all day and was exhausted. The Germans had been on the island for less than a day but in that small period of time they had invaded Zakynthos en masse. Wherever she looked there were grey uniforms, motorcycles, flatbed trucks, and small armoured cars. She had made her way straight to Bohali and stood under the cover of trees, staring at the activity in the busy harbour. Boats had been landing on the shore for hours, unloading troops, guns, hand grenades, cannons and other war paraphernalia. Dionysis was right. The Allies had not been able to protect them and there was nothing left for the Zakynthians. The enemy had arrived with full force, and the islanders were abandoned, alone and left to fend for themselves.

Elena had seen enough. She left Bohali and made her way north, back towards home. It would be getting dark soon. As she passed one of the Sarkis olive groves, she saw two carts coming towards her. She ran to them, wondering who it could be. She had to warn them to get off the road. As she neared, she was shocked to see it was the Sarkis family.

"Angelos?! What are you doing out here?"

Angelos pulled on the reins and the donkey stopped. He signaled for Maria in the other cart to do the same. As they came to a halt, Sophia, who was nestled in her basket in the base of Maria's cart, stirred and began to cry.

"The Germans are here, Elena. They have commandeered our house and land. Father tried to resist but..." he trailed off.

Pigi whimpered, tears falling down her face.

"I do not understand," Elena said.

Angelos could only point over his shoulder. Slowly she walked to the back of the cart to take a look, but she was not prepared for what she saw. Loukas Sarkis, her sworn enemy, lay cold and dead wrapped in an old rug. There was a hole in his head and the rest of his face was caked in blood. It was evident that he had been shot. Staggering back, she gripped the side of the cart, trying hard not to vomit. As much as she had hated Loukas, she was not convinced he deserved that.

"They killed him? But why?"

"Because he said no. They demanded our house. Father said no, so they shot him."

"What will you do now? Where will you go?"

"To Stelios's. There is nowhere else we can go."

"Okay, travel as quickly as you can, and stay safe. The Germans are everywhere. We must protect ourselves from the enemy. Do not worry, Angelos, we will keep fighting. I have to go and report this."

Before he had a chance to respond, she was gone. He flicked the reins and the carts continued their journey. The soothing motion of the cart settled Sophia and she once more drifted off to sleep. Angelos was the man of the house now and Elena was right, he had to get them to Stelios as soon as possible. While they were on the road, they were in grave danger.

~

Elena carried on. She knew where she had to go, but she was taking a long and circuitous route in case she was being followed. Tiredness was beginning to overwhelm her and she was starving, but she had to keep going. She was stunned by what she had learned from Angelos. She knew his relationship with his father had always been strained, but Loukas's death must still have come as a huge shock to him. She wished there were something she could do, some way of comforting him, but it was no longer her job. That task would fall to his wife. All Elena could do was her job, and hope that in the months and years ahead, the man responsible would be held to account. A few hours later, she had finally finished the climb up into the hills and entered the cave under cover of darkness. Dionysis was patiently sitting and waiting for her.

"Is Georgios safe?"

"Yes, Elena. He is fine. You did the right thing in alerting us. I have sent men out to gather information. The Germans are everywhere. It seems that we have a big task ahead of us, and I just pray that their invasion will be as peaceful as possible."

"They have already killed."

"They have?"

Elena explained about the Sarkis family and even Dionysis looked shocked.

"As much as I disliked the man, that seems terribly harsh."

"I agree."

"What will Angelos and his family do?"

"Go to live with Stelios Makris, if he will have them."

"Good. We need a plan of action. I fear that we have now entered the depths of hell and that no one on this island is safe. "

They both fell silent.

"Is the war lost, Dionysis?"

"No, Elena. Nothing is ever truly lost. There is always hope and that is what we need to keep hold of now," he said, and then paused. "I need you to do something, Elena. Regardless of what happens, you need to stay close to the Italian soldier. He is a captain, and if the Italians remain on the island, he will be party to a lot of information. He will still be of great use to us."

"Yes, Dionysis."

"We should go. But heed my warning Elena: these Germans are vile and dangerous people. You saw what they did to Loukas Sarkis and he was on their side. Take care and watch your back."

This time, he departed first and disappeared into the trees. Elena sat to catch her breath and take everything in. She knew that she was now playing a very dangerous game. The Germans, as they had already proven, would stop at nothing to get what they wanted. For the first time in her life, Elena was truly scared and she wondered how she was going to find the strength to carry on.

~

Mayor Vallis and Bishop Ioannou sat uncomfortably at the large dining table in Commandant Brandt's newly acquired house, waiting for him to appear. The German Army had set up their official headquarters just outside of Zakynthos Town, but Commandant Brandt liked all the pleasures in life and had heard about the good work that the Sarkis man had done with the Italians. It seemed the Sarkis family lived in luxury compared to most islanders, and the commandant saw that he was right when he finally got his hands on the house. It was filled with good furniture, and a lot of food and wine. There was plenty of space and he liked feeling as though he was lord of the manor. He thought about the two men who would be sitting and waiting for him to appear, but wait they would. He was having breakfast at his leisure and no one would rush him, not even a man of god, *if* the bishop could call himself that. He assumed that they had both heard the rumours of the Sarkis man's death. Captain Cipriani had told him much about the island already and it seemed that news travelled quickly here.

Sitting in silence, the two men continued to wait for the commandant. Their nerves were heightened, and the wait was beginning to get to them. When the commandant's summons had first arrived, they were both hesitant. They had seen the activity in Zakynthos Town and inwardly mourned the loss of the Greek flags as they were stripped from their poles to be replaced with the blood red flag sporting its evil swastika. Neither wanted to meet with the commandant and they wondered why they had been brought here instead of being taken to the German headquarters in town. They had been sitting at the table in relative silence for almost half an hour now, waiting for Commandant Brandt to appear, but as yet there was no sign of him.

"If he does not come soon, I am leaving. The Germans may think they are in control, but I am still mayor of this island, and they cannot order me around like this!"

"Hush. You will only antagonise them. Be still, my old friend. If they wanted to kill us, then they would have already done it."

Mayor Vallis sat back in chair sighing. "I know you are right. I just wonder when all of this madness will end. People are dying unnecessarily. Look what they did to Loukas Sarkis, and all because of one man's futile dreams."

The door suddenly creaked and swung open. A clicking of boot heel on wooden floor accompanied Commandant Brandt as he strode purposefully towards the table. Coming to a sudden stop, he raised his right arm and straightened the hand giving an emphatic "Heil Hitler!" Dropping his arm he pulled out a chair and took a seat opposite the bishop and the mayor.

"Thank you both for coming. I am hoping that this meeting will be swift. I understand that you are Bishop Ioannou and Mayor Vallis?"

Both men nodded agreement, as they absorbed the shocking gesture the commandant had just used to greet them.

"Welcome. I am Commandant Brandt,

Governor of Zakynthos, as decreed by the Führer. My instructions are simple. We are in charge and you Greeks will do as we ask. Those who resist us, and I know there are many, will be dealt with swiftly and severely." The commandant paused to open a silver cigarette case. He offered it to the two men opposite, but they refused. Taking a cigarette from it, he tapped it on the case before lighting it, and then placed the cigarette case on the table in front of him. "Now we get down to business. I need a list of all Jewish people living on the island. They must be identified as soon as possible and the two of you will provide me with the details."

The mayor leaned in to study the enemy before him, "Why is it you need these details, Commandant?"

"That is of no concern to you. Like you, I have my orders and I am carrying them out. I know that both you and the bishop will be able to assist me."

The mayor was not willing to let it go. He, like many of the other islanders, had heard the horrific stories filtering through the illegal radio sets. Jews rounded up, shipped off to internment camps and put to death by the Germans because they did not fit into Hitler's idea of a perfect world.

"You must understand, Commandant. On this island, the Jewish population is such a small number. They are poor people, they have no big houses, or expensive jewellery, there is no reason to single them out. Zakynthos is part of Greece and all her inhabitants are Greek people."

"Are you refusing to do as I ask, Mayor?"

The mayor and the bishop briefly looked at each other with unease. They had a duty to try and protect every man, woman and child on the island, but how could they possibly go up against the ruthless might of the German Army?

"We are not refusing, Commandant," the bishop interjected.

"But you need more time?" Brandt raised an eyebrow as he pulled on his cigarette.

The mayor and the bishop knew the commandant was toying with them, like an injured bird caught by a vicious cat.

"More time would be an advantage," the bishop agreed.

"Fine. You have twenty-four hours. Then I want the list. If you do not give me what I want, I will have to make an example of you both. You know what that means?"

"You will kill us."

"Yes."

Commandant Brandt stood and walked to the door and, as he reached it, he turned.

"Until tomorrow, gentlemen. I hope you make the right decision. I would hate to have to kill you both."

A moment later he was gone, leaving the

room in an uneasy veil of silence.

"What do we do now?" the bishop asked.

"We leave quietly without speaking, and then we head into town."

~

Elena had not seen Pietro since their interruption. She walked through the streets under as much cover as she could, heading towards his house. The Germans were now everywhere and islanders were unable to go anywhere without being stopped and interrogated. She carried a basket of bread and olives, feigning a trip to the market to cover her tracks. Each time she was stopped, the soldiers stole from her, and her wares were sadly depleted.

Turning a corner, she saw Pietro's house, but the sudden sound of thudding boots on hard ground reached her ears and she hid in the shadows of a doorway waiting for the line of marching German soldiers to pass. The very sight of them made her shudder. She was about to step out when a hand grasped hold of her, pulling her back. Her heart plummeted and she waited for a rough German voice to speak, but it never came.

"*Piccolina*! What are you doing here?"

"Pietro!" she flung her arms around him, shaking with relief. "I came to see you, I was so worried."

"I am okay, but you should not be here. It is

too dangerous. Come, but you must be quiet."

Looking out onto the road, he watched as the last of the soldiers rounded the bend. As soon as they disappeared, he grabbed Elena's hand, pulling her along behind him. When they reached his house, he pushed her inside and slammed the door behind him.

"Elena. I have missed you. I wondered what they would do to you after I left. Did anyone hurt you?"

"No. Your young soldier called me a whore before demanding I leave, but I am okay. I managed to sneak out the back."

"I will have words with him. He cannot talk to you like that!"

"No matter." She waved her hand in the air as though she did not care. "What happened when they took you away?"

Pietro sat heavily on the bed. "Everything has changed. The island is under German rule now. The man who came to collect me is Commandant Brandt, and he is the new governor of the island. They are making plans, Elena. I do not know all of it, but I did hear that the mayor and the bishop have been given orders to give the commandant a list of all Jews on the island. They have until tomorrow to provide it."

Elena felt sick. She sat next to him and took his hand. "Why do they want it?"

"They mean to take their property and ship

them off to the camps, Elena."

"The camps? Is that not where they kill them?"

Pietro shrugged, "I do not know. Maybe."

"And you agree with this? How can you, Pietro?"

Pietro looked at her with surprise. It was the first time she had ever let her feelings about the war show, and she knew in that moment that she had said the wrong thing.

"So you are truly Greek after all then, Elena. I thought you were on my side, but all you wanted was someone to fuck now that your precious Angelos is married. You really are showing your true colours. Does it make you feel like a big brave woman, knowing that you are sleeping with a captain of the Italian army?"

"No!"

"Do not lie to me!" he snarled as he advanced on her. He was so close now that it frightened her. "Maybe now you will be bored with me and move onto the commandant, or maybe you will just go back to Angelos and sneak around with him in the woods?"

Pietro had fire in his eyes and she had never seen him like this before. She knew she had all but given herself away, and only had the smallest chance of redeeming herself.

"Pietro. My darling Pietro," she cooed as she cupped his face with her hands and gazed lovingly into his eyes, hoping that he would believe her.

"You know I no longer care what happens to Angelos. It is you that I love. I would not care if you were an Italian peasant!"

"So why do you still wear this?" He snatched the locket from her neck and ripped it from her, throwing it across the room. In that moment, she realised that she was safe. Pietro was jealous, jealous of her relationship with a past love and that was all. Inside she breathed a sigh of relief.

"Please Pietro, do not be cross with me. We have all had a shock today. The German Army has turned the island upside down in such a short time and it affects us all. Please believe me when I say I love you."

Pietro sighed and pulled her close, wrapping his arms around her. "I am sorry. I worry what will happen now. I may get sent home tomorrow, I just do not know."

Pietro kissed her and then pulled back to look at her. He loved her beautiful face, but he hated that they had met under such circumstances. He wished the war would end so he could settle into a normal life. "I cannot talk about it anymore, Elena. I am so tired of it all."

"Then do not speak," she whispered, and placed a comforting hand on his chest and gazed up at him. He had seen that look before and knew what it meant. It was the middle of the day and he should be on duty, but he no longer cared. Reaching forward, he kissed her again, and swiftly unbuttoned her flimsy dress. Moments later she was naked under him and he finally felt safe once more.

~

Dusk was beginning to creep over the horizon as Elena did up her dress. Pietro was asleep and had been for an hour. She knew he would worry if he found her gone when he awoke, but there were bigger things at stake. She needed to get to Dionysis as soon as possible, and had wasted too much time already. The argument she had with Pietro had not helped either. As she turned to leave, she reached under the bed for her locket. The chain was broken, but it did not matter. She tucked it into a small pocket in her dress before turning to leave.

Running through woodland and brush, Elena made her way to the caves. It had been a difficult journey once the Italians had arrived, but now with the Germans on the island it was downright dangerous. She finally made it in one piece and Dionysis was already waiting for her.

"I have grave news."

"Elena. It is good to see you. Sit and tell me."

"The Germans have demanded a list of all the Jews living on the island and mean to ship them off the island as soon as they can. We need to help them, Dionysis!"

"How do you know this?"

Elena explained everything while Dionysis listened in silence. As they discussed the situation, other members of the resistance began to arrive, and the news was shared with these brave islanders who continued to put their lives on the line for the freedom of their families and their home.

~

It was late in the evening and Mayor Vallis was pacing the main room of his house. He and the bishop were in a difficult situation, with seemingly no way out. Whatever happened now, the Germans would make sure someone paid, and most likely it would be with blood - their blood. A sharp knock at the door made him jump and he crept over to the window. Curfew had begun hours ago and whoever was at the door was taking a big risk. In the shadows, he could make out the familiar stature of the bishop. Next to him was an unidentifiable figure.

Swiftly, the mayor opened his door and allowed the two figures in, guiding them into the main room. As they sat, he stepped back in shock.

"Elena Petrakis?"

"Yes, Mayor Vallis."

"What on earth are you doing here?"

Bishop Ioannou motioned to the armchair and the mayor sat. The bishop said, "Let me explain. It seems that we are not alone in our predicament.

The resistance already has a plan to help save the Jews, but we must still play our part."

"They do?"

The bishop nodded at Elena and she spoke up, "There are many of us on the island fighting for the cause. I know very few people who support the Italians or the Germans. We have a network of spies and fighters in the hills. The enemy hardly ever goes up there. We have discussed it and have agreed that, when you go to see the commandant tomorrow, we will move all of the Jewish families into the mountains."

The mayor listened intently with surprise, "But there are over two hundred and seventy of them! How on earth will you move and hide them all? Surely someone will notice?"

"We have a plan. I cannot tell you all of it, as I do not want the details to fall into the wrong hands. I mean no disrespect to either of you, but the less you know, the better."

The bishop only nodded, before turning to the mayor. "What do you think?"

"I think if they can do it, it is a good idea, but what of us, Bishop? We need to have our own plan."

"I have been thinking about this, and I have come up with something if, of course, you agree. We must first destroy the records of the existing Jewish families on the island. The resistance is willing to help." Elena nodded in agreement. "Then, Mayor, we must make the greatest sacrifice of all."

"And that is?"

"The commandant will get his list, but it will not be what he is expecting."

Mayor Vallis realised in that moment what the plan was, and he knew it was the only option. He sat back in his chair and thought about the life he had led. It had been a good one, and he had always been an honest and respected man. Tomorrow he and the bishop would go to meet Commandant Brandt and they would give him the list of names he so eagerly sought. In the meantime, the resistance would do their best to save the island's Jews. It was a brave but risky move, one that could go very wrong. Only time would tell if they succeeded.

CHAPTER TWENTY-THREE

Zakynthos, Greece, 2002

Five days after arriving on Zakynthos, Kate finally summoned the courage to go to Exo Hora. After speaking to Nikoloas, she had driven all over the island, sunbathing on beaches at Porto Zoro in the south, and Alykes in the northeast. She had gone into Zakynthos Town and visited some of the beautiful churches including the Church of St Dionysis with its imposing Venetian bell tower and explored the quirky side streets. Ambling along the harbour, she had watched an old man as he sat in what could only be described as a rowing boat, concentrating hard on mending an old fishing net. In stark contrast, a white shiny yacht that looked as though it had arrived straight from

Monaco was moored nearby. Old next to new, and neither looked out of place. Kate had even managed to locate the old Venetian castle at Bohali. She explored it taking in the history of the place before admiring the incredible view across Zakynthos Town.

The drive up into the mountains on the west coast was beautiful. There were very few cars about and the scenery was picturesque. Parking up in Exo Hora, Kate walked through the streets taking in the pretty village with its old stone houses and hanging baskets of fragrant flowers. It was not long before she came across a towering olive tree. It was enormous, with thick twisted brown branches that reached skywards and ended in shady green boughs. She stopped and sat on the wall next to it, and thought about her family. There were still so many questions and she wished she could have some of them answered. Now that she was here, where Angelos Sarkis lived, she was nervous. How could she tell a man, who probably did not speak English, who she was and why she was here?

She closed her eyes, breathing in the sweet aroma of sunbaked land, flowers and rich smelling coffee from a nearby café. She liked this place. There was something about it that made her feel at home, made her feel at peace and she was glad she had come. Instinctively, she clasped Athena's engraved silver locket that she had now taken to wearing, and wished for an answer to all her prayers.

"Elena!"

The loud unsteady voice startled her and her eyes flew open. An old man was staring at her, his face etched with shock and disbelief. Feeling uncomfortable, she rose and walked away but, despite his age, the man was quick and he placed himself in front of her.

"Elena?" It came out as a mere whisper.

"I'm sorry. My name is Kate." She hoped he understood English

He continued to stare, talking hurriedly in Greek but she had no idea what he was saying.

"Papa!" A woman ran across the road. Coming to the man's aid, she took hold of his arm. Kate studied her a moment before speaking. The woman had strong Greek features. The sun had kissed her ageing lined face, and her eyes sparkled. Kate noticed that her short brown hair was streaked through with grey and she guessed that she was in her late fifties or early sixties.

"He saw me sitting on the wall and keeps trying to say something to me." Kate explained, hoping the woman spoke English. Thankfully she did.

"I'm sorry, he is so old, he gets confused and unsteady on his feet."

The old man pointed at Kate once more. "Elena."

Kate heard it then for the first time. "Did he

just say Elena?"

"Yes." The woman said. "It is strange. He has been saying it a lot recently. We have no idea why. I am Sophia."

"Hi Sophia, I'm Kate."

"Nice to meet you, Kate."

Sophia turned to her father and spoke rapidly in Greek. He glanced up at Kate and confusion crossed his face again. He pointed at Kate and spoke frantically trying to explain something to his daughter.

"My father is convinced that he knows you or at least someone who looks a lot like you. Like I said, he does get confused. I should get him home."

"Do you need any help?" Kate spied the full bags of shopping on the ground that Sophia had dropped in her haste to get to her father.

"If you do not mind? Thank you."

"Not at all." Kate lifted the bags and followed Sophia as she slowly helped her father along the road. Their house was built of stone, had a pitched tiled roof and painted wooden shutters on every window. Kate followed them into their home and placed the shopping on the side while Sophia helped her father into a chair in the back garden.

When she came back into the house, Sophia said, "Thank you for your help, Kate. Would you like a drink before you go?"

"That would be lovely. Thank you."

"Have a seat outside; I will be out in a moment." Sophia motioned to the door and Kate stepped out into the small back garden. To the right was a large table surrounded by chairs, sheltered overhead by a wooden veranda. Sophia's father sat in a chair in the corner, his eyes closed to the world, lost in sleep or his own thoughts. Quietly, so as not to disturb him, Kate pulled out a seat opposite and relaxed back into it. Sophia appeared carrying a tray of drinks and she took a seat between her guest and her father.

"So how long have been on the island?" Sophia asked.

"Just over a week."

"Are you staying close?"

"No. I'm in an apartment in Kypseli. It's nice and quite secluded."

"That is a good choice. Much better than Laganas, not so much partying," Sophia laughed.

They fell silent but, as awkward as the moment was, Kate felt comfortable with them.

"How long are you here for?" Sophia asked.

"Only two weeks."

"A nice long holiday." Sophia smiled.

"Yes. Well it's a little more than a holiday." Kate had no idea why she was opening up to this woman, but she found herself spilling her heart out. "My life is a bit of a mess. I'm adopted and we think that my real mother was Greek. My real name is Katerina. My birth mother died years ago, but she left me a letter telling me I had family here on Zakynthos but she did not know much about them. Her dying wish was that I come here and find out where I came from."

"Ah, I see. And even though you have little to go on, you still came and are doing what you can to find out who you really are?"

"Yes. Something like that," Kate sighed.

"How very Greek!" Sophia laughed. "Maybe we can help? Papa has known many families on the island. What was your mother's name?"

"Athena. There's no surname in the letter, but it does mention a Sarkis family and someone called Elena Petrakis."

Sophia's hands flew to her face, disbelief fluttered in her eyes. She could barely speak. "Sarkis! Did you say Sarkis?"

"Yes. Why? Do you know someone of that name?" Kate's heart thudded in her chest and her mouth was dry. Sweat had gathered on her palms and she wiped them on her trousers.

"Papa's name is Sarkis. Angelos Sarkis. This cannot be." Sophia glanced at her father blissfully asleep and unaware in his favourite chair. "I am sorry Kate, this is a big shock. I need to speak with my father. You said he recognised you earlier, or something about you. If what you say is true, then he may be the person to help you. But he is old, Kate, and very unwell. I do not want to upset him. He looks stronger than he is, but he is not. This late in his life he needs to relax and rest, and does not need a great shock. I do not know what to do. You must let me think about what is best for him."

Kate nodded. It was as good as she was going to get. She looked over at the old man, the person who held the key to her family history.

"Of course, Sophia. The last thing I want to do is upset you, or him." Reaching into her bag, she pulled out a piece of paper and scribbled her apartment details on it. "If you change your mind, you can reach me here."

"Okay. I cannot promise you anything, Kate. I have to do what is right for my father. He is my priority."

"Of course, I understand," Kate said as she stood. "Thank you for the drink."

"You are very welcome."

Sophia saw Kate to the door and leaned against the frame, watching as the beautiful longhaired English woman climbed into her hire car and drove away. As she closed the door, she let out a long weary sigh. She had a very big decision to make, and really did not know what to do for the best. She knew her father had been in turmoil for some time. Many a night, she and her husband were woken by his pitiful cries, but never once had he confided in his daughter. Never once had she learned what pained him so. Now she had an opportunity. She had seen the look on her father's face. It was as though, when he looked at Kate, he was staring at a ghost. She had no idea what to do, but while her father was still pained by the secrets he carried, Sophia would always worry.

~

The following day, Kate had no idea what to do with herself. Nikolaos Makris had told Kate that Angelos was the person to talk to and by some fluke she had found him. Now all she could do was wait for Sophia to contact her. She felt she should stay near the hotel just in case Sophia called, but then she worried that if she stayed there, Sophia would not ring at all. She had her mum's voice going around her head: *"A watched pot never boils, Kate."* Eventually she gave up and decided to go for a walk. Maybe some fresh air and a change of scenery would do her some good?

Walking towards the small beach near her hotel, her mind turned over again. She wondered if Athena had been born on the island, and if so, had Angelos known of her? There were so many unanswered questions and they tumbled though her mind like pebbles caught in waves. She was desperate for Sophia to call her. The old letter had mentioned a Sarkis family, so they must have known about Athena? Or maybe the name Sarkis was like a Greek version of Smith? Maybe this place was filled with people called Sarkis and she would never find what she was looking for.

Letting out a frustrated shout, she kicked a stone along the road. Why was life so hard sometimes? Why could her life not have been simple?

Arriving at the beach, Kate sat down on the warm pebbles and crossed her legs, watching the waves swish back and forth. It was the same beach she had sat on when she first arrived on the island. The day she had thought long and hard about Fletch and cried over him. It was stupid really, but whenever she was close to the sea, it felt like she was close to him. She wished she knew where he was. He would have loved Zakynthos, and she wished she could have visited the sites with him. He would not have been able to surf here, but he would have swum in the crystal waters and dragged her in behind him, even if she had not wanted to. They would have talked and laughed, drunk Mythos beer and eaten delicious meals in small tavernas overlooking the sea, and walked hand in hand content in each other's company. They had always had so much fun together, and now it was all gone. Kate shook herself. Not again, she would not shed tears over him again. He was gone and he was not coming back. It was time to face facts and just get used to life without him.

Leaving the beach, she walked up the lane to the main road. It was lined with olive trees and wildflowers, and she stopped to watch a small lizard that was basking in the sun. They were fascinating creatures and looked so prehistoric and out of place in Europe. On the main road at the top of the lane was a small shop, where she bought some more bottled water and snacks to keep her going. She liked the walk up to the shop. The scenery was beautiful.

Michelle greeted her with a wave as she arrived back at the hotel.

"You had a phone call. A lady called Sophia."

Kate's heart leapt and she felt the excitement fizz within her. "What did she say?"

"She's spoken to her father and thinks you should go and see them at ten tomorrow morning. She said meet them at her house."

Sophia had said yes; she was going to allow Kate to talk to her father. Kate hugged a bemused Michelle tightly and ran up to her room filled with excitement.

~

Fletch had managed to get through five days of laddish behavior without much more than a few hangovers. The argument with Jase still weighed heavily on his mind. He had shaken Jase's hand and apologised for attacking him in the club, but only to make Shane happy. He was still furious with Jase, and he knew that once this week was over, it was the last he would see of either man. His excuse for not going to the wedding was already set. He would not even be in the country. His promise to stay in England and sort his life out was gone. As soon as he returned home, he was packing up his bags and leaving England for good. He would go back to California, and sort his life out. His pining over Kate had gone on for too long. He had to get over it and admit the fact that she was never going to be part of his life. This time he would start a new life and stick to it.

Looking across at Shane and Jase, he saw they were both asleep on their sunloungers. He was bored and could not wait for the holiday to end, as far as he was concerned, those two days could not go quickly enough.

CHAPTER TWENTY-FOUR

Zakynthos, Greece, 1943

Commandant Brandt was already seated at the table when Mayor Vallis and Bishop Ioannou walked into the Sarkis house. They took their seats opposite the German who was lighting a cigarette. The commandant had moved their meeting to the end of the day, which favoured the resistance. Their plan was already set in motion. The Mayor and Bishop just hoped that the resistance would be successful.

Outside, the sun cast an eerie glow over the olive groves as it began its descent.

"So, gentlemen, do you have my list?"

The mayor nodded and pulled a piece of paper from his jacket pocket. He handed it to the bishop first for him to read. Once he had looked at it, the bishop pushed it across the table. Pulling on his cigarette, the commandant opened the piece of paper and scanned it.

"What is this? It says Metropolite of Zakynthos Bishop Ioannou, and Mayor of Zakynthos Vallis. These are your names. Is this a joke? Where are the other names?"

"It is not a joke. That list is correct. Those are the names you are seeking, commandant." The bishop leaned forward looking directly at the German. "If you are not happy, you can arrest me. If this solution does not satisfy the Germans then I will be happy to go straight into the gas chambers with the other Jews."

Mayor Vallis sat in silence, allowing the bishop to speak. The atmosphere in the room was tense and he could see that the commandant was angry. Mayor Vallis knew that, at that very moment, the resistance were rescuing every Jewish family on the island and taking them to secret hiding places in the hills. Where exactly, the mayor and bishop did not know. Elena was right; it was safer for them not to know. He only hoped that they could get them all moved by the time the meeting with the commandant was over.

"If you do not believe that I am serious then you must do as you see fit, Commandant. I have also written this letter. It is for Herr Hitler himself. I trust you will pass it to him?"

The commandant took the small envelope from the bishop, and turned it over in his hands. He was rattled. The Greeks were playing a dangerous game with him, and it was one he had not expected. Now they mentioned writing to the Führer himself, which made him more than uncomfortable. Duty meant he was obliged to send the letter, and now his hands were tied. He did not want his superiors to think that a lowly bishop and mayor had outsmarted him, but what else could he do?

"And what does this letter say?"

"That is between me and Herr Hitler, but know this, Commandant, I am the Bishop on this island. Any Jews living on Zakynthos fall under my authority and therefore cannot be harmed by your army."

The commandant did not like being told what to do, but even he knew that a sealed letter for the Führer could not be opened by the likes of him. He could burn it and pretend it had been sent, but if the Führer ever found out, Brandt would be executed. He had no choice but to send it. He motioned to a young soldier and instructed him to see the letter on its way. He turned his attention back to the two men before him.

"You have played your hand very well, Bishop, Mayor. Your letter will be sent to the Führer and we will see what he says. Until then, you are free to go about your lives as normal. You will have this list back though. I do not believe it is correct. Know this, you will give me the full list of names when I next ask for it."

The bishop took the list and passed it to the mayor who put it safely in his pocket. The two Greeks stood and left the room, grateful to be leaving with their lives. The commandant stood at the window and watched them leave the house. Once they were out of sight, his temper boiled over. The commandant raged through the room like an infuriated bull. He lifted chairs, flung them at the walls, and watched as ornaments and pictures smashed, and wood splintered. Nothing was left untouched. His staff heard the noise, but no one dared to interrupt him; they feared him too much.

~

Elena ran through the streets under cover of darkness. She had to get to the next house as quickly as possible. Her heart was thudding in her chest, the adrenalin coursed through her and, despite knowing she would die at the hands of monsters if she were caught, she was enjoying every second. As she reached the house, she slowed to a walk. Hiding under the boughs of a small tree, she checked the area for the enemy, but all was quiet. Silently, she crept to the house and knocked on the wooden door. Moments later it opened and she squeezed inside, pushing the door closed behind her. In the hallway stood a nervous and frightened family: father, mother and a daughter who looked to be about eight years old. Quickly, Elena explained who she was and why she was there. She told them to get as many clothes as they could carry and any personal items of sentimentality. They would not be coming back.

"You have five minutes and then we must go. You must stay quiet on the road and do exactly as I say. You cannot speak or cry out and you must obey my instructions. If we are caught, the Germans will not hesitate to use us as an example. They will kill us. Do you understand what I am saying?"

Scared, the family nodded. Leaving the daughter with Elena, the father and mother moved around the small house, quickly packing what they could. When their five minutes was up, Elena beckoned them to be quiet before opening the door. She motioned for them to stay where they were. Once she had checked the street, they crept out into the darkness using the shadows and foliage for cover. As they rounded the corner into an old farm track, she walked straight into a tall figure.

"Halt!" said the male voice and Elena stopped dead, barely inches away from a gun that pointed directly at her. She heard the mother whimper behind her and motioned to the family to stay quiet.

"Elena?"

She recognised the voice and pushed the man back into the shadows, simultaneously pulling the family along with her.

"Angelos?"

"Yes. What are you doing here?"

"Nothing. What are you doing here?" She remembered Dionysis's words.

Trust no one.

"I have joined up, Elena. Dionysis thought you might need help."

Elena gauged him and thought for a moment. They were not safe standing here in the open with only minimal shadows and trees to cover them. She could hear the family getting restless, and knew they were sacred, but did not know what to do for the best. She had known Angelos for a long time. Angelos was the father of her child and she still loved him, but his father had worked with the Italians and it was not so long ago that Angelos had chosen to stand with Loukas. Could she really trust him?

"I know you are doubting me, Elena, but you *can* trust me."

"Can I?"

"Yes. I swear to you on Athena's life that I am on your side. But we cannot stay here and discuss it. We both know what will happen if the Germans catch us. We must get out of here."

The moment he swore on their daughter's life Elena knew that he was one of them. She motioned to the family and the five of them hurried as quietly as they could up the path to a field. She had already planned her route and, in a few hours, under cover of darkness, trees and hedges, the family would be safely hidden in the hills.

"I am glad you are here, Angelos," Elena whispered as they slinked their way through the trees. They had been silent for a long time and she felt the need to break it.

"Me, too. You are so brave, Elena. I could never be as brave as you."

"You are here now, that is what matters."

"That is true, but this is only one thing. You have done so much more."

"It does not matter, Angelos. Even if you only do one good thing in this war, it is better than doing nothing."

She paused suddenly, placing a finger to her lips and motioned for the family to stop. As they huddled under a canopy of trees, they heard an airplane fly directly overhead. As the final noise of the airplane engine disappeared, Elena motioned that it was safe for them to move again.

The village was deathly quiet as they sneaked in. No one was about and they lightly knocked on the door of the house that would become the rescued family's new home. Angelos handed over a basket of food to the homeowner before taking Elena's arm and disappearing into the night.

~

Pietro rolled over to find the bed was still empty. He had fallen asleep early and hoped that Elena would have come to see him by now. He knew he probably would not see her tomorrow. The Italians were under strict instructions to help the Germans search every home in Zakynthos Town. They were to look for Jews and, if found, remove them from their homes. What happened to them thereafter, Pietro did not want to know. He was sick of this war and wanted out, but he had to be careful. He was a long way from home and did not want to end up dying at the hands of madmen. He wanted a life, a life away from death and destruction.

He wanted Elena.

He wanted a house just outside his home town, one with a garden for Athena to play in, where he could picnic with Elena, where they could run hand in hand through the rain, bask in the sun, and watch the sunset. But he knew it would never happen. He was already married and he would never be able to leave his wife. He sighed and knew that while he was still serving in this war, his dreams were just that. Dreams. And every day when he woke, they fell further and further from his grasp. The only choice he had now was to join the Germans, take their orders and pray he came out of this alive.

The door creaked and banged, and he heard

someone pad across the room. He pulled his gun from under his pillow and flicked on his lighter.

"Is that how you greet all your women?" Elena's eyes glinted in the light of the single flame.

"Where have you been?" He placed the gun on the side before lighting the lone candle that sat next to it.

"Athena would not sleep; I have only just managed to get away." She stood at the side of the bed staring at him. He was a handsome man, and yet he was still the enemy. She hated every moment that she was with him, but slowly, very slowly, feelings were beginning to stir. She had tried so hard to suppress them, but they refused to stay down and her brain constantly battled with her heart. Would it be so very wrong to fall in love with him?

"Are you going to stand there all night?"

"Maybe." She grinned as she unbuttoned her dress, allowing it to fall to the floor. Removing her underwear, she climbed on the bed and crawled naked towards him. She could tell from the look on his face that she was teasing him, but she no longer cared.

Reaching forward, Pietro grabbed her and pulled her to him, kissing her hungrily. In that moment they both forgot about their predicament. The resistance fighter who, that very night, had helped save a Jewish family from almost certain death, and the Italian soldier fighting an unjust war firmly aligned with the enemy.

~

Commandant Brandt paced the main room of the Sarkis house. Everyone still called it that despite his insistence that it was now *his* house. He was frustrated, and angry. His men had spent the day searching homes in and around Zakynthos Town, and some of the outlying villages, but every property they visited was empty. The Jews, it seemed, had disappeared into thin air. To where, he had no idea, but he would find out. He ordered his men to arrest neighbours and friends of those who were missing and interrogate them until the Greeks were exhausted, bloodied and bruised. Two men had been shot for being members of the resistance and their bodies were disposed of over a cliff on the west side of the island. It was easier for the sea to get rid of them than the Germans having to worry about the stench of dying bodies piling up. He would do whatever was necessary to make these islanders understand that he was in charge. He was proud to be German and these pitiful Greeks meant nothing to him.

~

Life for the Greeks was hard. Food was still scarce and since the arrival of the Germans, things had become worse. The villagers had learned to be very careful about where they kept their supplies.

Most had opted for the safest way of storing what little food they had, by placing it in pots and burying them in their backyards. The Germans almost never came to the villages but they did not want to take their chances. They went about life as normally as they could, but they were no longer free to roam the island. If they did, they were stopped and checked for anything that may betray resistance support. Therefore, many islanders did as much as they could under the cover of darkness. When a donkey and cart had to be used, they bound the hooves with material so the animal's clopping was silenced. They ran through fields, using bushes and trees for cover. Others just chose to stay prisoner and remained where they were, hoping that others would come to their aid.

By now, all of the Jewish families on the island were hidden and their lives had been saved. Even Elena did not know where half of them were, and it was better that way. It had been a huge victory, and the bravery of Mayor Vallis, Bishop Ioannou and the island's resistance kept the Greeks strong. If they could pull together like this and achieve something so great, then there was hope for the future.

Elena was sitting in the cellar of a house in one of the mountain villages talking to Richard who was eating some much-needed food. The English airman had been moved there from the caves as soon as his leg had been strong enough for him to walk on. Richard put down the bowl and wiped his mouth with the back of his hand.

"I have good news for you," Elena said, smiling.

"You do? I am very excited. It is quite boring sitting here all day with little to do, so good news would make my day."

"I have spoken with Dionysis, and you are going home!"

"I am? Really!"

"Yes. It has been arranged. Dionysis has spoken with some resistance on the mainland. They are sending a boat over in two weeks' time. You will leave from a small cove in the north of the island, at a time of the month when the moon is at its thinnest. The plan is being finalised as we talk, but Dionysis wanted me to let you know."

"That is such good news. I cannot wait to see the green fields of England again."

"And Alice."

"Yes, and Alice. Do you know something, Elena? Being here has given me much time to think. I have missed Alice the most out of everything, and realise that I love her very much. I am going to marry her the minute I get home!"

"That is wonderful Richard. I am very happy for you."

"And you Elena?"

"Me?"

"How are things in your complicated little

life?"

"They are still complicated," she sighed. "I am still spending time with the Italian. I have hated him for so long, but recently, I have found my feelings changing. War does strange things to the mind, Richard. I do not know whether I truly love *him*, or whether it is just circumstance and the things he does to me that makes my mind play tricks."

"What does your heart say?"

"My heart." She sighed. "My heart is still broken. I can never change how I feel about Angelos, but I wonder if it can learn to heal by being forced to love another?"

Richard laughed, "For one so young, you think far too much. We may all be dead tomorrow, Elena. There is nothing wrong with making plans for the future but for now, why not just enjoy life?"

"But he is Italian. He is the…"

"…the enemy. I know all of that already, Elena, but if the war did finish tomorrow, what then? Angelos would still be married to someone else, but your Italian would be available. He could still be yours and you could be happy."

"Are you saying choose him, choose the Italian?"

"No, only you can make the choice, I am just trying to give you some perspective."

Elena stared at him, thinking hard. She knew Richard was only trying to help, but rather than making things clearer all he managed to do was confuse her even more.

~

Despite their bravery life had not been so fortunate for the mayor and bishop. They once again returned to see the commandant and passed the list to him, watching as he read it.

"This is the same list as before. I know there are Jews on this island, and yet you lie to me!" he bellowed.

Neither mayor nor bishop flinched. Both had agreed that if they needed to sacrifice themselves for the greater good, then they would. What were two lives as opposed to saving over two hundred and seventy men, women and children?

"It is the correct list, Commandant. It is now up to you to decide our fate," the mayor said.

"Very well."

The commandant turned to the two young soldiers behind him.

"Arrest the mayor and the bishop and take them to Bohali."

Glancing at each other, the mayor and the bishop stood and merely nodded to each other, as the young soldiers dragged them from the room. A few hours later, they were sitting in separate reutilised cells in Bohali's old Venetian castle awaiting their fate.

~

Pietro sat at his desk in the Italian headquarters, with piles of paper in front of him, but the last thing he wanted to do was deal with any of it. The commandant was a tough man to work for. The Germans had taken over everything on the island and, as the days passed, the Italians felt more and more sidelined. Because of his rank, Pietro was party to a lot of information and spent much of his time with the Germans, but he did not like the way they operated. Some of their methods made him shudder, but he carried on knowing that he had no choice in the matter. He was safer being aligned with the Germans. Hearing the door bang he jumped to his feet, and saluted the young Italian officer who entered the room.

"Captain, there is news from the island of Kefalonia."

"What news?" Pietro motioned to the seat opposite and the young soldier gratefully took it. As Pietro sat down, the man continued.

"It is the Germans, they have killed all of the Italian soldiers."

"Killed them? Are you sure?"

"Yes, we received an emergency broadcast. They have been slaughtered like pigs." The young soldier was agitated and Pietro could understand why.

"Thank you for telling me. You may go. Tell the chauffeur I need the car. I must go to see the commandant immediately."

"Yes, Captain." The young man saluted before hastily departing.

Pietro grabbed his cap and put it on, having already forgotten about the paperwork on his desk, and took the stairs to the main door two at a time. The car was already waiting for him. He quickly climbed in, and then watched the island scenery pass by as the car took him closer to the old Sarkis house. He shuddered as he remembered the day that the commandant had shot the previous owner. It was as though the deed was as natural as breathing to him. Pietro wondered if this was what had happened to the Italians on the next island. As they rounded a corner, he caught sight of Kefalonia in the distance, and it looked quiet and peaceful. He hoped the news about the d'Aqui Division was wrong, and that they were all still alive.

The commandant was sitting at his desk and Pietro was shown in straightaway.

"Captain Cipriani, this is a surprise."

"Commandant."

"Sit."

Pietro did as instructed.

"What can I do for you?"

"News has reached me of some kind of massacre on Kefalonia. Is it true?"

"I am afraid it is, but you must understand, it is not the will of the German Army, Captain.

Sometimes some people, how would you say it, take things into their own hands. The man responsible is not a true German soldier and he will be punished for his part in the deaths of the Führer's allies. For that is what you Italians are, you are our allies and you serve alongside us. We value you, therefore there is no need for us to kill you."

"My men are worried, Commandant. We need assurances."

"And I have given them," he insisted. "Was there anything else?"

"No, Commandant."

Pietro stood, saluted the senior officer and left the room, but his mood was sombre. He was not sure if he could trust the commandant anymore.

~

Elena sat on the bed watching Pietro change. Once he was done, he grabbed hold of her hand, pulled her from the bed and along behind him. Outside his door was a basket and he lifted it, placing it in the back of the jeep he had borrowed. Opening the passenger door, he helped Elena up into the seat.

Driving through country lanes, they headed south, a direction Elena had never before been to with Pietro.

"Where are we going?"

"Somewhere special."

"Where?"

"To a place that I have been told is the best place to watch the sunset. I think you called it Keri?"

"Yes. We do. How do you know about it?"

"One of my men heard about it from a girl he met. I thought that we could spend some time together, have a nice meal, sit at the end of the world and watch the sun fall on another day."

"It sounds nice."

Silence fell as Pietro concentrated on the road ahead. Elena stared out at the passing scenery, realising that despite living here all of her life, she always saw something new. The seasons always brought changes to the island, but it had changed even more since the arrival of the Italians and the Germans. Since the invasion, they had taken over government buildings, and put life back into the ancient Venetian castle, albeit as a prison. The Italians had built a small airstrip on land at the south end of the island, to save them from having to navigate the waters between Zakynthos and the mainland. The Germans were now turning it into a fully functioning airport. Almost every day, planes landed and took off, filling the air overhead with shuddering engine noises. The Germans had also chosen an old building just outside of Zakynthos Town as their headquarters. Lookout towers, checkpoints and barbed wire littered the coastal cliffs scarring the once beautiful landscape.

Slowly, they were taking over and changing things, and the island was no longer the happy, peaceful Greek paradise it once was, it was a prison, and it made Elena very sad.

It was not long before they arrived at Keri. Parking up, Pietro turned off the engine and got out. After helping Elena down from the vehicle, he reached for the basket and a blanket.

"What a view!" he said, stopping short.

"It is wonderful."

Carefully stepping closer to the cliffs, they peered over the edge. A white lime scale precipice fell away from them, dropping for metre after metre to the turquoise waters below.

"Careful that you do not fall, Elena." He pulled her back from the edge until they were at a safe distance and then lay the blanket on the ground. Pietro sat and patted the ground next to him before reaching into the basket to remove the contents.

Elena sat and took some village bread, dipped it in olive oil and nibbled at the edge. As usual there was more food in the basket than they needed and she wished there was some way she could get it to those who did. Like the Jewish family she had rescued, or Richard, who was still in hiding. Looking up at Pietro, she wondered what he would think if he knew about her secret life. Would he understand or would he march her straight to the Germans? She shuddered at the thought.

"Are you cold, *Piccolina*?"

"No, why do you ask?"

"You shivered as if you were cold."

"I am okay," she smiled at him.

"Once we have eaten, I will warm you up." He smiled, his eyes twinkling.

She smiled back and carried on eating. The food he had brought with him really was delicious and she ate ravenously. She could not remember a day when she had not felt hungry and knew she was thinner than she had been. When they finished, Pietro threw the remnants back into the basket before lying back on the blanket. Elena joined him, and stared up at the sky, which was beginning to show the first signs of the day coming to a close.

"Do you not wish you could lie here like this forever, Pietro?"

"Yes. If you were with me then, yes I do."

"It would be so nice. It would be just us, no war, no Italian army, no German Army, no horror stories. We would be free from it all. We would be free from them."

Pietro shifted uncomfortably. "What do you mean, Elena?"

She sat bolt upright, and took his hand. "Are you not sick of all this? Sick of all the hatred, the suffering and the fighting? Those German pigs killed your fellow men over on Kefalonia. Are you not worried that they will do the same to you?"

Pietro sat up. He had never heard her talk like this before, and it shocked him. "I have already had assurances from the commandant that it will not happen here."

"And you believe him? How can you believe a man like that?"

"A man like what?"

"A man whose only aim is to kill the innocent, to take their land, their lives and their freedom!"

"Yes I believe him! What is this about, Elena? You are scaring me. You sound like the resistance, the ones who fight against us, the ones who will stop at nothing to rid the island of me, my men and the Germans."

"Pah! You have no idea…"

In that moment, Elena realised that she had said too much. She shut her mouth and stared out to sea. The sky was now tinged through with yellow, orange and gold and it was a beautiful sight. Looking back at the confusion on Pietro's face, she knew she was on dangerous ground and in all likelihood had just given herself away, so she had to think and act fast. She bowed her head and burst into tears.

"I am so sorry, Pietro, I am so very tired. Athena keeps me awake, my parents are struggling, I am so very hungry and I just do not know where all of this will end. I am scared for you. When I heard about what happened on

Kefalonia, I ran to find you, but you were not there. I was so scared. I thought they had taken you to be killed, too. I love you Pietro, I never want to lose you!" She lifted her head. Tears etched her face. She did not love Pietro. She did not even care about him that much. She knew that now. In her heart, she only cared for Angelos and for her daughter, and it was for Athena that she was crying. But she had to protect herself, she had to make him believe.

Pietro pulled her into his arms and held her tightly. "I am so sorry, my *piccolina.* I did not mean it. Like you, I am sick of this war, and I do not know whom to trust. Come, dry your eyes and let us enjoy our evening together."

Pulling her back down to the blanket, he kissed her and she kissed him back. Elena felt the relief flood through her and inwardly sighed. Pietro stroked her head and tried to stop the nagging doubts from overwhelming him.

CHAPTER TWENTY-FIVE

Zakynthos, Greece, 1943

Two weeks after that night on the cliffs at Keri, Pietro found himself called to the German headquarters on the outskirts of Zakynthos Town. He was ushered into the briefing room to join a mixed group of German and Italian soldiers. He was instructed to take a seat at the table facing the officers. There was only one other seat next to him and he assumed that it was for Commandant Brandt. His assumption was correct and the commandant joined them a few minutes later, giving a brief "Heil Hitler", before sitting.

"Gentlemen. Our radio officers have learned that the Greek resistance have been hiding an English airman on the island, no one knows for how long. We have tried searching for him, but we have been unable to locate him. It seems these peasants are good at hiding people. I will not tolerate this! We are in charge here!" As if to emphasise his point, the commandant thundered his fist into the table. The sound reverberated around the room, making the occupants jump.

"Enemy forces are going to try and rescue him in the next few days, but we do not have any other information. I have gathered you all together as you will be the group that will help stop the rescue and capture the airman. Any resistance involved will be shot. I will not tolerate this on my island!"

The commandant stood, signaling the end of the brief meeting. "Captain Cipriani. Come with me."

Pietro stood and followed the German from the room. The commandant was stony and silent, and the only sound in the hall was the noise of his boots clicking on the wooden floor as they walked. Reaching an office, he opened the door and took a seat behind the large wooden desk.

"Shut the door and sit, Captain."

Pietro did as he was told and waited patiently for the commandant to speak.

"When I arrived on the island, you were a pleasant surprise, Captain. You had run your men with a firm hand and, despite some of them being a little unruly, you handled things well. Now I am not so sure."

Pietro shifted uncomfortably in his seat.

"I know that when men are away from home for a long time, they like the odd pleasure in life. It is what whores were invented for after all," the commandant laughed at his own puerile joke. "But to hear that a married man of your standing is running about the island for over a year with the same girl. It worries me. Did you know that you were fucking a member of the Greek resistance, Captain? Or had you just chosen to overlook the fact?"

"I…" Pietro had no words. He did not know if the commandant was testing him, or if indeed Elena really was resistance. He thought back to that night on the cliffs at Keri, and suddenly it all became clear. She had always been one step ahead of him, asking how his day was, gently prying information out of him when they were in bed relaxing. How could he have been so stupid? He knew the commandant was out for blood and, if he was not careful, Pietro knew it would be his.

"I never knew. I will do whatever you want, Commandant, just tell me."

"You must get the information from her about the rescue. Then you will tell us."

Pietro could only nod.

"Then, once you have played your part we will decide what to do with you."

"Yes, Commandant."

He motioned for Pietro to leave, but as he was

opening the door the commandant spoke once more.

"I hope she was worth the trouble."

Pietro did not answer and just carried on walking. He had two choices and both were very risky. He hated this damn war and wished he had never come to Zakynthos.

~

"I am going to be gone for a few nights, so I need you to look after Athena, Mama."

"Where are you going?"

"You know that I cannot tell you that."

"Is it safe?"

"You know that I cannot tell you that either, Mama."

"You risk your life too much, my little one."

"I do it for you and Papa, for my brother and my daughter, and for everyone else on the island, so that they have a future. Now, I must go or I will be late. Just remember that I love you. I will see you soon."

She planted a big kiss on her mother's cheek, and was about to lift her bag when there was a knock at the door.

Elena pressed her finger to her lips and peeked through the glass. Pietro? What on earth was he doing here?

"It is okay, Mama. I am going to open the door, but just be calm, do not say anything, just go about your business."

Pietro grinned widely as Elena opened the door.

"*Piccolina*, I have brought these for you," he said as he pulled a bouquet of wildflowers from behind his back. "I thought I could take you and your lovely daughter out for the afternoon?"

"Oh? Well I am not sure…"

"If there is something else you would rather do?"

Elena caught the glance from her mother, and knew she had to go with him.

"That would be lovely. I shall just get Athena ready. Mama, would you help me please?"

The woman nodded and followed her daughter into the other room.

Quickly and quietly, Elena gave instructions to her mother as she gathered up her daughter.

"Tell Georgios to go to the usual place. Dionysis needs to know I am unable to help. He has to cope alone."

"Okay," her mother whispered as she followed her daughter and granddaughter into the other room.

Turning to her mother, Elena kissed her cheek again. "Goodbye, Mama."

"Goodbye, Elena."

As her daughter left, Mrs. Petrakis sank to the chair, and cried for her daughter, before remembering she had work to do.

~

"So what made you want to see us, Pietro?"

"I have missed you and I thought that it would be nice to spend some time with you and your daughter."

They were trundling through the island's lanes heading towards the east coast. It was unusual to be so far north on the island; Pietro never came this way. It surprised her, but she pushed the nagging doubts down. It was not long before they reached a small cove, and Pietro parked up.

"Come, little Athena," he said lifting her from her mother's arms. "Let us explore."

Elena watched as they walked ahead. Her daughter ran unsteadily on her short legs and giggled, pointing at birds in the trees and anything else that moved. Left to her own thoughts, she smiled. How she wished that Angelos could have been like this with his own daughter. It was not to be though. Instead it was an Italian soldier, an enemy of Greece, that was making Athena laugh. The thought unsettled Elena and she ran to catch up with them. Pietro sat on the sand and watched Athena running barefoot, playing with rocks and pebbles she found. Sitting next to him, Elena kept a watchful eye on her daughter.

"Why did you come today?"

"Because I needed to talk to you, Elena."

"What about?"

"You."

"Me?"

He sighed. "Elena, I know who you are, I know what you are and I came here to tell you that you are in great danger."

Her heart hammered in her chest and she tried her best to keep her breathing as normal as possible.

"I do not know what you mean."

Pietro lifted her chin and turned her head to face his and, in that moment, she saw it in his eyes. He truly did know. Everything.

"You, my *piccolina*, are resistance and have been for a very long time."

"I…" she stammered, nervously looking about her, expecting to see Germans soldiers walking towards her with their guns held high ready to shoot. But none came. It was just the three of them, alone on the beach.

"You have no need to worry. No one is going to hurt you. I would not let them." Pietro took her hands in his and kissed each one individually. "Oh Elena. Why did you do this? I love you so much, but you know it is impossible for you to stay here on the island you love, do you not?"

"Why, why is it so impossible? You are not going to tell them are you?"

"The commandant already knows."

"He knows! You told him?"

"No! He told *me*. He knows everything. He knows all about the English airman, too. He knows that you mean to help him escape."

"Oh god." Elena felt the blood drain from her extremities and stared at her daughter. Athena was so precious to her and she would move heaven and earth to protect her. But how could she when the enemy was tracking her down, coming ever closer. She knew now that it was only a matter of time.

"Who gave me away?"

"That I do not know."

"What shall I do? If they kill me, they will kill Athena too. I just could not bear it, Pietro."

"I will help you."

"You will?" she looked up at him and saw friendship in his eyes. "Why would you do that for me?"

"Because I love you. Because I hate this war. Because I just want to get off this island and get as far away from Commandant Brandt and his ruthless comrades as possible."

"But how? How would we even consider getting off the island?"

"The same way as your airman. When you take him to the meeting point, you take Athena and me, too. We will go with him. Your resistance will help us."

"I do not know." Elena was confused. Pietro was the enemy, so how could she possibly trust him?

"Look at me."

She did as she was told and he pulled her close. He kissed her ever so lightly on the lips, small butterfly kisses that moved to her cheeks. Softly he whispered his true feelings to her and her heart finally melted. She knew then that her decision had been made.

~

Dionysis and Angelos made their way into the village under cover of darkness and waited for the signal. Once they heard it, Angelos rushed forward to help the lone figure into the back of the cart. They had put extra material around the donkey's hooves in the hopes of staying as quiet as possible. Traversing the back roads, they made their way east towards the coast to Xigia Beach. Just the thought of being back there again made Angelos think of the times he had spent there with Elena when they were younger and life was peaceful. A time when they swam and splashed in the water and lazed around, talking about their future. It now seemed like a lifetime ago.

Both men were scared to death of the rescue attempt. They knew that, if caught, it would be the death of them both, but they knew they had to do it. As they got close to the coast, Dionysis told Angelos to leave the donkey and cart in a field hidden behind a hedge. Angelos was to follow them down to the beach, but stay out of sight. If things went wrong it would be up to Angelos to raise the alarm.

As Dionysis neared the beach, he gave the signal and waited for one to come in return. When he heard it, he stepped out, with Richard following closely behind. Running down the edge of the beach, they kept close to the rocky outcrop. A boat was already moored with one man on board. Elena was patiently waiting next to the vessel, holding Athena's hand. Next to her stood Pietro.

Dionysis pulled up short when he saw the child and the Italian soldier. Carefully, he pushed Richard forward and told him to get into the boat. Without a second thought, Richard did as he was told.

"What is going on here?" Dionysis demanded.

"I am sorry, but I can no longer stay here. I am leaving tonight with Pietro and Athena." Elena lifted her daughter into the boat, as if to prove a point.

"You are leaving with him? He is the enemy. You cannot trust him, Elena."

"But I do. I love him and he loves me."

At that moment, Angelos, who had been watching in shock from his hiding place, let out a low whistle. Coming down the road were two vehicles: German armoured cars.

Dionysis heard the whistle and knew what it meant. He pulled his gun and pointed it at Pietro, but the Italian matched him move for move. It was then that Elena realised what was going on. Her worst fears had come true. As much as she had wanted to believe in Pietro, he had remained the enemy and had turned on her. Swiftly, she heaved her weight behind the boat, and reached over to Richard.

"You must protect my daughter, Richard. I beg of you. When she is older you must give her this." Reaching into her pocket, she passed him the locket and a small envelope, careful words written in haste, in case the worst happened. She had hoped she would never need it, but Pietro, it seemed, could not be trusted after all.

"Promise me!"

She was waist high in water now and Richard knew that he had no choice. He took them from her, and stowed them safely in his pocket.

"Come with us!"

"I cannot."

"Why?"

"I have to make sure Angelos lives. Now go!"

Elena smiled at her daughter, then turned her back and waded ashore. Glancing over her shoulder, she saw that the boat was making good pace on the water, and was slowly disappearing into the blackness of the ocean.

The beach was suddenly covered with men in grey uniforms and Elena knew it was over. There was nothing she could do but surrender.

Dionysis turned and began firing on the Germans but Pietro shot him in the back. As

Dionysis fell to the ground, Pietro grabbed hold of Elena and pulled her roughly up the beach.

Commandant Brandt stood on the shore, watching as they neared.

"So this is the resistance peasant who has been giving us the runaround," he sneered as he traced his finger down her cheek.

Elena glared defiantly at the German and spat at him.

"I have a lot of questions for you. Take her to headquarters." The Commandant ordered. "Captain Cipriani, you will ride with me."

CHAPTER TWENTY-SIX

Zakynthos, Greece, 2002

Kate walked into the already familiar house in Exo Hora and glanced around her, taking in the surroundings. She had not really paid attention the last time she was here. It was quite small, but felt very much like a well-loved home. She could tell that family was important to the owners; pictures of them littered the walls and furniture surfaces. She liked it very much.

"We are out the back, come this way," Sophia beckoned kindly.

"I can't thank you enough for allowing me to talk to your father," Kate said.

"Please, call him Angelos. It is easier than calling him my father. It is okay. I know how important this is to you."

Angelos was sitting in the same chair, under the veranda. Sophia went over to him and placed her hand on his arm, speaking to him in Greek.

He looked up at Kate, with eyes wide and unbelieving.

"Elena?" His voice was barely a whisper.

"Like I said, he gets confused sometimes." Sophia turned back to him and spoke in Greek, "No, Papa, this is Kate. You remember Kate from the other day."

Sophia turned back to Kate, motioning for her to sit. Kate took the chair opposite and studied the man again. Sophia sat next to her, and reminded her father why Kate was there. He nodded and occasionally glanced at the stranger across from him. Finally he spoke, slow meandering Greek words that Sophia translated.

"I never thought I would see you again, Elena. But here you are sitting before me. How can this be?" His eyes were glistening with tears.

"I am sorry, Kate. He really does get very confused."

"I understand. I don't want to upset him."

Angelos pawed at his daughters arm, trying his best to stand. He muttered insistently in Greek and Sophia helped him to his feet.

"Excuse us for a moment, Kate. He would like me to get something."

Kate looked out across the garden for a few

minutes as she patiently waited for Angelos and Sophia. As they reappeared and took their seats, she noticed the old man was carrying an aged shoebox. With unsteady hands, Angelos opened the box and rifled through the contents until he finally found what he was looking for: two aging black and white photos, which he stared at for a moment before passing them to his daughter.

"Elena," he said, pointing at the pictures, and then Kate.

Sophia looked at the photographs and then at Kate. The resemblance was remarkable, and it shocked her. Who was this girl that sat before her and how was she related to her father? Hesitantly, she passed the images to Kate.

Disbelief rippled through Kate as the woman in the pictures stared back at her, a mirror image of herself. She was dumbstruck and looked up at Sophia questioningly.

"She looks just like you," Sophia said, confirming Kate's own thoughts.

"She does," Kate breathed with barely a whisper. "Is she Elena Petrakis?"

Sophia turned to her father, speaking slowly. He looked at Kate and then back at the photographs. Kate allowed him to take his time. She could see it was hard for him. The memories that he was pulling from the furthest reaches of his mind were from a time he would rather forget. She allowed him to go at his own pace.

A faraway look on Angelos's face altered his

features; he suddenly looked younger, much younger. He had been transported back to a past memory, a memory that obviously meant a lot to him. He looked happy, but more than happy. He looked serene.

Slowly, Angelos began to speak and he told Kate everything: the first time he had met Elena Petrakis, how he had fallen in love with her, and how they had conceived a child together and called her Athena, but that they were never married, how his father had forced them apart, and how, against his own wishes, he had been made to marry Maria Makris. The serene happy look fell from his face and he began to tell them about the war. How they had been invaded and how they had been plunged headlong into a vicious bloody battle. His entire life story came out, in every minute detail.

Kate sat captivated and listened as Sophia translated everything for her. When Angelos had reached the part about the locket, Kate reached to her neck and unclasped the chain, handing it across the table to him.

"This is the locket you gave Elena, isn't it?"

Angelos took it in shaking hands and turned it over and over, tears falling down his face. He could only nod.

"Let us take a break," Sophia suggested. Her father had never told her about any of this. She knew he had been hiding something, but had not expected the secret to be this big. Something nagged at her, though, and she knew there was more to come.

Kate got up and followed Sophia into the kitchen, "Are you okay, Sophia?"

"Yes. I think so. It is hard to hear my father's past laid out so painfully. I never knew that he was forced to marry my mother. I never knew he was in love with someone else, and I certainly did not know that he had a child with her. He must have loved Elena very much; I can tell that much from his face. It seems that she is the ghost that haunts him. He has been that way all of his life, but I always figured it was because he lost our mother when I was so young. This has come as a bit of a shock."

"I am so sorry to have brought this hurt and upset to your house, Sophia. If I had known..."

Sophia turned and hugged her tightly. "You must not apologise. I am glad you are here. I am learning so much about my family's life. Things that I never knew. And I have met you. You are family now."

"I am?"

"Of course. Have you not yet realised? Angelos is your grandfather. That makes you my niece, and I am very happy that you are here."

Kate reached for a nearby chair and took a seat, shaking with shock. She thought hard about it for a moment. Sophia was right Angelos and Elena Petrakis were her grandparents.

"It can't be. Someone would have told me."

"Well I do not know for sure, until Papa tells me, but the evidence is pretty clear Kate. Your mother was Athena; Papa's daughter was called Athena. Athena's mother was Elena and you look exactly like her. I would say that is strong evidence."

Kate was lost for words.

"Are you okay?" Sophia sat next to her and placed a hand on her arm.

"I think so. I just didn't expect this. I knew that my birth mother said there was a family connection with the island, but to be honest, I didn't expect to find out anything. I never expected to find all of you. It's a shock. A good shock, but a shock nonetheless."

"I understand. It is a shock for me too. You need time to take it all in. Do not let anyone rush you, Kate. We will always be here for you, but take your time. Get to know who you are, get to know the island, then once you are happy, we will be here for you."

"Thank you Sophia." Kate smiled at her new aunt. "Did you know Elena?"

"No. I have heard rumours and stories about her from the locals, though. It seems she was a brave woman and, despite what my grandfather Loukas and others on the island thought, she most definitely was not a peasant, or the other things he called her. You have to understand, my grandfather was a breed apart. It was a different time and luckily for all of us, Papa turned out to be nothing like him."

"If Angelos decides it's too much, Sophia, I won't mind. I want what's best for him. I don't want to upset him or make him ill."

"I know you do not, but one thing you will learn about Angelos is that he is stubborn, and he will carry on until he tells you everything there is to know. And I have a feeling there is much more to learn."

Kate and Sophia stood and walked back outside. Angelos smiled up at them as they sat. He spoke in broken English. "You are as beautiful as your grandmother. She would have been proud of the young woman I see before me. I think she would want you to keep this," he said as he took her hand and pressed the locket back into it. She closed her fingers over it, holding her hand in his. "My granddaughter. I still cannot believe it. You must promise me that you will always wear the locket. You must keep Elena alive in you, never let her die."

Kate blinked back the tears, "I promise."

Angelos released her hand and patted the top of it. Once more he began to speak in Greek and Sophia translated.

"The war went on for years and our island was slowly torn to pieces. Families were pitted against families, friends against friends. My father forced me into an impossible position, making me spy on the locals for the Italians. My father thought of himself as an important man in the ranks of the new order, but it turned out he was wrong." Angelos's voice quieted. "When the Germans invaded, he was shot dead. His stupidity made us all homeless and we had to move in with Stelios, my father-in-law. I rarely saw Elena and had no idea that she had joined the resistance, although I had my suspicions. It was not long after the war began that she joined them, and she fought hard against the island's oppressors any way she felt necessary. The more the war dragged on, the further Elena and I drifted apart, but I always tried to look out for her when I could, even though she never knew it."

Angelos stopped to take a sip of his water, with trembling hands. But his voice was strong. "Not long after the Germans invaded, they demanded the names of all the Jewish people on the island. Elena and I helped to rescue them and hide them in the mountains. She would sneak food to them, and look after them any way she could. She also helped save the life of an English airman who was shot out of the sky. She helped him escape from the island, and he took Athena with him. His name was Richard and he was the reason Athena survived. Little did she know, Elena's involvement would end up being her downfall."

Angelos stopped for a moment and took another, longer drink of water, before continuing.

"Maria, my wife, had always been jealous of Elena; she had always felt threatened by her. Maria knew that I had always loved Elena and always would do. On the day that the Germans killed my father, Elena let slip in front of Maria that she was resistance. Maria stored that information away. When we heard about what happened with the Jews, the islanders were so scared. They knew there would be trouble ahead."

Angelos shook his head; he could barely look at his daughter. Sophia took hold of his hand.

"Papa. What happened?"

Angelos could not continue; he had already said too much. How could he tell his daughter what had happened?

"Please. Papa. We think no less of you. The war happened a long time ago. There is nothing that can be done now. But you need to release the demons you have been carrying all these years."

Angelos cupped his daughter's face in his hands and gently kissed her forehead.

"Maria, your mother, went to the Germans. She told the Germans that Elena was resistance. She sold her soul to the devil that had its stranglehold on all of us. I was furious. I had always wondered how the Italian Captain Cipriani learned of Elena's involvement. I thought she may have given herself away, but she had not. It was all down to your mother. I was there when the Germans caught Elena and took her away. She had been assisting with the rescue of the English airman. She thought she was going to escape the island with the Italian captain and Athena too, but the only person who ever made it onto the boat was Athena. The Germans kept Elena for days at the headquarters, torturing her for information, but she never gave them any. She was brave till the last."

"What happened to her?" Kate asked. "What did they do to my grandmother?"

Angelos stared out across the back garden. He thought of that day, standing near the German headquarters waiting to see if today would be the day that they released Elena. The modern world around him seemed to disappear and he was back in 1943 again. He could hear a ghostly echoing version of his own voice as he spoke.

It all happened in slow motion. The door opened and the commandant and Captain Cipriani marched down the steps with a battered and bruised Elena dragging listlessly between them. She was barely conscious and looked so thin. He knew where they were taking her so he jumped onto the motorbike he had borrowed and raced after them. Angelos wanted to help her. He needed to help her.

Eventually they reached Keri. Angelos stayed back in the hope that no one would see him. He ditched his motorbike, and made the rest of the journey on foot. He slowed to a walk and crept closer, hiding amongst the brush. As he peeked through some bushes, he saw Elena standing on the headland. Despite her neglected state, she was now conscious and her head was held high. She stared coldly and defiantly at the men who stood before her, the men whose very clothing was a symbol of hatred to almost everyone on Zakynthos and the rest of the world alike. Angelos saw that Elena's once beautiful hair was matted and dirty and had fallen from its pins. Small wisps of brown waves fell about her beautiful strong face. Her clothes had been ripped in places, in a struggled bid for freedom. Her feet and legs were scratched and covered with dust and dirt.

The Keri headland was a truly beautiful place. Angelos had heard the rumours, normally traitors were taken to Kambi. But Angelos knew that choosing Keri was a deliberate act. Pietro had been foolish to believe that Elena loved him, when all the while she had been a traitor to him. Coming to Keri was a way of Pietro showing her that he had all of the control. And it was here that she now stood facing down her aggressor. She had known the risks, but she thought Pietro was different, but he was not. Angelos hated him. Pietro Cipriani, the wolf in sheep's clothing. He had tried to warn her off the Italian but she had not listened and the wolf now showed his claws and bared his teeth. So now, Elena stood, the chase over, facing Pietro down in the cold light of day, not knowing what would happen next.

Outnumbered. Scared. Alone.

Angelos wished he could do something, but he was only one man. He knew if he broke from his hiding place, he would only manage to walk two paces before being shot. He was a foolish miserable coward, and could only watch as the commandant and Pietro stepped forward to mete out her punishment. Pietro ran his fingers down Elena's face, making her flinch. It was as if his touch was molten metal that burned the very flesh from her skin. Angelos watched in horror. Pietro slowly took hold of Elena's arm and walked her to the edge of the cliff. Evil seemed to emanate from every pore, seeping out of him, staining the grass, the sea and the sky around them, choking the island with its embittered madness.

Elena's limbs shook from fear and she shuffled her feet forward at Pietro's instruction. Angelos felt a single tear slide down his cheek. He knew that her view would be a beautiful one, a bright blue sea that stretched as far as the eye could see. Pietro released Elena's arms and his lips breathed a warm gentle breath at her ear, a feeling that was all too familiar. It made her nauseous and tremble with fear.

Despite being hidden, Angelos heard what he said to her.

"I will always love you, Elena, but you have betrayed us, and for that you must pay the price."

Unable to tear himself away, Angelos watched as she breathed in sharply at the touch of the cold metal barrel against the back of her head. Tears instantly escaped her eyes, staining her face, but she stifled back a sob, not wanting to show her terror to the enemy. Before she could even utter a word, the shot rang out. Her death was instantaneous and her lifeless body tumbled forward, falling over the cliff edge. It struck rocks as it fell, her blood staining the chalky white cliffs, finally landing with a splash, surrendering itself to the vast ocean depths.

Angelos stifled a cry, and remained hidden in the undergrowth. All he could do was cry. Cry for Elena, for his daughter who was lost to him, and for himself, the biggest coward of all.

He brought his attention back to the present - back to Sophia and Kate.

"It was dark and I was alone by the time I stopped crying. But only one thing remained true: my beautiful Elena was dead…murdered at the hands of the Nazis and their allies. I wanted to kill that damn Italian, I wanted to scratch his eyes out, but I did not get the chance. The commandant did it for me. I hate myself for it, but I was actually happy to see the fear and confusion in his eyes as the bullet left the gun. He was killed in the same manner and thrown over the cliff to join Elena. The Germans did not take kindly to one of their allies sleeping with the resistance."

Seeming a little more at ease, Angelos continued, "When I eventually returned home, your grandfather Stelios greeted me with terrible news. Maria had been taken away by the resistance and had been shot for being a traitor. The Germans rounded up the Petrakis family and executed them all, even poor little Georgios. I thanked god that Athena was with the airman. In one day, I lost the woman I truly loved and I also lost my wife. Worse still, both my children lost their mothers, and I had lost Athena forever. I never even knew if she had escaped, been lost at sea or captured by the enemy, but I prayed every day that she would find safety."

Angelos collapsed back in the chair and closed his eyes. The relief of finally being able to unburden his story was all too clear.

Kate turned to look at her aunt. Sophia had turned the palest shade of white and she was crying. Without a second thought, Kate threw her arms around her and held her as tightly as she could.

CHAPTER TWENTY-SEVEN

Zakynthos, Greece, 2002

Kate sat on the beach at Laganas. After she had pushed her way past the throng of tourists enjoying the highlights of the strip, it was not as crowded as she had expected. She was not interested in bars, clubs or souvenir shops. She wanted peace and quiet, if that was possible.

She had learned so much since arriving on the island. Her grandmother and her mother had been born here. She herself was Greek, and only happened to grow up in England by a fluke. By rights, she was a Zakynthian, which had come as a shock. But even more of a shock was the fact that her grandmother had been a very active member of the Greek resistance. She helped to save the lives of the entire Jewish population by helping to hide them from the Germans. She did everything she could to try and upset their plans. She was such a brave woman, but her bravado had cost her her life. She was shot dead by a man she thought loved her. Looking around her now, she could not even begin to imagine what it must have felt like to live through the war. It was hard to imagine a place so relaxed and idyllic overrun with German soldiers.

Kate desperately wanted to go to where her grandmother had died, but she could not do it alone. She just could not face it. As the merriment of Laganas carried on around her, Kate buried her head in her hands and cried. She cried tears for the mother she never knew, who had been taken from this life too young. There were tears for her grandmother, a woman who had been so courageous and had paid for her bravery with her own life, and tears for herself, for a life less lived and a man she had lost so many years ago.

~

As evening clouds began to drift in, they coloured with the fiery orange glow of the day's end. Kate finally stood up; it was time to find something to eat. She had missed lunch and was starving. She dusted the sand from her skirt and then picked up her sandals, swinging them in her hand. A group of drunken lads came running along the beach towards her. She stepped aside to avoid them, but only ended up clattering head on into one of them.

"I'm sorry," she mumbled, quickly sidestepping them to continue on her way.

"Katie?!"

The voice made her stop. She knew that voice. No, it could not be! It was just her mind playing tricks on her. She went to take a step forward, but felt a gentle hand on her shoulder.

The voice was barely a whisper as one word floated gently past her ear on the evening breeze. "Katie?"

Slowly she turned and the shock hit her.

"Fletch?"

"Yes. It's me."

She studied him. He still had a handsome face, but there were a few more lines and character to it. He was older now, they both were. What was he doing here?

As if he had heard her thoughts, he answered her question. "Stag do, Shane is getting married next week."

"Ah. I see." She did not know what else to say. It had been so long since she last saw him, since he ran into the waves, leaving her alone and upset on the beach. He had never come back to her and had just disappeared. It had hurt her so much.

"And you? What are you doing here?" Fletch asked. She looked even more beautiful, now that she was older. Her skin was kissed by the sun and looked as if she could pass for a local. He had missed her so much and just wished he had not abandoned her all those years ago.

"Fulfilling a dying woman's wish."

"Really? You finally did it?" Fletch was surprised.

"Yes. To be honest I didn't really have a choice. Mum and Dad kind of forced me into it!"

"Do you want to talk about it?" Fletch asked.

"Your friends are waiting. I don't want to spoil your evening."

That was a no then, and he felt the disappointment surge through him. "Right. Well it's nice to see you again."

"You too, Fletch."

He turned to leave and then stopped. "If you do want to talk while you're here, I'm staying at an apartment nearby." He pulled a pen from his pocket and scribbled the name on the back of her hand.

"Okay."

Silence fell between them. With nothing left to say, they turned and walked away in opposite directions, both regretting the loss of the other.

~

It was Kate's last full day on the island. She had still not been to Keri to see where her grandmother died and she wondered if it was actually for the best. After all, her grandmother died a long time ago, and there was nothing left up there except ghostly memories.

She sat on her hotel balcony thinking things over and her mind wandered back to Fletch. The writing was still etched on her hand and she was reluctant to scrub it clean. There was so much she wanted to say to him, but it had been so long. She was still angry with him for abandoning her, but she missed him. She wanted her friend back.

Without hesitation she grabbed her bag and car keys and drove to Laganas.

It was not long before she parked the car and was heading to his apartment complex. As she made her way to reception, she heard his voice behind her.

"Katie?"

The last decade disappeared in an instant and all she wanted was to feel her friend hugging her. Her Fletch. She ran to him and, not caring what happened next, threw her arms around him.

Fletch let her, and held her tightly, allowing her to take the comfort.

"I need to talk to you, Fletch." She looked up at him. "Do you have time?"

"I have all the time in the world for you, Katie, you know I do."

They walked in silence down the strip towards the beach. Once there, they sat on the sand, looking out over the crystal clear waters of the bay.

"I don't know where to start, Fletch."

"Start at the beginning, just let everything out."

Kate told him about her business in Bristol, her home, her lack of friends, the surprise birthday visit and present from her parents and finally the trip to Zakynthos, and all that she had learned while she was here. By the end of it, she felt exhausted.

"Oh Katie." Fletch took her in his arms, holding her tightly.

"I want to go and see where Elena died, but I'm so scared. I just don't want to do it on my own."

"Then let me take you."

"Why would you do that, Fletch?"

"Because I'm your friend and I care about you, and can see how important it is to you."

"But we haven't seen each other in so long. Everything has changed."

"I'm still the same person, Katie, I'm just older. I have no one in my life either. I still surf, I still bum around. The only difference is that I have missed my best friend. But she's here now, and trust me, I'm never letting her go again!"

Kate laughed. "I'm glad I found you again too, Fletch. But I can't ask you to do this, it's too much."

"I won't take no for an answer. Come on." He stood and held out his hand to her.

"Now?"

"Well there's no time like the present."

~

The winding country lanes got narrower the closer they got to Keri. Signposts were few and far between, but every now and again one appeared confirming that they were still heading in the right direction and it was not long before they reached their destination. After parking the car, Kate froze. Was this what she really wanted?

"Come on Katie. You can do this."

Fletch had already stepped from the car and was holding the door open, his hand outstretched. Trembling, Kate took hold of his hand, allowing him to pull her gently from the safe haven of the vehicle.

Turning, she stared out across the scrubby ground that ran all the way to the edge of the cliff. The horizon was filled with deep azure blue waters, the Ionian Sea. It stretched as far as the eye could see, eventually merging with the sky.

Looking down, Kate noticed Fletch was still holding her hand.

"I'm with you every step of the way," he reassured her.

Slowly, step-by-step, they edged closer to the precipice. Kate took in her surroundings, the stony scrubby ground underfoot, the bent and gnarled trees that were dotted about the clifftop, a mixture of unkempt waving grass that merged with what looked like thick heavy gorse. It was exactly how Angelos had described it. Glancing around her, she wondered where he had hidden on that fateful day.

They were almost there now and she held onto Fletch for dear life, stopping a metre short of the edge. She closed her eyes, trying to imagine how her grandmother had felt. Opening her eyes, she looked out across the sparkling waters, before looking down. Steep cliffs, a mixture of white and grey in colour, plunged directly to the sea below. This was where Elena had died. This was where a sadistic man murdered her before throwing her into the ocean below. The reality and pain of her grandmother's death hit home and Kate's knees buckled. She was unable to hold the weight of grief any longer, and she lay on the ground clutching stones and shrubs, as her tears stained the dust. Fletch sat next to her and stroked her head, allowing her to mourn, as she wept uncontrollably for the grandmother she had never known, and never would.

~

"Feeling better?" Fletch asked as he poured some more water into her glass.

They were now sitting in a small restaurant overlooking the sea.

"A little." She looked up at him; there were

not enough words to convey how thankful she was. “You didn’t have to do this Fletch.”

“I know, but that’s what friends are for.” He smiled. “I guess we should be heading back. I don’t want to get stuck out here on these country lanes in the dark.”

During the drive back, they were silent. Kate stared at the ever-changing views of the island as she drove. She would miss this place. It had wormed its way into her heart and now that she knew she was Greek, she could truly call it home. She glanced at Fletch. And what about her best friend? Would they remain friends once they left the island? She had missed him so much over the years, but they had both changed. Only time would tell.

In Laganas, the music from the clubs was already loud and enticing. Revellers were out enjoying the drinks and company. And it felt like she had arrived somewhere else. The change between day and evening was remarkable.

“Well, that’s me,” Fletch said.

“Thank you again for coming with me. I couldn’t have done it without you.”

“You’re welcome,” he sighed. “I had better go as the guys will be wondering where I’ve got to.”

“Of course. I don’t want to keep you. It was nice to see you again.”

“You too, Katie. Have a good flight home tomorrow.”

"Thanks."

Then he was gone and Kate was left sitting in the car alone. There was only one thing left to do, return to her apartment and pack.

~

Kate took one last look at the view from her balcony. She would miss Zakynthos dreadfully. It had been a rollercoaster of emotions, but it was the best decision she could have made. She had finally learned all about her past, and felt as though a big weight had been lifted. She could now return home and start her life over with a clean slate. It did not matter one bit that she was adopted. She loved the Fishers dearly, they were her parents and always would be. But she had discovered a new family, a heritage that made her understand a little more about who she was and who she was meant to be, and that made a big difference in her life.

Dragging her case downstairs, she waited for the taxi to arrive to take her to the airport. It arrived on time and she sat back watching the scenic countryside pass by. All too soon, they arrived at the airport. Once she paid the fare, she entered the building to check in. As she was queuing, she heard a shout. Thinking it was just a drunken holidaymaker, she ignored it.

"Katie Fisher!" The shout was even louder this time. She spun round to see Fletch running across the concourse.

"Fletch?"

"Thank god I caught you."

The queue shuffled forward and Kate shuffled with it.

"I need to talk to you, Katie."

"What about?"

"Can you come with me?"

"Fletch. I'm in the queue to check in, my plane leaves in an hour. Whatever you have to say, say it here."

"I can't."

"Well then, it can't be important."

The queue moved forward again and Kate moved with it, leaving Fletch behind; she did not have time for this. Fletch paced. This was not how he had planned things. Kate was next and stepped up to the desk. As she handed over her passport and ticket, she smiled at the girl behind the check-in desk.

"Good afternoon, madam," the girl greeted, as she took Kate's documents and began to tap away on her keyboard.

"I love you, Katie!"

Everyone in the queue and at the check-in desk fell silent. Slowly Kate turned and saw an anxious Fletch standing next to her.

"What did you say?" She could barely breathe.

"I love you." He stepped forward, and placed a hand on her cheek. "I always have."

Kate was thrown. She was about to get on a plane and fly home. How could he do this to her now? And with all of these people looking at her! It was so embarrassing!

"I can't do this now." She turned back to the check-in girl.

"And I can't leave things like this. I love you, Katie, and I know you love me too."

She spun on her heels. "I don't have time for this! For god's sake, Fletch." She was exasperated.

The check-in girl tapped her on the shoulder, passing her documents back to her.

"Why don't you go talk to him? You still have another twenty minutes before the desk closes."

Feeling like she had no other choice, Kate took the papers from her and dragged her suitcase away from the desk. Roughly, she pulled Fletch to one side.

"Why are you doing this?"

"I told you already."

"Yes I heard; apparently you love me. I haven't seen you for ten years Fletch, and then suddenly you turn up in my life declaring undying bloody love for me! You can't do this; I'm not some bloody holiday romance!" Kate was pacing up and down. She did not need this now. She needed to get home and see her parents.

"Katie, look at me." Fletch grabbed her

shoulders and turned her to face him. "I'm just trying to be honest with you."

She looked up at him. She could see from the look on his face that he really did love her. It shocked her. Had it always been there? Had she really missed the signs?

"I've been through so much, Fletch. I can't take it all in right now."

"You don't have to if you don't want to, but I have to tell you how I really feel, before you disappear from my life again!"

Kate was angry now. "Me? Me disappear from your life? You were the one who turned your back on me, Fletch. You left me sitting there on the beach when I was at my lowest. *You* turned your back on ME!"

"No, Kate. I gave you some straight talking and some time to think. Then you did what you always do: crawled into your shell. You stopped coming out and then I lost you. I may have gone to America but you were the one who left. You ran away to the city. You left me, you left your parents, you turned your back on everyone and threw yourself into your job." Fletch was angry now. "You did the running, Katie, not us!"

They were at an impasse, both too angry to carry on. Kate made the decision for them. Turning her back, she dragged her case over to the check-in desk. With sadness in his heart, Fletch knew it was over. He watched as she loaded her case onto the conveyor belt and took her documents from the check-in girl. Without looking back, she walked through the departure gate. He had tried. There was nothing more that he could do. Stepping out into the bright sunshine, he flagged the first taxi he could find.

~

In the departure lounge, Kate stared out of the window at the large expanse of grey tarmac. It would not be long before she was onboard the plane, departing for home. Fletch's words kept running through her head, going round and round, refusing to leave her alone. Was he right? She thought back to that time, when things had been in turmoil. She knew she had shut her parents out, that she admitted, but had Fletch not been the one to ditch her? The more she thought about it, the more it confused her.

A call came over the tannoy; it was time to board the plane. With a heavy heart and weary legs, Kate joined the queue, and moments later she was walking the same grey tarmac she had trodden two weeks earlier, every step taking her closer to the plane; the plane that would take her away from the island, and away from Fletch.

She stopped dead. She did not want to leave.

She loved him, too. More than she would ever be able to put into words.

In confusion, she stood on the tarmac allowing the other passengers to buffet past her, not knowing what to do next.

~

Fletch walked out to the pool area. He was so angry. He had bared his soul to Kate, only to have her tear him to shreds and blame everything on him. He wished he had never seen her again. He wished he were somewhere else halfway across the world, instead of here. Perching at the bar, he asked for a Mythos and, as the barman slid it across the bar to him, he heard a familiar voice.

"I'll pay for that." The barman looked over and took the notes, shrugging. "So. You love me."

"Aren't you supposed to be on a plane?" Fletch thought for a moment that he was dreaming.

"Yes. But I decided I couldn't leave until I told you something," Kate said. "Look at me, Fletch."

He did as she asked, and she saw it, pure love. It was written on his face, it shone in his eyes, it radiated from him. She knew it had always been there, but she had been too young and self-absorbed to see it. She took a step closer and their eyes locked. Slowly, she leaned forward, brushing her lips against his. In response, his hand slid behind her back pulling her closer, his lips eager to be part of her.

Once they parted, she pulled slightly back and stared into his eyes.

"You know I love you too, right?"

"I know. I've always known, Katie," he whispered.

"You were that sure?"

"Of you. Yes."

She laughed. "Shall we get out of here?"

"I thought you'd never ask!"

Acknowledgements

Thanks to my incredible team. Chris Joyce, for another great book cover, it's perfect. Dale Cassidy and Laura Barclay, the most patient editor and proofreader I've ever met. Thanks to both of you for helping me make this book what it is, I couldn't have done it without either of you!

My bestie Dee Thompson, thank you for everything, you're the most amazing friend! My writerly friends, Belinda Jones, Melissa Foster, Bella Witzenhausen and Sass Cadeaux, your continued support is much appreciated.

This book wouldn't have been possible without help from the following people: Niki Rozner Pavlopoulou, the Zante/war information you found was incredible, thank you for taking the time to help, it means a lot. Ailsa Burns, Katerina

Tsekouras, Angela Spinou, Sarah May Horan, Lesley Paterson Augoustinou, Bobby Goertz and Ken Spencer, your research tips and general information about Zante was invaluable, I really appreciate all of your help.

Sharon Voutou and Alexandros Bouas, thank you for reading the book during the editing process, your help with the intricacies of Greek life was great. I'm so grateful to you both.

To everyone in the *Among the Olive Groves* and *Zante Informer* facebook groups, you really are the nicest bunch of people, and I hope you all re-discover the island you love, as you turn the pages of this book. Your support has been truly overwhelming.

Finally, to my husband T, and my family. Thank you for your continued support, I love you all very much.

About the Author

Chrissie Parker lives in London UK, with her husband.

Twitter - @chrissie_author

Facebook – https://www.facebook.com/ChrissieParkerAuthor

Web – www.chrissieparker.com

20915243R00226

Printed in Great Britain
by Amazon